"AREN'T YOU CURIOUS NOW?" MICAH ASKED.

Lizzy couldn't get enough air. Her breathing had become short and shallow and she felt as if she were being crowded —even though the man in front of her hadn't moved.

"Be honest, Lizzy. You're burning with curiosity. I bother the hell out of you. Because I'm a puzzle missing some of its pieces. And you don't know whether or not to believe the picture that's starting to form. Am I the enemy? Am I a criminal? Or am I merely a victim of circumstance?"

She nervously wet her lips, and Micah's gaze darted in that direction, clung.

"I might have kept my word so far, but you're wondering if you can continue to trust me. If you should have trusted me at all."

He inched closer. She felt the inexplicable warmth of his body. His nearly *naked* body. The thought alone sent a shiver down her spine.

"You should never have kept me here, Lizzy," he murmured, touching her with nothing more than his eyes. "I'm dangerous to you. You should let me go and forget you've ever seen me."

"No."

"Yes. You know I'm right. Deep down, where it counts. Let me go. Before it's too late. . . ."

Books by Lisa Bingham

Silken Dreams
Eden Creek
Distant Thunder
Temptation's Kiss
The Bengal Rubies
Silken Promises
Sweet Dalliance

Published by POCKET BOOKS

For orders other than by individual consumers, Pocket Books grants a discount on the purchase of **10 or more** copies of single titles for special markets or premium use. For further details, please write to the Vice-President of Special Markets, Pocket Books, 1230 Avenue of the Americas, New York, NY 10020.

For information on how individual consumers can place orders, please write to Mail Order Department, Paramount Publishing, 200 Old Tappan Road, Old Tappan, NJ 07675.

LISA BINGHAM

POCKET BOOKS

New York   London   Toronto   Sydney   Tokyo   Singapore

This book is a work of fiction. Names, characters, places and incidents are products of the author's imagination or are used fictitiously. Any resemblance to actual events or locales or persons, living or dead, is entirely coincidental.

An *Original* Publication of POCKET BOOKS

POCKET BOOKS, a division of Simon & Schuster Inc.
1230 Avenue of the Americas, New York, NY 10020

ISBN 978-1-4767-1573-5

This Pocket Books paperback printing September 2004

10 9 8 7 6 5 4 3 2 1

POCKET and colophon are registered trademarks of Simon & Schuster Inc.

Cover art by Bill Dodge

Printed in the U.S.A.

To the survivors
and the fighters
who never cease
to inspire me:
Nancy,
Danice, Lyn, Sherilyn,
Shirleen.
And to my favorite critic,
Caroline.

.

Prologue

Mississippi
March 1864

Thunder crashed overhead, a simultaneous burst of lightning streaking to earth. In an instant, stinging shards of rain pelted the already saturated ground, cutting visibility to mere inches.

Peering up into the darkness, Micah St. Charles held a hand over his eyes and squinted at the blacker outline of the train trestle. Because of the deluge, it was difficult to see what progress had been made. Emergency repairs had been completed throughout the night and into the dawn in the hope that the way could be cleared for a supply train which would be arriving at five. The shipment had to get through.

"Captain!"

The shout barely pierced the din, but Micah had become so attuned to any noise that was out of place amid the hammering and pounding that he immediately sought its source. Turning, he lifted an arm over his head so that the soldier on the upper bank could distinguish him from the other muddy figures who worked to reinforce the supports.

Nodding to show he'd seen the gesture, the soldier scrambled down the hill. Mud slides and erosion had left very few handholds, and he all but skidded to a stop, waving his arms madly as he tried to keep his balance.

"What is it, Wheeze?" Micah demanded. "You're supposed to be at your post."

"Cap-tain!" The sentry could barely speak, he was so winded from the difficult climb down the bank. Long ago the men had given him the nickname of Wheeze since he'd taken a bullet in the lung. It was Micah who'd found him in the bushes and carried him to safety on that distant day. Since then Wheeze had been his constant companion, a sort of gruff-mannered, grizzle-haired watchdog.

Pressing a hand to his ribs, Wheeze gasped, "Captain, you've got to come. Quick!"

Micah absorbed the blank terror in Wheeze's eyes, one he'd seen only a few times before. It caused him to halt what he was doing and give the older man his full attention.

Wheeze's chin trembled as he struggled to control his erratic breathing enough to communicate. "Captain . . . there's a dozen men here who say . . . they've been sent directly from General . . . Bushing. They tell me they've been ordered to search . . . the premises for . . . spies."

Micah blinked against the rain, sure he couldn't have heard the words correctly. "What?" he shouted into the wind.

"Spies! They're looking . . . for spies!"

"Spies?" he echoed in disbelief. "Damn it all to hell, we haven't got time for their games of hide-and-seek. Can't they see for themselves that we're working hard and fast on the Union's behalf?"

Wheeze tried to answer, but Micah waved aside the

2

protest. "Never mind. They can wait. We've got to get this trestle finished. The train will be here any minute."

When Micah would have turned away, Wheeze grabbed his arm. "Captain," he said hesitantly, his voice softer this time, nearly drowned out by the storm. "Captain, they say they have proof."

"Proof? Proof of what?" he demanded impatiently. When Wheeze didn't immediately answer, a shiver of unease trickled down Micah's spine, mingling with the icy rain that soaked his uniform.

"That you . . . that you've . . ." Wheeze pressed his lips together then blurted, "Profiteering. Treason."

The words alone caused Micah to grow still, cold. As the war had progressed, idle gossip about informants and spies had quickly developed into suspicion, and suspicion into near hysteria. Evidently Micah was to be the next target of concern.

He didn't need to know what had fueled the allegations. The war had been trudging on for far too long. Supplies and tempers were growing short. Since Micah's unit had developed a reputation for completing impossible jobs successfully, his men were about to suffer for their resourcefulness. It didn't matter that their squad had continually been sent behind enemy lines and had been able to steal some of what they needed. It didn't matter that Micah had connections with a supply officer in Washington—a former classmate at West Point—who routed shipments his way every now and again. Because Micah and his men had what they needed, someone must have decided the man in charge of the squad was part of a profiteering ring. That man was Micah.

By now Wheeze had caught his breath. "You've got to come and talk to them, Captain. They won't wait. They told me that if you don't come right away, they'll haul all of us in for questioning."

"Dammit!" Micah bit back another string of expletives and threw a jagged plank into the mud, ignoring the splash of grime that splattered onto his already filthy uniform. "Continue on here!" he instructed the rest of the crew.

"What about the train?" one man shouted from a brace halfway up the structure.

"Let it pass over the bridge. It should hold. Hutcher!" he shouted to a stooped soldier on the top of the bank. "Light the signal lantern to inform the engineer that it's safe to go ahead. The rest of you, secure your repairs then get onto level ground. Judging by our earlier estimates, we've got less than five minutes until that shipment arrives."

Although time was ticking against him and his men, Micah felt sure that they had reinforced enough of the beams so the train could cross without incident. After that, they could worry about securing the bridge for future travel.

"All right, Wheeze," he growled, shoving the handle of his hammer into the waist of his pants. "Where's the fool who thinks I'm a profiteering son of a bitch?" He scrambled up the bank, his fury giving him more speed than Wheeze had displayed in coming down. "Who in *hell* does he think he is, and what proof does he think he has against . . . me . . . ?"

The words trailed into the turbulence of the storm as he searched through the rain, beyond the gloom, and located his accuser. Ezra Bean.

The chill Micah had felt a moment ago sank deeper into his bones, becoming more than a vague premonition of danger. Wheeze had been correct in feeling a certain amount of fear. The man Micah confronted now was the only person on earth who had ever looked at him with open, violent hate. Not even in battle had Micah experienced such potent antipathy from another person.

Ezra had not dismounted. He was still seated on a dun-colored mare, probably because he felt that abandoning the saddle could have been interpreted as a gesture of respect. The rain pounded on his shoulders and the crown of his hat, spilling over the brim and down his back, but if he felt any discomfort, he did not allow such petty concerns

4

to show. He remained motionless, silent, allowing Micah plenty of time to absorb the overt contempt that gleamed from the man's eyes.

Not willing to give Bean any more of an advantage than the element of surprise he had already employed, Micah dug his heels a little more firmly into the mud. Bean would have to meet him at least halfway.

"What do you want, Ezra?" he demanded, shouting loud enough to be heard by those who stood a good twenty yards away.

Bean's lips twitched ever so slightly, as if he knew the reason behind Micah's ploy, but he didn't comment. Nudging his horse, he approached, motioning for the half dozen men who had accompanied him to wait near the cluster of deserted tents. By their carefully schooled expressions, Micah supposed that Bean ran his soldiers with the same strict discipline he had employed with his family. One that bordered on cruelty.

"I am here on an official errand," the man finally said.

"Last I heard, your brigade was stationed in Pennsylvania. What are you doing so far south?"

Bean ignored him, refusing to explain.

"Don't tell me you're lost," Micah scoffed, knowing he was treading on dangerous ground. If there was one thing Bean had always prided himself on, it was his attention to detail, his scheming. The same qualities that had made him the wealthy owner of the B&B Iron Foundries in Ohio.

"No, *sir*," Bean stated deliberately, contemptuously. "I know exactly where I am." He paused significantly before finishing, "Just as I know exactly what kind of man I'm addressing."

"State your business, Bean," Micah said, suddenly weary of the verbal sparring. He had work to do. He didn't have time for Bean's games. "My man said something about an investigation directed at me."

Bean's jaw hardened, his pale gray eyes growing flint-hard. "An investigation that should have started the night you killed my daughter," he said, his voice so low that no one but Micah could hear.

So that was it. Micah sighed, raking his fingers through his mud-matted hair. "We went through all of this the last time I saw you." The subject was still too painful to talk about. His wife. Lili. Ezra's daughter. Her death.

"You stole her from me, damn your hide."

"She came willingly."

"She was my child."

"Good hell, man! She was nearly twenty-three! Old enough to make her own decisions."

"She belonged with *me*. She never should have left home for that fancy school back east, nor should she have stayed to teach. She never should have consorted with your kind. She never should have died."

Micah tried to take a breath to ease the invisible fist that clamped tighter and tighter over his heart with each word the man spoke. "I did everything I could."

"You *killed* her!" Bean quickly lowered his voice when his horse pranced skittishly at the outburst. "You killed her as surely as if you'd wrapped your fingers around her throat."

"She died of diphtheria," Micah said wearily. He'd explained Lili's death time and time again. He'd sent Ezra a telegram in those winter months before the war. He'd written a detailed letter describing the circumstances of her illness. He'd spoken of it to Bean just after Manassas and again after Shiloh. Each time, the man had grown more bitter, more accusatory. How much more caustic would he become if he knew the whole truth? That Lili had been six months pregnant when she died.

"You will pay for your crimes, Micah St. Charles."

Micah's hands balled into fists in sheer frustration. "She died, Bean. She died of a disease that could not have been prevented or cured. There was nothing that could have been done."

"Liar." If possible, Bean's posture became even stiffer. "You will pay. Beginning today, you will pay." His voice rose to a level that could be heard over the storm. "Micah Asherby St. Charles, you are hereby charged with profiteering and treason by order of General Albert Bushing. I have been instructed to take you into custody and escort you to Fulton Hill prison where you will be court-martialed. If you are found guilty, you will be hanged."

The distant pant of a locomotive filtered into the air, but only a small portion of Micah's brain acknowledged the fact. He wanted to brush off Bean's accusations as trivial, return to his work, assess future repairs, but he knew that it would be a mistake to turn his back on Bean now.

"Treason?" he asked mockingly. Not even Bean would go so far as to think he could make such charges stick. "No one will believe you if you make such a claim. I'm a decorated soldier of the Union army."

Ezra merely smiled. A humorless smile. "I have witnesses. Proof."

"Like hell. I—"

"Look out!"

"Jump!"

The shouts came from the trestle. The roar of the locomotive increased, thundering against the bluff but not completely drowning out an ominous whoosh of air. Then the morning was rent by a huge blast.

Micah was thrown onto the muddy ground. Beams and broken timbers showered over him. The screams of injured men were joined by the low huffing of a train that was coming too fast to stop in time. Micah covered his head with his hands as the screech of metal on metal filled the air. Then, forcing himself to look over his shoulder, he saw the trestle collapsing and the boxcars piling horribly one on top of the other in the riverbed. The bodies. His men.

Then there was silence, an awful silence. It stretched on for an eternity before he heard the *thwuck, thwuck* of a

7

horse's hooves picking through the mud. At long last they too were quiet, and Micah looked up, up, up, into the icy eyes of his father-in-law.

"Get up," Bean ordered harshly.

Behind them the shouts began from deep in the river gorge. The moans of pain.

Micah struggled to push himself upright, seeing the man's rabid hatred was directed at him. Bean had never accepted him. Not since his daughter had dared to run away from the school where she taught and marry a plantation owner's son. A St. Charles. She had disobeyed her father's orders, then had intensified that disobedience by dying before Ezra could punish her for her supposed sins.

Rising, Micah glanced from the wreckage to his father-in-law. He could not ignore the slight twitch of satisfaction that tugged at the man's lips.

Then the significance of the explosion dawned on him. "What have you done, Bean?" Micah whispered, knowing that the horrible damage had been deliberate, planned, the result of several carefully placed explosives.

Ezra made a *tsk*ing sound with his tongue. "I suppose this disaster is evidence of yet another of your crimes," he said, waving an arm to indicate the wanton waste. "Willful destruction of Union supplies. In my report I'll have to tell General Bushing that you blew the trestle up yourself. That you intended to sell the damaged goods to the enemy at an inflated price. That train was carrying food and medical supplies, you know. Its cargo was worth a fortune."

"Good hell almighty! No one will believe you!" But even as he uttered the words, Micah feared he might be wrong. Bean wasn't a man to gamble if he didn't think he could win. *"You* were the one who arranged this mess, weren't you, Bean? Which of my men agreed to do your dirty work?"

Bean ignored him, patting his saddlebags. "There's no need to point the finger at your subordinates. I have all the necessary documentation here to prove you are solely responsible. You can protest the charges if you wish, but your fate is sealed. After all, who would dare to trust you? A traitor to the beloved Union? A former slave owner masquerading in the federal army? A murderer." His voice dropped to a feral whisper. "Your only hope is a swift death."

Bean motioned to the soldiers around him. "Apprehend this man! Tie him up and gag him firmly. I won't have him spreading his talk and influencing our gallant boys with his lies. Come morning, we'll take him to Fulton Hill Prison where they can proceed with his court-martial. By the end of the week he'll be executed."

"No!"

The shout came from Wheeze, who had remained nearby during the interchange. He ran forward.

"No! He hasn't done anything wrong! He's our captain, don't you see? He's our captain!" The older man whipped his revolver from his holster. "I won't let you take him like this. I won't!" Coming to a stop only a few feet away, he lifted both arms, grasping the weapon firmly in his hands. "Run, Captain! Run!" he shouted.

Then he began to fire.

Chapter

1

Ohio
September 1865

I think he's dead. . . ."

"Can't be dead. He's breathing."

"Not so you could notice."

"Doesn't matter if you can notice it or not. All that matters is that he's breathing."

"Hmm . . ."

"Poke him."

"You poke him."

"It's your turn."

"Is not!"

"What's the matter? Are you scared?"

Micah blinked, his brow creasing in confusion when he attempted to focus his bleary eyes. Good hell almighty, his head ached. And his throat. He tried to swallow, but a dry scratchiness prevented the action. His tongue filled his mouth like a ball of cotton.

A scuffling occurred behind him, a host of guilty whispers.

"Look what you did!"

"Not me!"

Summoning the scattered wisps of thought and action that clung to his brain, Micah braced his hands beneath him. He had to get up. He had to get away. He couldn't stay now that he'd been found. He couldn't—

A childish scream pierced the air, stabbing through his brain and causing his head to pound. Moaning, he collapsed against the straw, covering his ears.

The squeals erupted again, followed by the mad rush of feet, the thump of boots on wood, then a woman's faint calls.

Micah could have ignored it all. He could have purposely forgotten that his location had been compromised. He could have avoided any sort of worry or unpleasantness and concentrated on the soft straw beneath his stomach, the sweet warmth that shrouded him, if it hadn't been for the fragment of a phrase that floated through the air: ". . . a man . . . there . . ."

His eyes popped open. This time more of his faculties managed to cooperate, testifying to the seriousness of his predicament. He remembered riding through a midnight storm, topping the rise alongside a riverbed and seeing a house, a barn, and the remains of a bridge shrouded in the murky drizzle.

The thought of finding rest in a place that was relatively warm and dry had been too much for Micah's tired bones to resist. He'd been worried that he might be experiencing a relapse into the sickness he'd caught the previous winter. One that recurred every month or so, bringing chills and aching bones, fever and sometimes delirium.

Hoping to ward off as much of the illness as possible, he'd tethered his horse in the woods and bedded the animal within the shelter of a bower of trees. He hadn't dared bring the mare into the barn for fear that her nervous snorting would cause him to be discovered, so he'd hidden her as best as he could, then crept into the yard and slipped through the shadows of the barn up into the dusty loft. He'd planned to sleep an hour, maybe two, allow his clothes to dry somewhat, and be on his way again. To hunt for Bean.

He closed his eyes again in pain. Dear sweet heaven above, when would the man be satisfied? For over a year now Micah had been listed as a wanted man, hunted not only by the North, whose officers wanted to hang him, but also by the South, whose generals believed the accusations and wanted to grill him for military information. He'd spent the war dodging from battalion to battalion in the confusion of battle, hoping to escape detection. Even at war's end, there had been no relief. The charge of treason was not about to be dropped merely because the fighting had ceased. But Bean had not been satisfied with making Micah's life an unending hell. He'd wanted more. So much more.

The emotional pain intensified, becoming almost unbearable as Micah remembered what else the man had done. Barely a week ago Micah had dared return to his birthplace, Solitude—just for an hour or two, to see how his brothers had fared. Bram and Jackson had long since left to fight in the war. In their absence, the house and its outbuildings had been ravaged, the land desecrated, the family fortune stolen. The caretaker had been given a message to relay to Micah and Micah alone: Bean was responsible, he and his squad. Micah knew that the destruction was the man's way of flushing him out of hiding, of forcing a confrontation. And by damn, Micah was more than willing to oblige him.

". . . utter nonsense . . . what man?"

The half-heard reply shot through him, infusing Micah's limbs with enough strength to help him rise to his knees. Ignoring the thud of his pulse against his temples, he staggered upright.

"If you're telling tales again, I'll thrash you within an inch of your life!"

Thump.

The sound of a foot being planted on the ladder caused Micah to whirl, then grip his skull as a lashing pain struck his eyeballs.

"I told you before what happens to little boys who don't tell the truth."

Thump.

Micah became acutely conscious of his surroundings. The crushed straw, the saddle and tack he'd brought with him, his clothes, his . . .

His *clothes?* Blast it all, where were his clothes? All he had on was a pair of underdrawers.

Thump.

He gazed about him in panic, but the faded army trousers, shirt, vest, and duster that he'd carefully laid out to dry were nowhere to be seen. Rushing toward his saddle and bedroll, he began to kick hay over them, hoping to hide them well enough so that they wouldn't be stolen.

Thump.

Dammit! Straightening abruptly, Micah whacked his head against the low center support beam. The sound echoed hollowly through the barn.

The regular cadence of footsteps paused. When she spoke again, the woman's voice was low. "Lewis, go into the tack room and get a rope, then wait here until I call. Clark? I want you to head into the house. Now. Take Oscar with you, do you hear? Then send Crockett to meet us in the barn."

"But, E-*liz*-abeth"

"Now!"

The stamp of childish feet retreated, followed by a distinct and measured snap. Micah had spent enough time in battle to recognize that sound—the stealthy click of a firearm being cocked.

Thump.

"Put your hands up!"

The order came long before Micah saw anyone, but he sensed the beginnings of a shadow bleeding into the wall above the loft's trap opening.

"Put them up, I say!"

Micah searched around him in consternation, not knowing how the woman could tell he hadn't moved. But he was reluctant to lift his hands from where they were cupped to shield his privates. His underwear covered him from neck to calf, but the fabric was old and gaped at the slightest movement.

"Damn you! Are you deaf?" The taut demand was followed by a woman's head appearing through the hole in the floor, then the shiny muzzle of a revolver.

Micah froze, his eyes widening in surprise. It was a *young* woman. A pretty one.

Something in his expression must have softened and given a clue to his thoughts because she became completely still. For several minutes there were no sounds as Micah studied the girl and she measured him with evident suspicion. Then she eased up another step, every inch of her stance reflecting the way she'd grown more cautious, more determined, and more angry.

He'd survived the war and a manhunt because he knew when to advance, when to retreat, and when to burrow into a hole and wait. He'd also learned to read a man's character and know immediately whether or not the person sighting down the barrel of a gun really meant to shoot him.

This woman, he knew, would pull the trigger at the first sign of trouble. A clear gleam of fury ignited the dark brown of her eyes with a spark of gold. Her gaze became intent, as if she could see right through him.

"Blast it all, I can see I'm going to have to get myself a dog," she muttered to herself.

Micah wasn't sure what she meant—unless she was referring to the way he'd managed to slip into her loft without anyone being the wiser.

She scrutinized his frame from top to toe, all without saying a thing, her face a perfect mask, completely blank of surprise or fear. Micah became abruptly conscious of his attire—or lack of it. He waited for some show of shock, the reddening of her cheeks, a catch to her breath.

Such a sign of weakness never came, but at least she didn't insist he raise his hands again.

She would have made a wonderful gambler, this woman. As she pulled herself the rest of the way into the loft, Micah had no hint of her thoughts. Not even so much as a grimace crossed her well-defined features. Indeed, had he not seen the way she'd paused upon her first sight of him, he would have thought she'd known she would find him dressed in little more than his drawers.

"I suppose—" Micah began, then stopped and cleared his throat. He didn't know what he should say—or if he should say anything at all. He'd been caught sleeping uninvited in this woman's barn, he'd frightened her children, and now stood before her in a most indelicate state. How could he even begin to explain?

"They stole my clothes!" Micah hadn't intended his first statement to be an accusation, but the words burst free before he could prevent them.

"I don't doubt it a bit." The woman's lashes narrowed thoughtfully over coffee brown eyes. Her hair was the color of rich aged honey and had been pulled back into a hasty knot.

An awkward silence ensued, one in which Micah devoutly wished he'd had the sense to cover his groin with something more substantial than his hands—his saddlebags, horse blanket, anything.

She crept closer, the gun still held at the ready. With each step she took, Micah became infinitely conscious that it had

16

been a long time since he'd been this near to a woman. His eyes kept straying to the beads of perspiration that clung to her throat, the way the homespun blouse she wore was draped across the contours of her breasts. He quickly noted the small span of her waist, the swell of her hips beneath the too-short skirt, and the cotton hose that covered her ankles, which flashed into view whenever she moved.

She wasn't a tiny woman like Lili. She gave an impression of height and stature, voluptuous curves. But judging by the fit of her clothes and the small span of her waist, there wasn't an ounce of spare flesh on her. This was a female accustomed to hard work, but looking at her now, he was quite sure that she couldn't have earned more than a score of years.

"What are you doing in my barn, mister?"

Had she known how much her question revealed, she probably wouldn't have asked it. Micah was immediately intrigued by the fact that she hadn't demanded his name or an explanation for his manner of dress. Instead, she'd asked what he was doing in *her* barn.

"You're alone here, ma'am?"

He'd said the wrong thing, putting her even more on guard. She held the revolver a scant half foot in front of him, aiming for the spot right between his eyes. "You might think this gun is an idle threat . . . but you're wrong."

The deadly intent behind her words was unmistakable, but Micah couldn't resist asking, "You'd shoot me?"

"In a heartbeat." She stamped on the floor with the heel of her shoe. "Lewis!"

"Yes?"

"Is Crockett here yet?"

"He's just coming."

"Tell him to bring that rope up here. Then round everybody up and meet us in the parlor."

"Yes, ma'am."

Within minutes, a young boy with a thatch of curly brown

hair scrambled up the ladder and took his place beside her. There was a marked similarity to their features; clearly they must be brother and sister.

"Tie him up, Crockett."

"Who is he?"

"Just tie him up!"

The boy shrugged. "Yes, Lizzy."

Lizzy.

The boy named Crockett moved to do as he'd been asked. Realizing that he was about to be trussed up like a goose, Micah hurriedly said, "If you'd wait a minute, I'd be happy to explain—"

"I don't want to hear your lies." Her lips pursed in open contempt. "What's the matter? Did they abandon you? Did you fall off your horse and get stuck in the mud? Or did they decide they didn't want you riding with them?"

" 'They' who?"

"Union thugs. Your *friends.*" She fairly spat the word, her eyes blazing with a barely submerged fire. "They came *requisitioning* our supplies, just as they did at the other nearby farms. As far as I'm concerned, that's just a pretty word for stealing."

Micah opened his mouth to respond, then paused. Requisitioning? His heart beat a little more quickly. The war was over; there was no need for such measures anymore. Yet he'd heard that same story before, usually from those who'd had the bad luck to run into Ezra Bean and his men.

"When were they here?"

She made a sound of disgust. "As if you didn't know. Tighten those knots, Crockett! We can't have him getting loose."

The boy tugged on the loops he'd wound about Micah's wrists and chest, pinning his arms to his sides. The action caused him to gasp as the cords bit into his flesh.

"Good hell, if you'd just let me—"

18

She jerked the revolver ever so slightly to remind him of its threat. "Shut up."

"But I—"

"Shut up!"

Stomping toward him, she used her free hand to whip a rag from her pocket and shove it into his mouth as a makeshift gag. He grimaced when he caught the faint taste of soap—and something more. Something distinctly unpleasant and oily. The whiff of horse liniment that wafted to his nostrils made him blink. His tongue began to burn.

The woman planted her feet mere inches from his own and dug the revolver into his stomach.

"You should have run when you had the chance. As it is now, you're on my property, in my barn. And I've just requisitioned *you* for a little labor on *my* behalf."

Chapter

The woman led him through the muddy yard, all the time holding him in her sights. He could feel each step she took behind him, the hairs at the back of his neck prickling from the intensity of her stare. Her attitude was yet another result of war, he supposed. What else could have made this woman so suspicious? So . . . hard? She was far too young to have such old, wary eyes.

"Up those steps."

Micah did as he was told without argument. Partly because of the presence of the revolver, but partly because he felt a curiosity build within him.

There was something strange about this house, this yard. He hadn't sensed it the night before. The rain and the blackness had left very little room for investigation. But now the sunlight streamed down, revealing the ruin and decay that should not have been there. True, Ohio had been involved in the war, its men had left, its women had been forced to cope. But there was something about this place that was almost . . . haunting.

Yes, that was the word. Haunting. Evidence of a successful farm surrounded him, fairly pummeled him with all the little details he'd taken for granted in some of the surrounding towns. There were outbuildings, fields, stables, chicken coops, and storage compartments. But even though this family obviously lived here—had probably lived here for years—the land had an air of abandonment. As if its spirit had been beaten into the dust.

The thought caused him to stumble and he stopped, his scrutiny growing intense. Although the farm didn't reek of the obvious damage he'd seen at Solitude, his own home in Virginia, the silence was palpable, the desperation tangible. He could see the remains of a broken bridge that hung like a skeleton across the water. The barn where he'd hidden was devoid of life, of the most common repairs. The outbuildings appeared unused.

Even the main house glowered down upon Micah in disapproval. He could tell by the simple architecture, the wide wraparound porch, and multipaned windows, that this had once been a grand place, but it had fallen into even more disrepair than the rest of the buildings. The porch steps were rickety and crooked, the small upper windows dirty and partially boarded shut so that they stared his way like mean narrowed eyes.

"Stop your gawking and get inside."

Micah turned ever so slightly, catching what he thought was a glimmer of embarrassment in the woman's gaze, a sheen of defiance, as if she'd guessed his thoughts and felt the need to explain herself.

If that was the case, she resisted the urge with great success. Prodding him with the muzzle of the revolver, she reminded him again who had the upper hand in this affair, and since he was dressed in nothing but his underwear and trussed up like a holiday package, there wasn't a good deal he could do except cooperate. Not yet.

Following her tacit commands, he moved up the steps, picking his way gingerly around the gaps in the boards and the rough slivers that threatened to pierce his feet. At the entrance he paused, waiting for Crockett to open the huge door with its frosted glass inset, an incongruous reminder of better times. As he passed inside, he caught a glimpse of a wooden sign leaning against the porch wall. It had once been elaborately painted but was now faded and worn. It read simply: Wilder's Ferry Landing and Inn. The board had been tucked behind a rickety rocker, one of several placed side by side on the porch.

"Watch your step as you go inside," the woman ordered. "There's valuables about, and I don't want you breaking anything."

Micah couldn't help shooting her a quick disbelieving glance. As if one broken item would matter anymore. The place—an old inn and stage stop if the sign was accurate— had long since gone beyond any need for concern over the condition of a few vases. Prospective customers would take one look at the outside of the buildings and run for cover long before they discovered he'd damaged anything inside.

But Micah said nothing. He was too busy looking, assessing, studying. It had been his manner for the past year to look at the world around him with suspicion and calculated care.

From the porch he was ushered into a dull, ominously dark entry. An oak floor, bare of most of its polish, extended to a scarred staircase and a worn scarlet runner. A cramped hall led past the steps to the interior of the house, but most of the space was taken up by a huge, dusty, moth-eaten stuffed bear.

Micah's eyes widened in disbelief. The animal—for it had obviously been a real animal—must have been a fearsome foe for whoever had killed it. True it stood on a carved wooden pedestal of sorts, but even without the base, the bear would have measured well over eight feet tall on its hind legs.

"My pa shot that," Crockett said, grinning.

Lizzy merely poked him again with the gun. "In there," she said, gesturing to his right and pulling open a door to allow him to see the room beyond. "That's the sitting room. Once you're inside, I want *you* to sit too, nice and easy."

Micah moved slowly, still trying to take in his surroundings, still feeling an unaccountable puzzlement, as if all was not as it should be and he would be wise to remember that.

The parlor was simple, small, and would have been quite elegant in its heyday. Now it appeared tired and sad, like an old woman stripped of any sort of artifice. Horsehair-covered settees and chairs cluttered the space. Tables were layered in dust and had been left to rot quite visibly in the heat of the airless room. Mice had nibbled on the tattered antimacassars and faded piano shawls. The windows were obscured by dirty lace curtains and faded brocade portieres, while the brittle remains of potted ferns stood as silent sentinels on tarnished brass stands.

His hostess pushed him into a chair, causing a puff of dust to form a cloud around his head. She removed his gag, then backed away, allowing Micah a moment to get his bearings and study his adversaries.

There were eight of them in all. The woman, Lizzy, was by far the oldest of the bunch, and much like the house, there was something about her that was out of place and . . . hollow. Yes, it was there in the eyes, in the absence of feminine coquettishness and flirtation. In the way she regarded him as an enemy, not as a possible conquest. It was not the sort of reaction Micah was used to receiving from women as pretty as she.

As for the boys, they were a motley assortment. Micah guessed they ranged in age from about five to nearly seventeen. Crockett, the boy who'd tied him up, was obviously the eldest male. Another lad, the next in line, had dark curly hair and black shoe-button eyes that blinked at him from behind incredibly thick spectacles; Micah estimated his age at close to sixteen. Then there was a boy with blackened britches and a bandage wrapped around his hand who looked about fourteen, a pair of bright-eyed identical twins wearing what looked like loincloths and war paint, another fellow about nine who carried a bulging sack, and a young boy of about five who clutched a worn rag rabbit and stared at Micah as if he might jump up and murder them all.

"Is this some kind of orphanage or home for boys?"

Lizzy scowled in annoyance. "Just keep that mouth shut or I'll be putting the gag back," she said.

Crockett nudged her in the arm. "Who is he?"

"We found him in the loft," one of the twins volunteered.

"We think he's a spy."

A distinctly predatory gleam entered the twins' eyes.

"We were the ones to discover him."

"Sleeping."

"In the straw."

"Just like an enemy patrol."

"Or a Comanche war chief lying in wait."

They began to creep toward him, one boy's hand tightening around a crude wooden tomahawk; the other twin wielded a spearlike stick.

"Now that he's tied up—"

"We could put twigs under him—"

"And light 'em—"

"Then scalp him—"

"Then—"

"Enough!" Lizzy stamped her foot and glared at the pair. "This is not one of your games. This is a *real* man. A *real* intruder! For all we know, he could be responsible for all the thieving and 'requisitioning' Mr. Ruthers reported on his last visit."

"But—"

"Hush up. Both of you. I need to think."

The room grew silent. Painfully so. Crockett stood with his feet braced apart, his arms folded, looking very adult, very menacing. The twins still held their weapons at the ready.

"We could torture him until he talks. Put matches under his—"

"Bridger! We'll have none of your bloodthirsty ideas either. My lands! I don't know where you and the twins get these things in your head."

Staring at them all in disbelief, Micah wondered what kind of asylum he'd stumbled into. The twins wanted to scalp him, Crockett obviously wanted to throttle him, and the boy named Bridger was ready to torture him until he gave them the answers they sought. He could only imagine what thoughts were brewing in the mind of the boy with the glasses or the youngster who held the rag rabbit in a death grip.

"We've got to tie him up."

"He's already tied up," Bridger scoffed. "I say we should—"

"Bridger! Quiet!"

"Yes, ma'am." But in Micah's opinion, the boy was far from cowed.

Lizzy's brow furrowed in concentration; then she turned to the oldest boy.

"Crockett, go get Mama's trunk. Bridger, fetch a length of chain from the barn and those old slave manacles Daddy hung on the wall."

Crockett disappeared again. The younger boy who'd wanted to torture Micah ran outside, his bare feet pounding against the boards of the porch.

"Boone, take Lewis, Clark, and Johnny into the bedroom until I call for you."

"But, Lizzy—"

"Do it!"

The boy with the spectacles nodded and shepherded the other children down the hall.

"Close the door!"

The soft thump of a lock bolting home was her answer.

Lizzy released her breath in a whoosh, then inched toward him. "Stand up, thief."

"I told you I'm not a—"

"Stand up!"

Since Micah hoped he could improve her mood by complying with her demands, he did as he'd been told.

"Whatever you might think, I'm not a fool, mister."

"I didn't say you were."

Her mouth pursed in annoyance at his response, but she didn't chide him. Instead, she dug the revolver into his ribs and muttered, "Don't move."

He wanted to make some sort of pithy reply, but the words died in his throat the moment her hand spread wide over his chest, testing, searching.

"What—"

"Just keep your mouth shut, you hear?"

As if he could say anything, as if he *wanted* to say anything. He was struck by the fact that this woman, this pretty, vital woman with the wary eyes had touched him, quite deliberately, quite intimately.

And she hadn't finished.

That same hand rubbed at his sternum, slipping ever so briefly beneath the wool of his underwear before backing away again and roaming down one side of his ribs then straying to the other side.

Micah stared at those fingers, those long, surprisingly supple fingers, and murmured, "What the hell?"

He'd disobeyed her, and a brief gleam of anger sparked deep in her eyes. "Don't take me for a fool. Just hold still and do as you're told. If you're carrying a weapon of any kind, I'll find it."

He had no idea what she meant by uttering such a statement—after all, what could he hide in a pair of baggy drawers?—but he was beyond caring overly much. For the first time since being found in the barn he was beginning to wonder if being caught might not have its advantages.

She looked up then and must have guessed a portion of his thoughts, because those eyes, those expressive eyes, grew an even darker brown, almost black. The hand that touched him trembled ever so slightly, then grew firm. Determined.

"You will not frighten me," she whispered so softly that he wondered if she'd really said the words at all or if he'd merely heard them echoing in his head. But then she said, "You will not weaken me," and he knew that what he'd heard had been real.

Never in his life had he experienced such a woman. He'd known her less than a quarter of an hour, yet here she was, touching him most intimately, watching him quite carefully, and he found himself intrigued by her boldness, her strength, even as he caught the far more gut-wrenching vulnerability that she couldn't completely hide.

As if daring him to think her weak, she ran her palm quite deliberately down his side, her fingers spread. At that point he noted the way her lips were unconsciously parted, moist. Her breath tickled him with its warmth. He could smell the ever so elusive scent of flowers on her skin and her hair.

He would have said something. He would have dared to break the silence, but at that very moment, boldly, so very boldly, she swept her hand around his back to cup his buttocks.

All thought scattered from Micah's head as the action caused her hips to press slightly against his thigh, the folds of her skirt to flatten against him.

Micah fought to maintain his composure. Dear heaven above, did this woman know what she was doing? Did she know what havoc she created through his body? For what possible reason? *What?* There were far simpler ways to

ensure that a man was unarmed than to sweep her hand—
that long, elegant hand—down the length of his body.

"Turn around."

He barely had the presence of mind to do as she asked.
She was causing him to remember things that he'd purposely purged from his brain the moment his dear Lili had been
lowered into the earth. He squeezed his eyes shut, but the
images came, fast and strong. A bed, rumpled linens.

A woman's breast.

When Lizzy made another sweeping investigation of the
opposite side of his body, his knees trembled. The ache in
his loins became nearly unbearable. His arousal was beyond
any attempt at concealment. The images in his head stole
his breath, becoming more powerful, more intense, shifting,
altering. Not a bedroom. A parlor. A rug. A fire.

His eyes sprang open in horror when he realized he was
beginning to imagine this room and . . .

That woman?

No.

No!

She stepped into his line of sight, and he prayed that she
couldn't read his mind. His mother had raised him to be a
gentleman. His father had taught him to keep all baser
thoughts buried beneath a layer of respectability. Females
were not to be exposed to a man's needs. Not even one who
held him at gunpoint and explored each hill and valley of his
body in great detail.

"You've no hidden weapons, I see." There was a slight
breathlessness to her statement. "At least, none that I can
find. Yet."

Had he imagined the wispiness of her tone? Had she
felt anything at all? There was no way to judge. No hint
of a blush tainted her cheeks; her eyes were curiously
guarded. But the hand that held the gun trembled ever so
slightly.

"If you'd asked, I would have told you I was unarmed."

"Why would I do that? Why would I believe anything you said? You've got your own secret purposes, I'm sure."

For one brief instant he thought her gaze flicked to a point below his waist, but he couldn't be sure. He didn't want to consider such a thing. The thought alone was more arousing than he could bear. It didn't matter that she was a stranger.

"Where are they, mister?"

"What?" The word was nearly indistinguishable as it rasped from his throat.

"Your weapons. You've got to have a private arsenal of some sort."

He shook his head, too dazed to talk, but she obviously didn't believe him. Fortunately for Micah and the blood that still rushed to parts of his body where it shouldn't, Crockett chose that moment to drag a heavy trunk into the room, making such a racket that no one could be heard for several minutes.

When he'd left the heavy wood and metal box by Micah's side, Lizzy nudged the boy with one hand. "Run back to the loft. Search the straw for guns—but be careful. If you find any, they're probably loaded."

Crockett's eyes grew dark and angry at that ominous possibility, but he hurried to do as he'd been told, leaving Micah and the woman alone.

She glared at him, seeming to dare him to do something rash so that she would have an excuse to shoot him, but Micah refused to offer her such a remedy. Indeed, he decided to test her control and sank slowly, deliberately, into the chair.

She wasn't pleased by the show of defiance, but she didn't make him stand again—a fact for which he was grateful. At least in the chair the fabric of his underwear wasn't as closely molded to his body and he could struggle to gather his control.

"You shouldn't have come back, you know," Lizzy said suddenly. "You shouldn't have taken our pig."

She waited for an answer, some confession of guilt, but even had he known what she was referring to, Micah wouldn't have been so foolish as to admit anything.

Her gait became a near-swagger as she circled the chair. Once back at the place where she'd started, she waved the revolver beneath his nose. "You must have thought we were fools, that we wouldn't have taken measures to protect ourselves from future 'requisitioning,' but we caught you unawares, didn't we?" When he didn't even grunt in response, she jabbed the gun into his ribs. "Didn't we?"

"Lizzy, I got it!" Bridger bounded into the room, carrying an armload of iron chains. The metal clanked and rattled as he skidded to a halt. At about the same time, Crockett thundered inside.

"He's got two revolvers, a rifle, and a bowie knife."

Micah could have sworn aloud. Until a week ago he'd been nearly out of ammunition. Then, mere miles from his home, he'd stumbled over the long-forgotten body of a fallen soldier and found the means to protect himself. In one instant he'd lost it all again.

Lizzy tipped her head in satisfaction. Whirling to face her captive, she pinched Micah's jaw with her thumb and forefinger, forcing his mouth to open wide enough for her to shove the gag in place. Then she turned to her brothers.

"Bridger, untangle those chains and bring them to me."

"Yes, ma'am." The reply sounded much too eager to Micah, given Bridger's earlier suggestions.

For the life of him, Micah couldn't fathom why they considered such equipment necessary, but in less than five minutes, he had his answer. His legs were quickly locked in the manacles, then attached to several lengths of chain. These in turn were padlocked in three separate places to the hardware of the trunk. Only when he was well and truly bound did Lizzy step forward to remove the gag.

He spat the bitter taste from his mouth and frowned. "Have you lost your ever-lovin' mind?"

"No, sir." She stabbed him in the chest with her finger. Since he was still bound by the rope as well as by a heavy chain, and shackled to a blasted trunk, there was no way to escape her poking. "I'm merely seeing to it that you pay for what you and your cohorts have taken."

"Cohorts? I'm a stranger to these parts."

She sniffed in disbelief. "That's what I'd expect you to say."

"Dammit, I rode in last night! Alone. It was raining. I looked for some sort of shelter and saw your barn and . . ." In an instant, Micah realized his mistake.

Her eyes narrowed in delight. "Bridger, I want you to scour the hillside. Find his horse."

"Lady, I—"

She shoved the gag into his mouth again. "There'll be no more talk from you. Not until we find your mount, not until we see what you've been doing in my loft, and *not*"—she shoved him again in the chest—"until I find out how many more of your friends are waiting to steal another of my animals!"

Chapter

3

Damn. *Damn, damn, damn!*

Lizzy stomped from the house, slamming the door behind her. Nearly tripping on one of the loose planks of the porch, she stopped, folded her arms under her breasts, and glared unseeingly at the muddy barnyard.

What in the blasted name of heaven was she supposed to do next?

After much scraping and grunting and sweating, they'd managed to drag the trunk into one of the storage rooms where they'd left the stranger lying on the floor. Then they'd abandoned him in the darkness of the boarded-up chamber. Lizzy had insisted on such measures, not just because it was the only place where they could keep him quiet, secure, and out of sight for the day, but because Lizzy had to think.

She wasn't a rash woman. She'd learned long ago the danger of making snap decisions, and this was definitely one time when every issue had to be carefully weighed. It was up to her to ensure the safety of her family, and in some way, keeping this man at their farm might serve as a twisted sort of protection. If she could hold him as her prisoner, she might, just might, be able to ward off another requisition strike, should it occur. Surely even that band of rogues and thieves wouldn't threaten one of their own kind. As soldiers, they must have a code of honor. She could use the man as a shield. A bit of insurance against the future demands by the unethical band.

But she had no guarantees.

Especially if they were the ones who had abandoned him here in the first place.

Blast. What was she supposed to do?

Lizzy stared into the yard. Dusk was quickly approaching. The sky was layered with a wisp of soot, causing the vibrant colors to be slightly muted and feathered at the edges. Tucking the revolver more securely into the waistband of her skirt, Lizzy left the porch, wandering aimlessly onto the front path.

This was her favorite time of the day. The younger boys were in bed, Crockett would soon send the older ones on their way. Evening chores were finished, the dishes were washed, and she had a few minutes to herself. She could take the time to grow calm, breathe deeply of the night air, relax . . . relax . . .

And weigh her alternatives carefully.

When she'd heard the boys' screams earlier, she hadn't really stopped to think about marching into the barn to confront their supposed intruder—she hadn't really believed there could be an honest reason for the boys' hysterics. The twins, Lewis and Clark, were prone to whooping and hollering and tearing about the yard as if the hounds of hell were after them. They would get Oscar and Bridger to join in and make even more noise. Having long since tired of their mysterious games, Lizzy tended to ignore the commotion.

She shook her head. Little had she known when she agreed to check the loft that she would be confronted by a tall—no, a *huge*—overgrown ox of a man wearing nothing but his underwear, sporting a thatch of wheat-colored hair and a scruffy beard littered with straw. If she'd had any warning at all that the threat of a stranger in their barn was real and not just a figment of the twins' vivid imaginations, she would have waited for some kind of help—or at least loaded her revolver with one of their two remaining bullets. She could only be grateful the stranger hadn't called her bluff.

So what was she going to *do?*

The question kept reverberating in her brain. Her hands balled into fists, relaxed, then tensed again. Not so much because of her predicament . . . as because, over and over again, she was tempted to bend this situation to her advantage.

Lizzy had tried to squelch the idea as soon as it came, but with each minute that passed it fed on itself, growing stronger and stronger until she couldn't ignore it. Great balls of fire, had she no shame? No caution? How could she even think of using this man—this soldier—in such a fashion? How could she even consider the possibility that his obvious brute strength could prove an asset?

She turned, staring at the shadowy reminders of all that had been, wondering when she had changed so much. Had the war done this to her? Had it made her so hard that she would think of her own kind first and others last?

Or had the brittle emptiness come because she'd thought to escape this place, journey into a land of privilege and excess as the bride to a man of consequence . . . only to discover, mere hours before her marriage, that politics had taken away her groom, her future, and all she had thought would occur?

Her jaw hardened and she turned resolutely toward the house. Her broken dreams didn't matter. Her place was here, her future was set, her aspirations simple.

She would see that her brothers were given the means to leave this place and make a life of their own elsewhere or to stay, as they wished.

Because it was a horrible thing when a person couldn't look to the future with any kind of longing.

"Lizzy?"

The childish voice startled her, she'd been so deep in her thoughts. Glancing up, she discovered that five-year-old Oscar had tentatively poked his head out the parlor window. When his sister didn't scold him for interrupting her thoughts, he crawled outside the narrow aperture onto the porch and approached her, leaning over the railing, the hem of his nightshirt flapping around his skinny legs.

"Liz, can I ask a question?"

Oscar's tone was so serious, so hesitant, that Lizzy forced herself to take a deep breath and relax her rigid stance. "Sure."

"Why'd you tie that man up to a trunk?"

Lizzy wasn't sure if she knew the answer to that question herself. Had she been warned of this predicament ahead of time, she wouldn't have dreamed of employing such methods. But when she'd climbed up to the loft and found a man—a no-good, scruffy, up-to-trouble man—she'd been overcome with fury. After all that those soldiers had done to their farm, she'd known she had to protect her family, and the only way to do that was to ensure that their prisoner was kept as immobile as possible. He wouldn't be put off for long by a woman holding a gun. The trunk had been the only thing she could think of that might prove unwieldy enough to prevent his escape and keep her family safe for a day or two. Yet, when she'd run her hands over his body, searching for weapons, she was shamed to the bone to admit that she hadn't been thinking of her brothers. She'd been unable to think of anything at all as a strange effervescence settled into her blood.

Dear heaven above, her own fiancé had never felt like that. Of course, he'd never allowed her to touch anything more than his elbow.

"Is he one of those soldiers that killed the pig?"

Oscar's sudden question pulled her mind back to the matter at hand, and Lizzy damned the way it hadn't come quickly enough to prevent a slight heat from seeping into her cheeks. "Yes. I'm sure he is."

The little boy rocked back on his heels. "Why'd he come back here? We haven't got any more pigs for him to kill."

Lizzy didn't know how to respond to that remark. No, they had no more pigs. Only a handful of chickens, a mule, and one temporarily missing goat were left.

As the silence grew thick, Oscar's eyes widened. "He hasn't come for the chickens, has he?" He didn't wait for an answer. "Damn him, I won't let him get them. I won't!"

Before Lizzy had a chance to catch him, he ran down the steps and into the barnyard. Lizzy suspected that he was heading for the grassy knoll behind the chicken coop, his own private place to think and play. He would stay there for an hour or two and ponder his problems.

If only life were that simple. If only Lizzy could lie in the grass, her head in her hands, believing that the solutions to life's dilemmas would come to her as if in a dream.

Sighing, she wondered when her own childhood had drizzled away, leaving her to wrestle with the troubles of adulthood. She had still been able to cling to the playful wisps of adolescence when her mama died in childbirth. She'd still clung to her youthful dreams the day her daddy brought his second wife home for her to meet. She'd been so excited. They were all going to be a family again—and so they were, for a few years. She'd been given a younger brother to play with, another and another, then the twins, then Johnny and little Oscar. As the only girl, Lizzy was assigned chores of her own, taught to read by lamplight, and shown how to run a line of stitches.

Then she'd met Bill Hutchinson and life had taken on an even rosier glow. The youngest son of a Baltimore merchant, he had come to Catesby to investigate the possibility of expanding their trade in the area. He and Lizzy had met, grown to care for each other, and made plans to marry. She'd been so excited, so filled with joy.

But that little world came crashing down around her ears in the winter of 'sixty-three. First—mere days before her fiancé was to journey back to Ohio for their wedding—word was sent that he had been killed by a sniper in Kentucky. Within a matter of weeks, her father had been drafted into the Union army. Not having the blood money to hire another to go in his place, he'd marched east, leaving Sally, Lizzy, and her younger brothers a farm, a broken-down inn, and a dilapidated toll bridge to run. Even so, they'd been able to eke out a modest sort of living until Sally had died in a fire at a fund-raising social in town. Life had grown more challenging without her step-mother's help. Lizzy could only pray that they would last until Pa returned and could help put the place to rights.

If he returned, a tiny voice whispered, and she silenced it immediately. She wouldn't think that. She couldn't. Even though, deep in her heart, she knew he wouldn't come back. It had been over a year since he'd been listed as missing. Two years. If he were alive, he would have sent word to them somehow.

Her lips pressed together. Damn the war—and damn all the trouble it had brought with it! The little valley she lived in had once felt like such a safe place, but in the past few months the area had become a sanctuary for thieves and deserters. The woods provided a haven for secret activities as well as game for hunting, and fresh, clear water. Whenever the outlaws got tired of that fare, they somehow found their way onto Wilder land. If they weren't enough of a problem, the Union squad that had been sent to the area was just as destructive. Just the day before, they'd returned again and taken two horses, a pig, a handful of chickens, and a goose—treasures indeed during times like these. Worst of all, Ruggles the nanny goat had turned up missing, and Lizzy suspected they'd stolen that animal as well. Since Ruggles had been with the family for a dozen years, Lewis, Clark, and Johnny were especially attached to her—indeed, she'd been more of a pet than a barn animal. Lizzy, fearing the loss would be a severe blow to them, had tried to convince them that Ruggles was only hiding, but her reassurances were wearing thin.

The front door squeaked open, and Crockett eased outside. Lizzy glanced his way, noting the too-long hair, the dusty cheeks, the patched and faded trousers held up to his bare, skinny torso with a pair of knotted suspenders. Sally Wilder would not have approved. Through all the years she'd lived on this Ohio farm, the woman had seen to it that her children were smartly dressed and the inn well tended while she remained as spry and pretty as a young girl. But Lizzy . . . she'd never developed a real knack for any of those things. Her spirit had always been too practical for such measures. In her opinion, if a war raged a few yards from a person's back door, what did it matter if all the mantels had been dusted? If there was no money for food, why spend what one didn't have on fancy clothing?

"So . . . what are we going to do, now we got him caught, Lizzy?" he asked, tucking his fingers beneath the worn leather braces. At seventeen, he was already far too old, far too wise. There should have still been a touch of fun in his manner.

Lizzy opened her mouth to lie to him, offer him some halfhearted reassurance, but the words wouldn't come. Crockett wouldn't be fooled by such measures to protect him from the truth.

"The twins said they found a blue uniform in the straw. Is he one of them soldiers that took the pig?"

"*Those* soldiers *who* took the pig," she automatically corrected. Her stepmother would have been appalled at the way the boys were swiftly losing what education she'd given them.

"Is he?"

"Well, I . . ." She nodded her head. "Yes. Yes, he is."

She could tell by the spark in Crockett's eyes that he didn't quite believe her.

"Do you *really* think he helped kill the pig?"

"It doesn't matter. He's part of that band. He did nothing to stop them when they came to loot us. He should pay for his crimes."

Crockett absorbed that statement in the slow, deliberate way he always did, as if he chewed and savored each word. Then he hugged the porch support with one arm, and scratched his neck. "How are you going to make him pay? I doubt he's got any money at all, judging by the state of his drawers."

"He can work off the price of a new sow."

"At market rate?"

"Market rate."

Crockett whistled under his breath. They both knew that the prices for beef and pork had skyrocketed as the need for food escalated.

"He'll be here for a while, then," Crockett remarked.

"As long as it takes."

"Why?" His brown eyes had the power to hold her where she stood. "Why keep him? You could turn him over to the troops in Catesby for trespassing."

"If he's part of the group that robbed us, he'd be out in a day." She sighed. "Besides, we need help, Crockett." She waved in the general direction of the farm. "We've done all we can alone. We *need* this man."

39

Crockett stared hard at her. "This has nothing to do with the pig at all, does it?" When she didn't respond, he added, "You're going to make him rebuild the bridge." It wasn't a question.

Until Crockett put the nebulous idea into words, she'd been afraid to admit her intentions to herself. Now they couldn't be denied. "We need the money it could bring. People will be moving west—much as they did fifteen years ago, I'd say. Not all of the travelers will be able to afford a train ticket."

She eyed the dilapidated toll bridge that had paid for the Wilder farm during the last land rush. The rickety boards spanned a crook of the Ohio River that lazed its way around the bend. The glassy surface effectively concealed the deep, treacherous currents that ran beneath. Lizzy had seen men and animals alike try to swim its murky depths only to be pulled under and lost without a trace.

When her father first built the bridge, it had been a godsend to folks in the area, and they'd been more than willing to part with a few coins to use it. It was the Wilders' only hope of restoring all that they had lost in the war. The nearest ferry landing was forty miles upstream, the nearest bridge sixty. Lizzy and Crockett could operate the old ferry for a time to haul wagons across the murky depths, but that was only a short-term solution.

"How do you plan on keeping that man here and making him work?" Crockett poked a thumb in the stranger's general direction.

"Any way I have to, Crockett." Her jaw grew hard. "Any way I have to." Then she marched toward the barn. As she closed the door behind her, she refused to admit that what she was about to attempt might not be completely moral—let alone feasible. No. It was time she banished all thoughts from her head except the most important of all.

Survival.

Chapter

Once in the barn, Lizzy climbed the ladder to the loft, gazing around her at the spot where this entire situation had begun. She wasn't really sure why she had gravitated here. A niggling detail was buried deep in her mind, and she couldn't quite bring it to the fore. She knew she was overlooking an important point. But what?

What?

Returning to the place where she had found the man was the only way to ease the nagging sensation. Lizzy could still see the impression of the stranger's body in the straw. It was easy to tell by the displacement of the piles where the man's weapons had been found, yet she saw no evidence of the clothes he must have been wearing at one time—not that she was surprised by such a thing; according to Crockett the twins were responsible for that. It would be their way of helping to protect her. If the man had nothing but his underwear, he wouldn't be going very far. Underwear . . .

Of course! He had to own more than one set of clothes. Even the most battle-weary soldier had an extra shirt or a spare pair of drawers. But if so, where had he hidden them? As far as she knew, the boys hadn't found any personal items.

In the corner Lizzy noticed the way some of the straw had been carelessly kicked into a pile, and she ran to the spot, pushing it aside to reveal a saddle and a set of leather bags. She knelt, pulling them close to her and running her fingers over the scuffed surface as if it could tell her everything she wanted to know. Within seconds, she paused. The cases were army issue. *Confederate* Army.

Lizzy froze. The man was a Reb? It wasn't possible. Not this far north. Her brow creased. His speech did have a certain languor, a certain unhurried elocution that many southerners had. Stars and garters! Had she captured herself a Rebel soldier? True, the war was over. But she'd seen enough of the restoration process to know that it would be some time before the sins of the war were forgotten. There were still brief skirmishes when factions of fanatical troops caught southerners isolated and unarmed. There were still bands of deserters roaming the countryside as well as thieves and refugees. It would be a long time before the average citizen felt safe again.

Was this man southern? she wondered again. To be honest, it didn't matter if he was from the North or the South. If he was a Union officer, he shouldn't have been a member of the group that had been stealing from their own kind. If he was southern . . . Well, if that was the case, she couldn't help thinking that her conscience might be salved a little for what she was about to do. After all, the South was responsible for starting the war, a war that had taken her father away when she'd needed him most.

Sure that the saddlebags would provide some clue to the

identity of the man in her storeroom, she delved inside. But the contents were disappointing: a few strips of dried beef, some slabs of hardtack, a nearly empty bottle of whiskey, a needle, a spool of thread, and a pocket-sized daguerreotype case that was worn and sweat-stained, as if he had kept it close to his body for some time.

Her fingers trembled ever so slightly as she picked up the hinged leather case. She knew that most soldiers carried photographs into battle. Many considered them a talisman against harm. What would this man carry, this big, brash giant?

Her thumb flicked the lock out of place. Slowly, almost afraid of what she might find, she opened the portfolio.

On the left-hand side was a group picture, probably of his family. An older man who could have been his father sat on a chair in the middle. To his left and right on the floor knelt two younger men who bore a remarkable resemblance to the man she'd found in her barn. Behind and slightly to the right of them stood her stranger. The picture must have been taken some time before the war broke out. He looked so much younger, softer . . . happier?

Her gaze drifted to the woman who was the subject of the picture on the right-hand side of the case. One finger traced the delicate form, the coronet of braids surrounding the ethereal features, the will-o'-the-wisp body, and the tiny feet peeking from beneath her skirts. Without rancor Lizzy realized that this woman was every man's dream and every woman's ideal. Just by looking at her, Lizzy knew she was the type who could create masterpieces with a needle and an embroidery hoop, who could pour tea without spilling a drop, who could calmly soothe a fevered brow. She was the sort that men adored, worshiped, the kind who inspired duels and reams of poetry. She was . . . beautiful. She was everything Lizzy had once hoped to be.

A strange sadness pierced Lizzy's heart. Sally had been that sort of woman. Although her stepmother had loved her without reserve, Lizzy had always known that Sally felt a certain amount of pity for girls like Lizzy. Those who couldn't quite tame their hair into the newest styles, who struggled with their sewing and had little talent in the kitchen. Lizzy had always been more interested in bookkeeping and organizing. Her dresses might have been of the finest lawn and lace, but they were often smudged with ink or traces of dust. She might have owned the proper trappings, but never in her life had she looked so . . .

Perfect.

Shoving the case into her pocket, she threw the saddlebags over her shoulder and stood. What did it matter that this man carried a picture of a woman with him? It was no concern of hers. Soon enough her bridge would be fixed, the man would be gone, and so would this unknown woman's picture.

But as she slipped into the house and tiptoed to her room, Lizzy decided not to tell her brothers about the picture. At least not until she'd had a chance to ask the man who this woman was, what she meant to him, and whether she was waiting for him to come home. Otherwise, her brothers might try to persuade her to let the soldier go.

The boys had long since gone to bed when Lizzy considered following through on her plans for a confrontation. She frowned a little when she heard the parlor clock strike ten. She knew it was awfully late for her to be prowling into the storeroom where the stranger had been locked up, but it had taken time for her to heat the flatirons and tidy up one of the few dresses she owned where the print had not been worn off at the hem and the cuffs. Then she'd had to comb her hair, carefully braid it, and secure it in a loose knot with a silver butter knife.

Twisting her head, she tried to see the effect in the mirror, but with no success. Normally she wouldn't have worried so about her appearance, about her hair, about the lack of hairpins, and about her wilted apron. But she wanted to look her best when she talked to the stranger again. Not out of vanity—heavens, no. She merely wanted to keep her air of authority, to make him see that although she lived in an isolated area, she was not completely without an appreciation of the finer things in life. She'd once worn satin and lace. She'd sipped tea from fine china cups, studied sewing and housekeeping. She hadn't completely let herself go.

Nodding to herself in the mirror to underscore that idea, she rushed to the door, paused, then returned to the bureau. A fine runner of crocheted lace was about the only remembrance she had of those days when the inn had been thriving and there had been the time and the money for feminine frippery. Hesitating only a moment, she pushed aside her comb and the broken hand mirror, grasping the bottle of French toilet water that had been a gift from her fiancé. When she removed the stopper, she was flooded with memories of how life had been before the war. The parties, the socials. Sleigh rides in the winter, hay rides in the summer. She'd had little else on her mind then but marrying well and escaping the drudgery of the Wilder ferry landing. Bill Hutchinson had promised to take her away from all that.

Now he was dead. Like so many men. So many boys.

Pursing her lips at her own foolishness in remembering dreams that were gone forever, she replaced the stopper and thrust the bottle back onto the lace runner. The time had come to get on with the business at hand.

As she stepped into the hall and made her way toward the back of the house, Lizzy knew she should be more cautious in talking with the man. Earlier, with the boys' help, they'd released the man of everything but a set of manacles chaining him to the bed. Even so, with his hands free, she should at least bring Crockett with her. But she didn't bother to call him. Not this time.

Detouring through the kitchen, Lizzy picked up the

scarred tray she had fixed earlier. It held a small kerosene lamp, a plate of bread, and a bowl. Ladling a full measure of soup into the bowl from the pot on the stove, she fussed over the arrangement of the spoon, the crockery, the linen napkin, then propped the tray against her hip and carried it to the room where the stranger was being kept.

She moved as quietly as possible, wanting to employ as much of an element of surprise as she could. Setting the tray on a hall table, she lifted the lamp with one hand, leaving the food where it was for a time. Then she carefully unfastened the padlock they'd fastened onto the storeroom door and tugged the revolver from the deep pocket of her apron.

The door swung open, creaking slightly. She winced a little at the sound, but she needn't have worried about startling the stranger. The man was awake, his eyes trained her way, brooding, dark, as if he had known for some time that she was coming to talk to him.

It was a little disconcerting to discover that he'd found her so predictable. She could only pray that he didn't see the slight heat that stung her cheeks or notice the way she'd primped for his benefit.

Needing to be the first to speak, she said briskly, "Good. You're awake."

He didn't respond to her statement. He merely continued to stare. His eyes looked slightly glassy, and his skin was beaded with sweat. She wondered if an escape attempt was at the root of his appearance, but he seemed curiously lethargic.

Lizzy set the lamp on a shelf near the door, then returned his gaze, refusing to be intimidated. But she couldn't deny, despite her bravado, that his unwavering scrutiny unsettled her; she felt as if he could interpret far too much with that glance.

She'd meant to speak to him calmly, rationally, but his whole manner put her on edge. Drat it all, how dare he? This man either was part of the group who had raided her home in the name of patriotism, taking most of their meager stores and leaving them to starve, or he was the enemy. A Rebel soldier. A traitor to his kind.

"Who are you?" The demand for information pushed itself free from her dry throat in a raspy whisper.

He didn't immediately respond. He sat on the floor, his back propped against a shelf support, one arm draped carelessly over a bent knee.

"I thought you'd already decided who I was," he stated, his tone dark and low. "As I recall, you accused me of being part of some sort of Union pig conspiracy."

Said in that manner, her earlier supposition sounded a bit preposterous. But he refused to acknowledge that she had a right to feel angry if he had really been one of the dozen men who had ridden into the yard—men who were obviously battle-hardened, determined, hungry. They'd handed her a document filled with words she couldn't understand, then had proceeded to strip the farm of almost anything they felt might be of value. They were federal soldiers, sworn to protect the families in the area, but instead of helping them, they had stolen their property with little or no regard for their welfare.

Lizzy's hand slipped into her apron, and she withdrew the daguerreotype case. Tossing it into his lap, she waited for his reaction.

He surprised her. She'd expected astonishment, perhaps a bit of defiance. But no. A strange gentleness settled over his features. His thumb traced the case with a simple tenderness. Then he tucked it inside his underwear next to his hipbone as if that was the only place he could think to keep it where it would not be misplaced again.

"Thank you."

Lizzy stiffened. She didn't want his thanks. She hadn't wanted him to react this way at all. She wanted him to fight, to argue, to protest, anything that would keep her in a position of control.

LISA BINGHAM

"Who is she?"

The question popped free of its own accord.

He didn't answer, but there seemed to be an odd sparkle to his eyes, as if he were secretly amused. She could only pray that the lamplight was responsible for such a phenomenon.

"Are you hungry?" she asked, then could have kicked herself for voicing her concern. Every time she opened her mouth, she sounded less like a captor and more like an uncomfortable hostess.

Not waiting for his answer, she retrieved the tray and set it on the floor a few feet away from him, then backed away again as if he were a strange dog one of the boys had brought home.

One of his brows rose. "Are you that afraid of me?"

She couldn't answer. She wouldn't. He was taking control again.

"Eat."

He didn't seem inclined to argue with her—or even to balk at the command. In fact, after pulling the tray closer with inestimable slowness, he took one look at the thick slices of bread and the chunks of vegetables in the soup, and laid the tray on his lap with a certain eagerness. The way he started to eat—like a starving man—made a pang of something akin to sympathy pierce her chest.

"When was the last time you ate?" Drat it all? Why had she asked? His comfort didn't concern her.

To her further consternation, he answered quietly, openly. "I've had nothing but what I could find along my travels. I can't remember the last time I had real food."

"Which army?"

He paused in the act of stuffing a piece of bread into his mouth.

"Which army?" she asked again when he did not respond.

He chewed slowly, but she knew it was a stalling tactic.

Lizzy made an obvious show of slipping her thumb over

the hammer of her gun. "The saddlebags and revolver you carry are Confederate issue, but your rifle and ammunition cases are more along the lines of the Federalists."

"How would you know which army issued what items?"

His none too subtle slur against her intelligence did not go unnoticed. "I've made it a priority to become aware of such things. What are you? A Reb or a Yank?"

He set the tray aside and slowly rose to his feet.

Lizzy immediately stiffened. She mustn't drop her guard now. Not when he towered over her, so big, so solid, so . . . real.

"Well?" she prompted when he didn't respond.

"What does it matter? The war is over."

"Is it? The battlegrounds might be deserted, but there's still a great deal of fighting. Fighting for survival."

"I see."

"Do you? Do you know what the loss of that pig will do to us? It was more than our last supply of meat. It was to provide us with the makings of candles, soap, lard. How am I supposed to replace those things now?"

He took a deep breath, exhaling it slowly. "I'm sorry about your . . . loss. Truly I am. But I am not responsible."

"Prove it."

"How can I do that?"

"My point exactly."

He frowned in confusion.

"Of the two of us, I seem to have the better case," she said. "I can attest to the fact that you were found in my barn not twelve hours after the raid. Since the twins finally surrendered your clothes just before bed time, I can attest that you were wearing the same type of uniform and that you bear a striking resemblance to the men who attacked us. You have nothing to add to the contrary."

"I give you my word—"

"Which, since I don't know you, means nothing." She pulled back the hammer of her revolver. "Who are you?"

She held the weapon straight, true, aiming it right between his eyes.

He stiffened ever so slightly, realizing that this was not a bluff.

"My name is Micah St. Charles."

"Yank or Reb?"

He didn't answer.

"Yank or Reb?" she demanded again, more forcefully this time.

"Which would better serve my purpose?"

She huffed in impatience. "The truth. Just tell me the truth."

"I'm neither. The war is over."

"Then I suppose you wouldn't mind if I checked into your identity."

She was taken aback by his immediate anger.

"Damn you!" He tried to lunge forward, the tray and dishes toppling to the floor, but the chains that still bound him to the trunk held him an arm's length away. When Lizzy shrank back against the wall and raised the revolver, he offered a placating gesture.

"I'm sorry. I didn't mean to frighten you."

She barely heard the words. She was too busy absorbing the implications of his reaction. The mere suggestion of inquiring into his background had caused him to react with a very real fear.

"Who are you?" she demanded again. "Who are you really?"

"I gave you my name."

"Your *real* name?"

He didn't answer.

"Why would an investigation into your background upset you so much?"

Still he didn't answer and she huffed in impatience. "Tell me! Otherwise I'll be taking you to the authorities myself." It was a bluff. She couldn't take him anywhere until she knew who he was. She'd seen enough injustices during the war to know that the people in charge weren't always honest. If he *was* involved in the raids on the nearby farms, she couldn't turn him in to his own people. They would only retaliate against her family. Then again, if he was a southern criminal fleeing retribution, she couldn't afford to keep him here, either.

Why had she been so impulsive? Why had she so foolishly invited danger into her own home? She'd been so naive, thinking she could trap this man and force him to help her family.

"Don't go to the authorities."

She started when the man spoke without prompting. "Why?"

He opened his mouth, stopped, then shook his head. "I can't go into that."

"You'd better. I won't put my brothers in danger."

"You're in no danger from me."

"Why should I believe you? A man who won't even answer a few simple questions."

He sighed, propping his hands on his hips and looking heavenward as if for a sign. Then bit by bit, he relaxed, looking at her. Reaching inside the gaping edges of his drawers, he withdrew the daguerreotype case that had been causing the cloth to sag slightly over one hipbone.

"Take this," he said softly.

"Why?"

"Other than my weapons and my horse, which you already have, it's the only thing I own."

"What good will it do me?"

"I want it back. It's important to me, it has great sentimental value. If I hurt you or your brothers, you'll never give it to me."

She should have laughed at such a preposterous suggestion—holding a photograph as a security measure. But she found she couldn't say the words. She'd seen the way he reverently touched the case. She'd seen the tenderness in his eyes, the longing. Such emotions had not been an illusion.

"Is she waiting for you?" Lizzy all but whispered the words, unable to keep them from spilling free.

"No. Not in this lifetime."

The reply held such an unspoken sadness that Lizzy felt her own throat tightening ever so slightly.

"We can sort this whole mess out, you and I. I will convince you that I had nothing to do with your family's current problems. Until then you have my guns and the photograph. I won't harm you. You have my word of honor."

Heaven help her, she believed him. She shouldn't have, but she did.

"You're not a guest here. You know that."

"Yes, ma'am."

"You'll work for your keep until I can determine whether you're to be trusted."

"Agreed."

"You won't be left unguarded."

"If that's what you want."

"You won't be released until I'm satisfied you've worked off the price of the pig."

"Fine."

Still she hesitated. But she could see no guile in his gaze.

She reached out, took the case, and put it in the pocket of her apron.

"You won't go to the authorities?" he asked, his body still tense.

"No."

Only then did the rigid line of his shoulders ease ever so slightly. Broad shoulders. Taut. Well defined.

"Will you tell me why I shouldn't?" she asked after he sank to the floor and propped his head against the shelf, his eyes closed in patent weariness.

"No." His single-word response was implacable.

Lizzy opened her mouth to argue, but she knew that to press the point would prove fruitless for now. She would have to uncover his identity in another, more subtle, way.

But she *would* find out who he was.

Of that there was no doubt.

Chapter

Micah felt something pressing against his nose. Something cool, soft, small. Wet. The horrible battle-tinged nightmares that had haunted him for most of the night faded away, leaving him suddenly and completely awake.

His eyes popped open, but the blackness that surrounded him allowed no hint of what had roused him. What had left a moist spot on his cheek as if he'd been . . . kissed?

"Lili?" he whispered. But even as the word slipped from his lips, he remembered that Lili was gone. Solitude was gone. His brothers had gone to war, and he alone was left to right the wrongs that had been done to the St. Charles family.

He heard soft breathing next to his ear. A low huffing sound much like a sigh.

"Lizzy? Is that you, Lizzy?" he asked a little more

hesitantly, the events of the past day flooding back and leaving him feeling shaken and disjointed. His head ached, his body ached, his lungs ached, and that woman was to blame for a good measure of it. She'd left him to sleep on a hard drafty floor to catch his death. Now she'd tiptoed into his room without lighting a lamp and stood close to him, breathing softly next to his ear, the warmth of her body seeping into his own.

"Dammit, woman, what are you trying to do to me?" There was no answer. He felt a slight pressure at his shoulder, the softest of touches. A horrible suspicion began to infiltrate his thoughts. Surely when she'd said he would have to earn her keep, she hadn't meant that she would have him . . . that they would . . . that he . . .

"Lizzy? Is that you?"

Her breath became more insistent, her touch more brazen. She was nuzzling at his shoulder, nipping. Biting.

Biting?

Micah reared back, shouting. There was a snort, an animal-like snuffling, then the sound of hooves pounding on the wooden floor. Damn it all to hell! What had this family done to him now?

Jumping to his feet, Micah crouched low as he heard the rattle of the lock—an action bred out of years of caution. The door flew open, and a rush of light spilled in from the hallway.

"Ruggles!"

At the same instant Micah realized some of the younger boys had come to set him free, he recognized his assailant as none other than a small, very pregnant nanny goat.

The goat's bleat of pleasure was drowned out by the twins' whoops of joys.

"She must have been hiding under the shelves!"

"What a smart goat."

"I bet the soldiers frightened her into coming here."

"She's been here before, you know."

"I told you she hadn't been taken."

Before he quite knew what had happened, Johnny and the twins had taken the goat out through the hall, leaving Micah and the bespectacled Boone alone.

Boone's gaze darted from Micah to the empty dishes on his tray on the floor. Sometime during the night, the leftovers had been licked clean. Micah hadn't even noticed.

Straightening, he stared at the boy in disbelief. "The goat was in here the entire time?" he asked.

Boone blinked and shrugged, adopting a stern, nearly-adult-looking attitude despite his boyish features. He had to be only a few years Crockett's junior. "I doubt it. There's some loose boards leading onto the back porch. She probably spent the day in the woods, then came back when she got hungry. I guess she got in the only way she could."

"I see."

"She's a very intelligent animal."

Micah saw no reason to disagree.

"Lizzy said you were one of the men that took our pig."

"Do you believe her?"

"I don't have any reason not to."

"What if I prove her wrong?"

The boy shrugged as if that was the least of his concerns. Then his expression grew quite sober. "My sister never hurt anyone."

Micah didn't quite know how to respond to the abrupt change of subject.

"Don't you be guilty of hurting her," Boone warned. Then he went out and slammed the door shut, leaving Micah in darkness.

He stood where he was for some time, musing over what had just happened. Had any of it really happened? Had he really been kissed awake by a nanny goat, interrogated by an adolescent boy, then locked in a dark storage room without so much as a hello, good morning, or go to hell?

Where in the world had he landed himself? For months

now he'd been trailing Bean and his squad. He sighed, knowing instinctively that the destruction had been Bean's way of forcing Micah to follow him.

He massaged his aching temples. Any sane man would have surrendered to Bean by now—or fled to Canada and made a new life. But Micah had found such solutions unacceptable. After months of assumed names and identities, moving from squad to squad involved in front-line battles, he'd hoped for just a few hours rest to gather his strength. At Solitude. Home. But when he'd returned to Virginia and seen what Bean had done, he'd known he had to find the man and stop him. The hunted had become the hunter.

If he'd only returned to Solitude a few days earlier, he might have prevented Bean from exacting his revenge on the rest of the St. Charles family, from stealing the family fortune, which had been so carefully hidden away in trunks before the war. Unfortunately, by the time Micah had arrived and seen the ruins Bean had left behind, the man had arranged for his squad to return to their home state of Ohio.

It was a trap of sorts. Micah was not foolish enough to think otherwise. His home had been violently ravaged, obvious clues left for Micah to follow. Bean had made no effort to conceal his trail home to Ohio. In fact, there had been a host of examples where Bean's men had "requisitioned" supplies and destroyed nearby farms whose occupants refused to cooperate. Then Micah had somehow lost the trail. Until now. Bean had been here. Micah knew he had. Bean was responsible for the missing farm animals.

He pressed a finger to the bridge of his nose. If he could only think clearly, he could devise a plan. But this damned fever was wreaking havoc on his senses. Why else would he have given his word not to escape? Why else would he have handed over Lili's picture so easily?

Micah sank onto the trunk. He was losing his mind. That

was why he was hesitating when he was so close to his quarry, why he was so tired of running, so weary of fighting. Otherwise, what in the world would have possessed him to linger here, where a young woman and a band of young boys were about to hold him hostage in the name of a dead pig?

He had to get away. Tonight. Otherwise he might be tempted to stay long enough to discover why Lizzy Wilder's eyes held such a glint of brittle sadness.

It took some time for the furor over Ruggles's reappearance to die down and the boys to disappear outside, but once Lizzy and Crockett were alone, she spoke.

"Unchain the soldier from the trunk, Crockett."

Long before she'd said the words aloud, Lizzy had known that the announcement would gain her a curious look from Crockett, but she hadn't thought he would stare at her with utter disbelief. His breakfast lay forgotten in front of him, the fork suspended halfway to his mouth.

"What?"

"You heard me. Unchain him."

"Why?"

"He'll need something to eat this morning. Then I plan to put him to work, see if he has a talent for building. If not, he's of no use to us."

The fork dropped to his plate. "That's a bit cold-blooded, Lizzy."

"I know." Her admission was low. Guilty. "But that's the way it has to be."

It was clear that Crockett wanted to argue with her, but the stubborn jut of her chin must have changed his mind. He merely shrugged and stood, grasping the rifle he'd propped against the wall and moving into the hall to release their captive from his chains.

Lizzy waited anxiously, wondering if she'd made a mistake in trusting the stranger, if there would be the sound of a scuffle, a shot. But she heard only the squeak of the distant door, then the muted creaks of the hall floorboards.

Micah stepped into the kitchen. Heavens above, he was big. He was forced to duck his head to get through the door.

For a few seconds he paused just past the threshold, making her aware of the brilliance of his eyes, the tattered state of his underwear. The cloth molded each hill and valley of his legs with disconcerting thoroughness. He didn't look much better than he had yesterday—still flushed, still perspiring.

She cleared her throat. "As I told you last night, the twins gave me your clothes, but I took the liberty of washing them. I doubt they'll be dry for hours."

"Thank you." The words were simple, quiet, but obviously sincere.

"Do you have a change of . . . underthings hidden somewhere?" she asked as delicately as she could.

"No."

"In that case, you can wrap that blanket around your body." She nodded toward a folded bedcover that lay on a bench nearby. She didn't know if he'd accept the offer, but when he hesitated, she gestured to his drawers, "I'll be needing to wash those as well. Crockett will lead you into the parlor so you can take them off. I've put a few of my sewing pins there if you'd like to use them, but I'll want them back. I don't have many left."

"Fine."

As he and Crockett disappeared from view, Lizzy wondered if her captive's docility was a ploy, a way to trick her into lowering her guard. Steeling herself against her own weak will, she ladled some porridge into a bowl. She would not be fooled by his civility. She wouldn't trust him. Not until she knew exactly who he was.

Lizzy knew the precise moment he reentered the room with her brother. She didn't bother to turn around, needing a minute to distance herself from her own wayward imagination, one that created images of the stranger swathed in nothing but a blanket.

"Sit at the table, please."

She knew he had complied, because she felt the tickling at the back of her neck ease a little, as if he'd looked away. Then she heard the scrape of a chair.

"We haven't got much in the way of breakfast, just porridge and scrambled eggs, but I won't put you to work on an empty stomach," she announced in a tone that made it quite clear he should be grateful. Unfortunately, she ruined the effect by nearly dropping the bowl on the floor as she turned to face him.

Dear sweet heaven, hadn't the man heard her when she'd said the blanket was to be used to *cover* him? She'd meant for him to employ it from neck to toe, not merely wrap it around those narrow hips. As it was, she was confronted by his naked chest—broad, firm, completely masculine, and dusted ever so lightly with hair the color of corn silk.

Her mouth became unaccountably dry. Try as she might, she couldn't seem to move, didn't want to move. A part of her brain told her she mustn't get any closer to him than this. It wouldn't be wise. It wouldn't be prudent. She'd never seen a man's bare chest before. Certainly not one this young, this hard. This close.

Stop it! Shaking herself loose from such thoughts, she managed to walk forward so that she could put the bowl in front of him. "Eat," she croaked.

He didn't bother to look at her, to comment. He took the spoon and began to hungrily devour the meal while Crockett watched her with evident curiosity.

She folded her arms, trying to remain casual, unconcerned, but Crockett's glare was making her edgy, and the stranger's bare chest was making her skittish. Unfortunately she'd made an error by tidying up the kitchen before sending for the man. Now she had nothing to occupy her hands. Sighing in impatience at her own lack of poise, she marched to the table to set a plate of eggs in front of him.

"You never told me what you do."

When Lizzy spoke, Micah raised his eyes briefly from the mush.

"Do?"

"Your work."

"Work?"

"Surely you've made a living for yourself."

"I've been a soldier for years."

"What did you do before the war?"

He scooped up the last spoonful of thick porridge and finished his eggs. "I was a . . . farmer of sorts."

"A farmer of sorts," she echoed, dissatisfied with such a vague answer. "Are you good with tools?"

His brow creased, and she suspected that she'd somehow touched a nerve with that question.

"Why?"

"I told you that you'd have to earn your keep until I could decide what to do with you."

"Why don't you let me go?"

She shook her head. "Not until I'm convinced that you've done nothing in the past and will do nothing in the future to hurt my family."

"I didn't harm your pig."

"Perhaps. But maybe your real reason for being here is even more sinister."

Micah's eyes flicked to Crockett who stood a few feet away, his boot propped on the seat of a chair, Micah's rifle draped over his knee, one of his revolvers tucked in his waistband. He seemed to be wondering how much she'd told Crockett about their interchange, and he was obviously not pleased to think that yet another person might know he had something to hide from the authorities.

Lizzy didn't bother to reassure him. "Come with me."

"Where?"

"You agreed to work. I think you'd better see what you're going to be required to do."

Signaling for Crockett to follow them, she marched from the room and out the front door, taking it for granted that Micah would follow. He did. Probably as much from the existence of the rifle in Crockett's hands as from the fact that he'd given his word to follow her orders.

She marched outside, down the steps, and onto the worn path. Once at the riverbank, Lizzy motioned for the man to stop. He watched her curiously. Obviously it had not yet dawned on him what job she intended him to perform.

"Can you fix it?" Lizzy's heart pounded in her breast as she waited for his answer. Her palm grew sweaty around the revolver in the pocket of her apron. She had worked hard to provide for her brothers the last few years. She'd learned how to shoot, how to hide her animals, how to till the gardens she'd sown in the forest by night. All of that had brought the Wilders this far, but only the toll bridge could help them to move on to better things.

"Fix what?"

"The bridge."

His eyes widened, darkened with some unfathomable emotion. "What?"

"Can you rebuild it?"

Lizzy had to admit that the ruined bridge was a sorry sight indeed. Where once it had been a lovely wooden structure with arched supports, a smooth plank base, and a whimsical picket railing, it was barely recognizable in its current state. The state militia had ripped away the center planks toward the beginning of the war as a precaution, storing the boards in the Wilder's barn. Since then, the structure had been pummeled by the river, devastated by weather, and looted for firewood, until only its supporting beams were recognizable for what they were.

Micah turned to stare at her, hard, and she was startled by

the fury in his expression. "What are you trying to do to me?"

He took a step toward her. "Who are you? How do you know Bean?"

"I don't—"

"Damn it it all to hell! Was this all some kind of trap? Are you one of Bean's minions?"

His hand snaked out, closing painfully around her wrist. But when he would have yanked her closer, the unmistakable sound of a rifle being primed split the air.

"Let her go."

Micah whirled, and Lizzy was able to see over his shoulder. Crockett held the man firmly in his sights.

"Let her go, damn you, or I'll shoot you here and now!"

Slowly, carefully, Micah released his grip.

"Back up, nice and easy."

Micah was forced to comply.

"Now return to the house. As far as I'm concerned, you've had enough freedom for today. You can spend the rest of the morning in the storeroom waiting for your clothes to dry."

Lizzy didn't contradict the order. She couldn't. She was trying to still the sudden thump of her heart and the wildfire heat of her skin. She stood in something of a daze as Crockett marched Micah back to the house. She was astounded by her reaction to his nearness. It was not fear that thundered through her. It was more than that. Much more. The emotion was more disturbing than she would have thought possible.

Purposely refusing to analyze the exact emotion Micah had inspired, she turned toward the house, prepared to take charge again. But it wasn't Micah who was the first to confront her. It was Crockett. He stepped onto the porch just as she was hurrying to the door.

"Just what in hell do you think you're doing, Lizzy?"

"I'm trying to get the bridge repaired."

"You're trying to get us all killed!"

"Nonsense."

"The man was a soldier not so long ago! Why do you think he'll submit to your orders without a fuss? What's to keep him from revolting and putting us all in danger, and who's that Bean person he's so worried about?"

She pressed her lips together.

"Liz-zy," he drawled a warning.

"He won't hurt us."

"You have no guarantee of that."

"I have his word."

"His *word?*" he asked incredulously. "That man's word isn't worth the breath it took to give it."

"I also have something he wants," she admitted reluctantly. "Something he owns. Something . . . valuable to him."

"What?"

She hesitated, knowing her brother wouldn't understand. "A picture."

"Of what?"

"A woman."

"What woman?"

"I don't know. But the daguerreotype is obviously precious to him."

Crockett stared at her for several long, uncomfortable moments, then shook his head. "You've lost your mind."

"I have not!" she retorted indignantly. She pulled the daguerreotype case from her pocket and handed it to him.

He opened it, looked inside, then sighed. "Do you honestly think that a photograph will keep that man in line?"

"Yes, I do."

"Then I have serious doubts about your sanity."

She snatched the picture back. "Just never you mind, Crockett. Don't you be forgetting that I'm the eldest Wilder here. I'm in charge."

"Only because Papa hasn't come home yet."

"And probably won't come home!" The moment the

words escaped, she regretted them. For a long time she'd feared her father had been killed, but she'd never voiced the thought. To do so would force her to begin accepting it as truth.

Not waiting for Crockett to comment she said, "Go unearth Papa's tools. Once that man has his clothes again, he'll be spending all of his time at the bridge."

It was an order that Crockett was not given the opportunity to refuse because she turned on her heel and stormed past him into the house, slamming the door behind her.

Chapter

6

Lizzy busied herself the rest of the day with household chores.

The inn seemed to be falling down around their ears a little more with each day that passed. First, the shingles had started to decay, then the paint, then the shutters. Now the interior was deteriorating just as quickly.

Until her death, Lizzy's stepmother had hired local women to keep up with the daily tasks. In those days the woodwork had been oiled weekly, carpets aired monthly, linens replaced daily. There were fresh flowers in the summer and everlastings in the winter, vases and vases of them decorating every nook and cranny. The smell of soups and fresh bread had permeated the air. There was rarely a day when less than three dozen pies had been left at the windowsills to cool.

There was none of that now. Except for the necessary bedrooms and the kitchen, the rest of the inn was quite inhospitable. The boys did their best to help with the chores, but they didn't really understand even the most rudimentary reasons behind sweeping and dusting, and Lizzy couldn't blame them for their limited vision of how things should be. They spent most of their time outside trying to care for the remaining livestock and the garden planted deep in the woods. The vegetables weren't growing well in the intermittent sunlight. There was no water near the plot, forcing the boys to haul bucket after bucket from the river.

Lizzy sighed softly to herself. They tried their best. She couldn't fault them for that. But sometimes she longed for another female to talk to, someone who would understand the hopes and dreams she still harbored deep in her soul.

If Sally were alive . . .

That idle wish had fluttered into her mind at least a hundred times. Sally would have understood. She would have known how to cope with their current situation with style and grace. She would have been fearless, soothing, loving.

The clatter of a horse's hooves drawing near caused the nostalgic thoughts to vanish beneath a sudden urgent awareness. Someone was coming up the front drive.

In a flash, Lizzy coped with a host of questions: Where were the boys? Was the stranger hidden? Where was Ruggles? What if the raiders had come back?

Wiping her hands on a dish towel, she touched the gun in her pocket and warily made her way to the front door.

"Afternoon, Lizzy."

She relaxed a little when she recognized the man who had brought his mount to a stop at the base of the porch steps. But she did not drop her guard completely. She had learned from the increased cautiousness of the townsfolk that even a former friend could become a foe after so many years of struggling. The men especially were to be regarded with

67

suspicion. War had not treated its victims kindly. Many of the returning soldiers had grown bitter, hard. Disillusioned.

"Mr. Ruthers."

The visitor had served as postmaster for years in the nearby town of Catesby. He'd returned from the war blinded in one eye to find that his wife had taken over his position and wasn't inclined to surrender it to him.

"I've been asked to spread the word that the school won't be opening again until November," Ruthers said.

"I'm sorry to hear that."

"I figured you would be, what with all those boys."

"I'd like to see them back with a real teacher."

"Yep, yep. I know just what you mean. But come next month, we should have the funds to hire us a schoolteacher. She can board with families while she's here. I suppose you'd be willing to take a turn?"

Lizzy nodded, but at the moment, it was difficult for her to believe that at any time in the future she would be worrying about boarders instead of finding a way to get through the coming winter.

"How are you getting on all alone here?"

The man's question caused her hackles to rise. She wasn't sure, but she thought he'd put a bit too much emphasis on the word "alone."

"Just fine, Mr. Ruthers."

"Your brothers are minding you well enough?"

"Yes, sir."

"No word from your pa, then?"

Again, the barely veiled curiosity. He was trying a little too hard to make his questions sound casual.

She stiffened, her hand slipping a little deeper into her pocket. The query could have been voiced out of simple concern, but she felt suddenly vulnerable. The Wilder ferry landing had once been so busy, so lucrative. Was that why Mr. Ruthers was asking all these questions? Would she next be guarding her fence lines as well as her animals?

"I only ask because we worry about all of you, out here by yourselves."

"There's no need to concern yourselves. Crockett is quite handy with a rifle should it ever come down to that."

She didn't think the reference to a weapon had gone unnoticed.

"Good, good." Ruthers straightened from where he'd been leaning on his pommel. "You be careful, you hear? The Union troops stationed in town have been chasing down rumors that there's a wanted man roaming around the area."

"A wanted man?" she asked weakly.

He nodded, quieting his horse when it became impatient to leave. "I didn't hear all the details myself. I doubt he's dangerous, personally. From what I understand, he's being sought for questioning in regard to charges of profiteering and treason. If it were me, I'd be halfway to Canada by now, but that colonel fellow in town swears the culprit has got to be somewhere nearby."

"Colonel? What colonel?"

"That new one who just transferred here with his squad. Dean . . . Ream . . ."

"Bean?"

"Yeah, that's the one. Colonel Bean." He touched a finger to his hat. "I'll be stopping by another day soon to check on you. Let me know if there's anything I can do."

She offered a halfhearted wave to the departing figure, but her mind was trying to assimilate all that had just been said. Drat it all, it was nothing but gossip and hearsay, but she couldn't deny that this was the second time today that she'd heard the name Bean uttered aloud.

Was Micah the man being sought? He had to be. How else would he have known the colonel's name?

It could be coincidence, a little voice argued. But Lizzy didn't think so. Micah had been upset with her this morning. What had he said? Something about wondering if she was one of Bean's minions.

She wound one arm tightly around a porch support as her knees began to tremble. Dear Lord in heaven above.

What had she done?

Darkness pooled in the hall as Lizzy made her way to the back storeroom. In her arms, she carried a clean pair of trousers, a shirt, and a suit of long underwear.

Night. She liked the anonymity of the blackness. She always had. Only at night could she dare to roam the paths in back of the house. Only at night did her responsibilities ease. Only at night did she have the freedom to do as she liked.

Only at night did she dare confront the soldier again. Away from her brothers' prying eyes and curious ears.

A tiny sliver of light greeted her from under the door. Crockett had been here sometime in the past hour or two. He'd been assigned to bring their prisoner some food, and Lizzy thought he'd stayed to talk, or to stand guard. Lizzy wasn't exactly sure which. She only knew that she'd heard voices melting through the walls. She'd had to wait for some time before her brother locked the door behind him and padded up the stairs to bed. Now it was her chance to seek some answers.

She unfastened the padlock and twisted the knob. The hinges squeaked slightly as she opened the door. She'd have to see that they were oiled, she thought idly. Then the door swung open, she met the stranger's eyes, and there were no more idle thoughts.

Micah sat where he'd been this morning, on the floor, his back propped against the shelves, his foot re-chained to a post, but there was something different about his posture. Something vulnerable. He looked so tired. Almost ill.

"I brought your clothes," she said softly. Her voice

sounded intimate in the quiet of a house that was often noisy. "You can change into them now."

"Thank you."

"The boys had hidden them in the chicken coop, but I washed them as thoroughly as I could, and I did a little darning . . ." The words trailed away and she shrugged, not knowing what else to say, not knowing if she should say anything. Who was this man? Why had he stumbled into their barn? He had to be the man being sought for treason and profiteering.

Profiteering? What exactly did that mean? The extent of the crime could range from the sale of inferior ammunition to the overpricing of a slab of bacon.

The stranger still had the blanket wrapped around his hips, but his bare shoulders gleamed in the lamplight. The effect was disconcerting to say the least, especially when she was trying to harden herself against him.

Lizzy set the clean laundry on one of the shelves, then stood in indecision, one hand rubbing the butt of the revolver in her pocket. Should she ask him now? Should she demand answers?

"You ate?" she said instead, not wanting to put the man immediately on the defensive.

"Yes."

"Did you get enough?"

"Yes."

It was an odd conversation. One which should have taken place with a guest, not a man she held prisoner, not a man she suspected was wanted by the Union army. Lizzy knew that if she was smart, she would leave. She shouldn't antagonize him with questions. She should send word to town that the missing criminal had been found.

But she didn't move.

She couldn't.

The air became thick. Hard to breathe. She felt as if she'd

been caught in a web of intrigue that she didn't entirely understand. Something involving this man. This stranger. This soldier.

"Who is Bean?" The words tore from her lips.

He immediately stiffened, and Lizzy wished she'd held her tongue. But this afternoon, when he'd grasped her arm, he'd seemed sure that she knew the man. Now that she knew there was a Colonel Bean hunting the area for a wanted man, she couldn't hold her tongue any longer.

"Who is Bean?" she said again, more firmly, when he didn't answer.

"A man I once knew."

When he didn't elaborate, she pressed further. "Why are you afraid of him?"

"Afraid?"

"This afternoon, you were worried that I might know someone by that name."

"It seems obvious now that you don't."

She deliberately waited a moment before saying, "Perhaps I do. The Bean family is not completely unknown in this county. They own a foundry not fifteen miles away. I've also been told, quite recently, that a Colonel Bean has been stationed in Catesby."

She couldn't miss the way some of the color bled from his features.

"Is that the Bean you were referring to?" she asked.

Micah didn't answer.

"What did he do to you?" She quickly amended, "Or perhaps I should ask, what did you do to him?"

His eyes narrowed ever so slightly, and she became aware that she was alone, so very alone, with this strong, powerful man. A man who could jump to his feet and rush toward her as far as his chains would allow.

But he didn't.

He'd given his word that he wouldn't hurt her. He appeared inclined to honor that vow.

"Was that the man you were referring to?" she asked again.

"The Bean I spoke of was someone I met during the war."

His answer was purposely vague, and they both knew it.

"On which side?"

He narrowed his eyes to mere slits. "You appear very concerned about my loyalties."

"After what I've been through the past few years, I have a right to such concerns, don't you think?"

His lips twitched in rueful acceptance. "The war's over. There are no more sides."

She was frustrated by his answer, but since she'd managed to get him to talk, at least a little, she didn't want to antagonize him into reticence. Not until she'd satisfied her curiosity.

"Then at least tell me what you're doing here. Why did you come to my farm?"

"I thought you'd already determined that I was one of the Union soldiers who took your stores?"

"Since then I've discovered that you carried Confederate supplies. Are you a Reb?"

"Would it matter?" he countered. "Or would you simply keep me prisoner for another set of reasons?"

She opened her mouth to refute such a preposterous idea, but found she couldn't. He was right. If he was a Rebel, and not the wanted man, she would be even more inclined to keep him here to build the bridge. It was the least he could do. The South had begun the war. They'd been ultimately responsible for her father's having to leave, for his continued absence, for the state of the family finances, for the lack of supplies. She was not above admitting that she held a grudge against all southerners—including the slow-talking blue-eyed giant she'd managed to apprehend.

"Just as I thought," he murmured, his lips taking a slightly hard edge. "You'll keep me here, no matter who I am, no matter which side I fought for."

Her chin lifted to a proud angle and her shoulders squared. "Is this some sort of ploy, Mr. St. Charles?"

He lifted one of his brows in silent inquiry.

"Are you trying to make me feel guilty?" she asked. "Are you trying to make me think that what *I've* done is wrong?"

"Isn't it?"

"No, by heaven, it isn't," she said firmly. "You're the one who trespassed. You're the one who slept in my barn. You're the one who frightened my brothers and nearly scared me to death."

"You weren't scared." He slowly rose to his feet, and she took a quick step backward. "Alarmed, perhaps, but not frightened."

"How do you know what I felt?" she demanded with more bravado than the question deserved.

"Because even when you stood there, with your weapon primed and your eyes blazing with fury, you were curious."

"Horse feathers!"

He took a step closer, another, another, until he stood within arm's reach, the chains taut. But he didn't touch her. He didn't grab her. That was the most startling thing of all. Because she had expected him to lash out at her. She had expected him to attempt to escape. But he didn't. He merely stared at her, long and hard. His gaze slipping from the top of her head to her face, her neck, down, down, down, to the toes of her shoes.

"Aren't you curious now?"

Lizzy couldn't get enough air. Her breathing had become short and shallow, and still she felt that she was being crowded, even though the man in front of her hadn't moved.

"Be honest, Lizzy. You're burning with curiosity. Deep inside where no one's looking, I bother the hell out of you. I'm a puzzle missing some of its pieces, and you don't know whether or not to believe the picture that's starting to form. Am I the enemy? Am I a criminal? Or am I merely a victim of circumstance?"

She nervously wet her lips, and his gaze darted in that direction, clung.

"I've kept my word so far, but you're wondering if you can continue to trust me. If you should have trusted me at all."

He inched closer. She heard the clank of chains, felt the inexplicable warmth of his body. His nearly naked body. The thought alone sent a shiver down her spine. Here she stood, only inches away from a man wrapped in nothing but an old blanket, one who might be responsible for crimes she couldn't begin to understand, and she didn't have the sense to back away.

"You should never have kept me here, Lizzy," he murmured, touching her with nothing more than his eyes but making her heart thump nonetheless. "I'm a danger to you. I'm a danger to your family. Let me go and forget you've ever seen me."

"No."

"Yes. You know I'm right. Deep down, where it counts. Let me go. Before it's too late."

A tightness clutched Lizzy's throat, a dryness, and she tried to swallow. How could this man, this stranger, read her thoughts so completely, so accurately? How could he delve into feelings she hadn't even examined herself and pull out the truth? Could he hear the little voice deep inside her? The one that kept uttering the same warnings? That she should release him. That she would regret her rash actions if she didn't.

The words trembled on her lips, the words that would free them both from the strange situation that had developed during the past two days. But then she remembered the bridge. She remembered her brothers. The farm. The soldiers who had come and taken their food.

"Damn you," she whispered. "You will not escape so easily. You will not talk me into handing you the keys to your manacles so that you can walk out of here free and clear." She quickly stepped out of the range of his grasp and whipped the revolver from her pocket.

"You wouldn't really shoot me."

"Yes," she said with deadly sincerity, "I would." She drew the hammer back beneath her thumb, snapping into place. "You see, I'm like you. I've been at war for nearly five years. It's hardened me. It's made me incredibly suspicious. But more than that, it's made me selfish. So damned selfish that I don't really care about you. I don't care if you're a corrupt Yankee soldier, a profiteering bastard, or a Reb traitor. I don't care if the man you fear is the same Colonel Bean who's in town or whether he's on the right or the wrong side of the law. All I care about is seeing my brothers through the coming winter—not the way they survived it this year. Not pinched and hungry and cold. When the first snow flies, they'll have food in their bellies and shoes on their feet—and I don't give a damn if I have to put you or anyone else to work to see that it happens."

With that, she marched forward to unhook his manacles and reattach them to one wrist. "See that you're dressed by morning," she ordered. Then she blew out the lamp, shut the door behind her, and twisted the lock.

Leaving Micah alone. In the dark.

He stood where he was for some time, absorbing the stillness, listening hard for the retreat of her footsteps down the hall. Then there were no more sounds than his own breathing, making him feel isolated and infinitely regretful.

He hadn't meant to frighten her. Not really. He'd only been trying to make her see that by keeping him here she would endanger herself and her brothers more than she could ever know.

Dear heaven, after her experience with Bean's men, she had decided Bean must be quite ruthless, quite unethical, to prey on his own allies. She must have thought that if such a man were to find Micah and to think she had been hiding him, there would be no protecting her from Bean's

76

fanaticism—and she was right. Micah had to get away from here. He had his own plan—to find Bean and to locate the missing St. Charles fortune. His brothers would need the capital to rebuild their home.

Micah sighed and sank to the floor, cradling his aching head in his palms. His body was proving the traitor, surrendering to the illness he'd tried to push away. It took all the strength he possessed to reach for his underwear bottoms, slip into his trousers, then huddle beneath the blanket on the floor.

But as sleep teased the fringes of his mind he couldn't forget the disturbing way Lizzy had responded to him, to the situation. Through the years of war, he hadn't thought much about the women who'd been left behind. But now he had seen how the conflict had changed their lives. They'd been forced to do men's work, to test their endurance. This woman did not seem inclined to forget the lessons she'd learned from such experiences now that peace had been declared.

Dammit! He had to get out of here! He had to leave before this family became embroiled in his fight for survival.

But even as that noble urge came to the fore, he realized that another part of him, a baser, more instinctive element of his nature, was whispering thoughts as selfish as those Lizzy had expressed so fervently. If he stayed, this family could unwittingly help him.

Chapter

7

The dream came again that night, as it always did when he was cold or hungry or ill.

It began with a blackness, a deep impenetrable wall of ebony that closed in on him, covered him, hugged him like a woolen shroud until he was sure he would suffocate. Then, like a pinpoint of mercury, a light appeared high above him, glowing, spreading, becoming a brilliant ball, a face, a form.

"Lili?" He called to her, knowing that this was a dream, that she wasn't real, but holding his arms out, wanting her, needing her.

"Lili, please. *Please!"* he cried, his anguish echoing in his own ears. But she came to him less and less often now, even though his very being longed for her gentleness. "Lili!"

The images remained the same. She would hover just beyond reach, smiling gently at him, wearing the ivory gown in which she had been married. She would extend her arms, but she would never touch him. He would try to move forward, try to embrace her, without success.

But this night there was a difference. This night it was Lili who took the step forward.

Micah felt his breath lock in his chest, burn there. She was so beautiful—she had always been so beautiful. In her presence he'd never ceased to feel a curious sort of reverence, as if she were too good for him. An angel in disguise. For the longest time after meeting her, he'd been afraid to touch her, afraid he might bruise her velvety skin. Even after they'd married, he had kissed her, caressed her, with the utmost care so that he wouldn't frighten her. So that she wouldn't grow wary. She'd been like a daffodil to him— golden, sweet, fragile.

"Lili?" he extended his arms, beckoning for her to draw close. "Lili, come here. Please."

She took another step, raising her hands to the back of her head in a lethargic, seductive gesture that he'd never seen before. Her eyes took on a curious glow, one that was hungry and just a little wanton. The emotions caused her cornflower blue eyes to deepen in color, change, become rich, dark. Brown. Her hair became less brilliant, less fine, darkening into a beautiful shade of honey. Then her hands moved away from her head, revealing the glint of a butter knife before her tresses fell free, spilling over her shoulders and down her back.

He was afraid to move toward her, afraid she might vanish as she had so many times before. But the image did not go away. It lingered, growing less delicate, less childlike. The woman he saw became much more voluptuous. The ivory gown melted away, and she stood before him in a flowing silken shift. The light around her penetrated the fabric, leaving the impression of a woman who would not need to be revered but would welcome his passion, his need.

"Lili?"

But no.

This wasn't Lili.

"Lizzy!"

Lizzy groaned, rolling into a sitting position and pushing her hair from her eyes.

"What?" The clipped query was tinged with irritation and worry. In her experience, nothing good ever woke a person in the dead of night.

"He's calling for you."

She squinted at Crockett in confusion. "What?"

"The soldier. Micah. He's calling your name."

Lizzy didn't move. Her mind was having a difficult time grasping such an odd statement. "He's calling," she repeated woodenly. "For me?"

Crockett nodded. "Over and over again. I can hear him through the door."

She sighed, swinging her legs over the edge of the feather mattress. Blast the man. What in the world did he want? And why couldn't it wait until daylight?

"All right. I'm going," she said, mostly to assure herself that she was awake and ready for a confrontation. "Go back to bed."

His mouth settled into a stubborn line. "I'll go with you."

She shook her head, taking the rifle from his hands. Since finding that rifle and Micah's revolvers, she rarely saw Crockett without them. "Sleep. The only way we can keep guarding him every minute of the day is to get our rest at night. The man has probably dumped his chamber pot all over his feet or tangled up his chains. I'll take care of it."

"But—"

"Sleep," she ordered again.

Crockett still hesitated, waiting until Lizzy shrugged into her wrapper and checked the rifle chambers for shells. At least they could thank Micah for that.

"Go on, Crockett," she said when he didn't move. "I'll

talk to him, then lock him up." She stared out of the window, thinking she could see a faint lightening in the east. "It will be morning soon enough anyway."

He didn't obey her right away. She knew that, because he gazed at her as she padded down the hall. Sure enough, after descending the stairs and moving within a few feet of the doors, Lizzy could hear the cries, garbled, guttural noises that did sound like her name.

"Blast and bother," she muttered under her breath, knocking on the door with her fist. "What do you want?"

The noises continued unabated, low, haunting sounds that gave her the shivers. Suspicious of a trap, she released the padlock and eased the door open, cursing the fact that the storeroom was black as pitch.

"What do you want?"

No sensible reply followed, merely a moan that seemed wrenched from his soul.

For the first time Lizzy felt a twinge of concern mixed with a healthy dose of caution. The lamp stood on the shelf by the door. Beside it she'd left a canister of matches. Leaning the rifle against the wall, Lizzy lit the wick and replaced the chimney. Even then, the air was rich with shadows, smelling mostly of must—a thought that saddened Lizzy, since she had always associated this storeroom with the scent of potatoes and onions, smoked meats, leather, and brine.

The groans came again and she took two steps, moving close enough to bathe the man in the fringes of light. The boys had made a bed for him by placing an old mattress on the floor near the shelves and covering it with fresh linens. She must have caught his attention, because his head rolled against the pillow and he looked at her.

Never before had she felt such a reaction to a man's stare. The bottom dropped out of her stomach, leaving her breathless, disturbed.

"Lili?"

Not her name. Another's.

He extended a hand, beckoning to her, his fingers slightly curled and moving in a come-here gesture. All caution fled from her body beneath the strangest yearning to touch those fingers, feel the strength of that palm.

Slowly, carefully, Lizzy moved forward, all the time waiting for him to rise, to strike out, to attempt an escape. But nothing of that sort occurred. He merely stared at her. His eyes were glassy, like Johnny's, when he walked in his sleep.

"Are you awake or not?" she asked bluntly, but to her dismay, some of the edge had left her tone.

"Lili?" he whispered, his face, his eyes, filled with joy.

The arm still tempted her, called to her, the muscles corded and firm, the hands broad and powerful.

"Lili, come here."

Never in all her life had a man used such a soft, velvet-over-gravel tone with her. Never had a man looked at her with such need, such want. She knew he was in a strange state of dreaming wakefulness, but she still took one step forward. Another. Another.

He grasped her wrapper with such swiftness and force that she jumped, immediately thinking she'd been duped. She remembered the rifle that leaned against the wall and cursed herself for being so careless as to leave it out of reach.

But Micah didn't attack.

He didn't confront.

"You're real," he breathed as his fist opened and he released her, sliding his hand around her knee, urging her closer, infinitely closer. She could feel the heat of his body seeping into her nightclothes with an almost feverish intensity, as if he were ill.

He swung to a sitting position, trapping her between his legs, wrapping his arms around her hips. The chains at his wrist still bound him, but he didn't appear to notice as he rested his head against her stomach.

"I thought you were dead," he murmured against her, the words barely recognizable. "But that was the dream. A horrible dream. You're here now. My wife."

Lizzy's breath was trapped in her throat at the stark pain she heard in his voice. She didn't want to feel anything more for this man than anger and distrust, but she found herself touching his hair, hesitantly at first, then softly, soothingly, experiencing an aching pity for him. His distress would return. Come morning, when he realized that she was not Lili. The woman in the picture. That had to be who he thought she was. What had he said to her? That the woman wasn't waiting for him? Not in this lifetime?

She felt a pang of sadness when the significance of those words sank into her heart. Dear sweet heaven above, this man thought she was the woman in the picture. He thought she was his wife.

She squeezed her eyes closed beneath the sting of unexpected tears—not for him, not for this man, but for herself.

The pain was sudden, unexpected, stealing her breath away. She had once longed to be married. She'd waited until she was nearly twenty before accepting Bill Hutchinson's proposal, after hoping beyond hope that a man would step into her life. One who would love her. Like this . . . she'd wanted one who would love her like this.

Her fingers curled into the softness of his hair, tugging him unaccountably closer even as she knew she should push him away and run from this room. She didn't want to be reminded that she'd settled for second best in accepting Bill's proposal. Moreover, she didn't want to remember that even second best had been denied her. She'd cared for Bill. She'd even loved him in a way. But not like this.

Not like this.

Micah's head moved, his nose shifting the nightclothes, rubbing, tickling, leaving a path of warm, moist air. Her skin was pebbled with gooseflesh in the wake of his movements. It became nearly impossible to breathe.

What had this Lili been like? Had she loved this man as much as he obviously adored her? Had she struggled to control a raging passion whenever he entered the room? Had she thought of him night and day, done all in her power to please him? Had she offered him her heart and her mind and her bed?

The questions couldn't be spoken aloud, but in that moment Lizzy needed to know the answers. She needed to know how much Lili had adored him. She needed to know how much of this man Lili had taken with her when she died.

Lizzy didn't pause to examine why she sought such intimate information about this man. Framing his face in her hands, she forced him to look up at her. She wanted him to see her. Really see her.

He stared at her for long anxious minutes, his hands still warm against her hips, their heat burning through her worn nightclothes.

"Micah?" His name sprang unbidden from her lips.

He pressed his face into her stomach again whispering, "You're so beautiful." His fingers curled, tightened, bringing her closer, closer, so that not even a space of air remained between them. "I've been gone so long, so long. I thought I would have forgotten you. But I see now that I'll never forget your scent, your sweetness, your feminine wiles."

Stunned by the words, spoken next to her, into her, Lizzy couldn't move, couldn't speak. Why? Why did such things have to be said to another woman? No man had ever talked to Lizzy this way. No man had looked at her with such utter desire. No man had clutched at her as if he would wither away if he let her go.

What had she done in life to be denied such things? She was not a cold person. She was not a selfish person. What element of her nature had kept her from this? *This.*

The realization that these emotions were the very thing

she had been craving all her life was humbling, nearly devastating. She'd always thought herself a little above the women in town who'd whispered about their husbands behind their fans, proclaiming to one and all in a hundred silent ways that their happiness revolved around a man's affections. Now Lizzy was learning that she wasn't really so different. She wanted to be loved. Body and soul. Was that really too much to ask? She was so lonely. Lonely clear to the bone. Would it be so terrible to indulge herself this once?

Just this once.

Slowly, hesitantly, she took the key to his chains from her pocket, unfastened his manacles, and pushed them away. Other than a soft sigh, he gave no reaction. When she stood, Micah lifted his head, trailing his lips over her ribs, her arms, and she trembled in the embrace, her own hands slipping across his back, to caress him in turn, and because she needed an anchor, something to keep her from falling to her knees.

"You are so lovely, so lovely . . ."

The words sank into her consciousness like water into parched earth. When he stood to kiss her shoulders, her neck, she could only tremble, soft, incoherent sounds escaping her mouth as she struggled to draw air into her starved lungs. Was this what it was like to be worshiped?

His hands cupped her head, his fingers feathering through her hair. Something disturbed him, caused his brow to crease, and she feared he might come to his senses, realize that she wasn't Lili, but he shook his disquiet away visibly.

"Kiss me," he said.

How could she refuse? She wanted to kiss this man more than she had ever wanted to kiss anyone else. With Bill, such displays of affection had been forbidden until after marriage. She'd nearly died of curiosity, wondering what happened when a man's lips met a woman's. She was about to find out. With this stranger. With Micah.

"Please kiss me," he whispered again, against her cheek, her chin.

It took only a slight dip of her head for their mouths to brush. Even with so simple a joining, the trembling in her knees grew nearly violent. A white-hot wave of sensation rushed deep in her body. She didn't know what would happen next, she didn't know what more *could* happen. Then Micah, this huge towering giant, deepened the embrace.

He was incredibly gentle, coaxing her with soft brushing caresses and tiny nibbles. She clutched at his bare shoulders, sure she would fall as the strength fled from her body leaving her weak.

Soon his clothes lay in a puddle at his feet. His hands, never still, brought her closer and closer until there were no secrets between them, no shy spaces. She could feel each swell and hollow of his body, the way her breasts flattened against the hardness of his chest. He was hot to the touch, from fever, from desire, from the close airless room, but she didn't think about that. She couldn't. His arousal lay between them, rubbing, delighting, frightening a tiny part of her, but causing the rest of her body to burn with an uncontrollable fire.

Her head fell backward as his lips trailed over her neck, following a sensitive path of nerves she hadn't known existed, then lower, lower, to the hollow between her collarbones, her breastbone, lingering there, causing her to gasp for breath.

"I've been gone so long." The words were said more to himself than to her. "I've been gone too long." Then he wrapped his arms around her shoulders, searching, delighting. He pressed her to him with a feverishness that could not be ignored or denied.

Lizzy knew this was wrong. She knew she should draw away. Her own emotions were raging out of control, while he . . . he was becoming too passionate. It had been years since she'd been needed in any way other than as a surrogate mother. It had been an eternity since she'd felt like a woman. A strong, beautiful, whole woman.

She could not stop him.

She could not stop herself.

In that instant, as the thoughts flashed through her brain, it was Lizzy who became the passionate one, Lizzy who became the aggressor. She might never have another chance. She might be damned in hell forever for what she was about to do. But she had lived through hell before and she could survive it again. As long as she had this moment. This memory.

Her hands slid down his body. Each portion of her skin became highly attuned to the sweep of muscles, the dusting of hair, as she explored the expanse laid bare to her gaze. She delved into the soft curls of golden hair.

With each caress, each deliberate embrace, she grew a little more frantic, a little less conscious of anything but this man, his body, her own. She had never imagined that touching a man could prove to be such a feast for the senses, that there were so many different textures, so many intriguing details.

The air she breathed became fraught with an electric anticipation. A fire burned deep in her loins, radiating out, out, out, filling her body with a delicious languor.

When he sank back onto the pallet, she did not resist. She fell willingly, her body settling over his own, absorbing its hardness, its unique scent, its maleness. Her lips clung to his, their gasps mingling together in a melody that was uniquely theirs.

Only once did she draw away, forcing him to look at her, willing him to really see her. A frown appeared between his brows, his eyes gleamed with a bittersweet longing, one that was enervating, yet at the same time heartrendingly sad.

Then he drew her closer for his kiss, rolling with her, pressing her back to the blankets.

She clutched at his shoulders, at his waist, his hips. Her body strained toward him. Lizzy was not naive. Sally had prepared her well for married life. She knew what occurred between a man and a woman. In her mind there was no mystery, no artifice. Sally had been quite blunt. There would be pain. A little, perhaps a lot, depending on the fashioning of Lizzy's own body. But if the man was right for her, in time there could be pleasure.

Lizzy grew nearly savage, clutching Micah to her breast, absorbing the tiny nips, the loving kisses.

Time.

Time?

Was that something she wanted with this man? Was that something she could afford?

It was the last thought to take root in her mind. Then she was inundated by sensation, fierce, elemental sensation. His palm cupped her breast, the thumb rubbing circles around the nipple until it grew hard and wanting. His hips ground against her own, firmly, insistently, so that her body began to pulse, to gather inward toward the very center of her being. Then his hand slipped down, rubbing the line of her ribs, the dip of her waist, before wedging between them where his thumb began a tantalizing rubbing, a sensual pleasuring.

Lizzy's mouth opened, taut gasps filling the air. She wanted to moan—to scream—with the pleasure that thrummed through her body, but she didn't dare. Instead, lifting her head, she sank her teeth into his shoulder. He uttered a short guttural cry and parted her legs with his own. A warmth, a hardness pressed against a part of her that had never known a man's touch. She squeezed her eyes shut, panting, wanting this. Wanting him.

Then he was pushing inside her, slowly, deliberately. She had to silence an instinctive cry at the sensation of tightness, a slight internal tearing, before he was in her, plunged to the hilt.

For long moments he lay propped on his hands, breathing heavily, gazing down at her with a mixture of astonishment and joy. Just when she feared this was all there was to the act, he began to move, slowly at first, then making each thrust more deliberate.

Lizzy had prepared herself for the pain she'd experienced, but not the pleasure. Sally had told her it might take many such experiences for a woman to feel anything but a slight unpleasantness. But what she was feeling now was far from unpleasant—the crispness of his hair against her softer skin, the warmth of his body, the weight, and the fullness. A taut cord deep within her began to draw tighter, tighter, in a pleasure-pain that she could never have anticipated.

Lizzy knew she would never forget this sensation, one of being . . . complete. Her fingers dug into his shoulders. Her eyes squeezed closed. Her whole identity centered around those feelings, that singularly pleasurable point deep in her body. Then, when she feared she would not be able to bear it any longer, her body shuddered, rocked, and she felt as if she were bursting with light and color, shattering into a thousand tiny pieces of joy.

Above her, she felt him moan deep in his throat, felt his own body grow tight. He was arching back, his hair spilling about his shoulders as he opened his mouth in a soundless shout of pleasure.

After that, time suddenly ground to a halt, each minute becoming an hour, each hour an eternity. Lizzy became conscious of the hard mattress beneath her back, the fabric of her gown tucked up around her waist. And this man.

This stranger.

Immediately she braced herself for the rush of guilt, the wave of second thoughts. She had made love with a stranger. She had allowed him to touch her in warm secret places, and through it all, he'd thought she was someone else. Lili. She should feel humiliated, soiled. But such emotions didn't come. Not yet. Perhaps they would storm her defenses in the clear light of day, but for now all she could feel was a sense of triumph. A sense of completion. Her decisions might not have been completely wise, but she knew she could never truly regret them.

As the man above her sank to her side and lay with his head pillowed next to her own, she brushed the damp hair away from his brow. His skin was hot and dappled with perspiration. Once again she was struck by the fact that he did not look at all well, but for the first time since finding him in her barn, Lizzy thought she detected a certain peace in his manner, a slight lessening to the lines of strain around his eyes and on his brow.

"Micah?" she whispered.

He answered with an unintelligible mumble of words. Delirious. He was probably delirious. That was why he'd been dreaming of Lili. His wife.

Immediately she chilled, squeezing her eyes closed at the unexpected stab of pain that gripped her heart. She doubted he would remember what had happened. If he did, he would think it all part of his dream. His dream of Lili.

Very slowly she rose to her feet and straightened her gown, all the while telling herself that she was glad he wouldn't remember. This had merely been a learning experience on her part. A chance to prove to herself that she hadn't become as empty, as brittle, as cold, as the war had made her feel.

But as she straightened, wincing at the slight twinge between her legs, she couldn't deny that the effects of the war had not melted away. Not entirely.

Moving to the door, she took a moment to wash herself with water from the pitcher and basin left on one of the shelves. She didn't look at the slight swirl of blood that lingered in the water when she was done. She couldn't think about that. Not now. As soon as she could, she would strip the lining off his pallet and erase what other evidence remained.

Sighing, she turned to look at her soldier, her stranger. Of their own accord, her feet began to move, bringing her back to him so that she could kneel and place a kiss on his cheek.

"Why did you ever come here?" she whispered. But there were no easy answers. Just as there were no easy answers to the question of what she should do now.

His eyes flickered, and he looked at her. Lizzy grew still. Tense. There was a clarity to his gaze as if he actually saw her. As if he knew just what had occurred between them.

He reached out, clasping her wrist. The mere touch of his skin against her own reminded her all too clearly of all she had done, of all she had given this man.

Gasping, frightened, she jumped to her feet, striding purposefully to the door. Just before blowing out the lantern, she made the mistake of looking his way one last time. He still stared at her, his arm outstretched as if he could summon her back to his embrace. With each passing second, his expression grew bleaker, more haunted, hollow.

"Lizzy?"

She choked on an instinctive cry. Her name. *Hers.*

"Lizzy," he whispered again, then closed his eyes, turned his face to the wall. And slept.

Slept.

Lizzy stood stock still, gazing at him in utter disbelief. Shock. Want. Her back rested against the door and slowly, ever so slowly, she sank to the floor. Gulping for air, she gripped her legs, burying her head in her knees. The tears came then, tears she had not shed when informed of Bill's death, of her father's disappearance. Tears she had denied herself, and had kept locked deep in her heart. As she fought them, tried to force them away, she wondered briefly if she could ever be the same again. This man had awakened her to all the thoughts and passions and dreams she'd shoved aside during the war. Could they ever be controlled so fiercely again?

Please, please, she prayed, knowing she was weak to even allow such thoughts. But then, admitting to herself just how much she had allowed this man to upset her well-ordered life, she finished the plea: Let him know it was me.

Chapter

Micah felt the warm sunlight against his cheek and smiled slightly to himself, rolling his head a little deeper into the pillow. What an amazing sensation that was. A soft pillow. Sweet-smelling linens.

Turning a little on his side, he luxuriated in the texture of the covers layered over his chest, the fluffy feather tick under his back.

Feather tick?

Sunlight?

His eyes blinked open, hesitantly at first, due to the bright pool of warmth that spilled through the window at his side.

He wasn't in the storeroom. That was the first complete thought to settle in his brain. He'd been moved to a real room. One with a bed, a dresser, and a wardrobe. A chair stood sentinel by the window, a pile of carefully folded clothing on its seat. His clothing.

Strange. He remembered changing into his drawers, his trousers. The chains. He shifted in bed; his feet were obviously unencumbered. One iron manacle still banded his wrist as if to be ready should he need to be restrained again, but the chains had been removed.

His eyes roamed around the room, taking in the simple furniture. Then he saw them. The iron links had been draped over the top of the dresser.

When had they let him go?

He rubbed at the ache in his forehead and squeezed his eyes shut. Almost immediately he was flooded with a tide of images. The storeroom. Darkness. Lizzy. Passion.

Lizzy?

He blinked, staring at his clothes again. Just the sight of them made the memories of his dreams grow stronger. He'd been experiencing the familiar images of Lili, then the pattern of those dreams had become so real, too real. The woman had ceased to be Lili and had become . . .

Lizzy.

No. It couldn't be true. He couldn't have actually kissed her, caressed her . . . made love to her?

There was a slight squeak and he stiffened, then peered at the small face peeking through a slit in the door.

"Lizzy, he's awake!" The piercing shout was followed by the thundering of bare feet down the hall.

Within a few minutes he heard another set of footsteps. When they paused, the door opened a little wider, revealing the woman who had embroiled him in this household's affairs.

Lizzy didn't move immediately into the room, but lingered just outside, her eyes dark, watchful. A tense stillness invaded the air, pushing aside the simple joy he'd felt in waking to a few creature comforts. Try as he might, Micah couldn't explain the sensation, just as he couldn't explain why he'd gone to sleep in a storeroom and awakened in a soft bed.

He drew the covers a little more tightly around his chest, realizing that he was quite naked beneath the sheets. The way this woman was looking at him didn't help matters much. He felt a stirring in his body, an intense awareness. An odd feeling of intimacy kept creeping into his consciousness. As if somehow, in the last little while, he and this woman had crossed the boundary from strangers to . . . what?

As the minutes ticked by, Micah had the strangest sensation that Lizzy was waiting for him to speak, but he wasn't quite sure what he was supposed to say to ease the awkwardness. He was still trying to fathom how he could have been moved from one room to another with no real knowledge of the change.

"You're awake," Lizzy commented when it became apparent that he wouldn't talk.

Micah struggled to a sitting position, gasping slightly when his head pounded at the effort. "What—" he gestured to his surroundings.

"You've been ill."

The fever. Dammit, was that why his mind felt so cloudy, why the oddest thoughts kept popping to the fore? He rubbed his brow, squeezing his eyelids closed in an attempt to remember clearly. But his brain seemed intent upon recalling only the strange and erotic dream he'd had. Dreams about this house. This woman. Her skin. The kisses.

"How long have I been sick?" he asked abruptly when his own consciousness was determined to take an inappropriate detour.

"A little over three days. You've had a bad fever, the shakes. The boys helped haul you in here the day before last—you're in a room across the hall from where you were before. Every now and again you decided to take a walk."

At that, his head darted up—a rash action he quickly regretted.

"No need to worry," she assured him. "We've put Oscar in the hall to keep you from going too far. Every now and again, he takes the cane we use with the livestock and shoos you back to bed."

The rather humiliating practice must have offered her a certain amount of satisfaction. But unlike their last few bouts of verbal sparring, there was no latent hostility in her tone. Only an unusual tinge of wariness.

"I suppose you're hungry."

He nodded. In truth, his navel felt as if it scratched his backbone, but he wasn't sure if that was something he should admit.

She nodded. "I'll put something on the stove. But first I'll be putting some water on to heat. You'll want to bathe the last of that fever away."

"Lizzy?"

Micah didn't know what had prompted him to speak. He only knew that when she began to turn, he had to stop her. "Has anything . . . happened?"

She grew still, so very still, and for the first time since meeting her, he noticed that the expression in her eyes had become guarded. "What do you mean?" She uttered the words so softly that he could barely understand them.

"Did anyone . . . come here while I was ill?" Had Bean found him? Was she in danger?

His question seemed to disappoint her.

"No. No one came. Not into the house, anyway. A few people came by to use the ferry to cross the river, but that was all."

"I see."

He rubbed his face with his hands again. Something was wrong here. The more time he spent in this woman's company, the more he sensed it. But the instincts he'd honed in battle and sharpened on the run, didn't seem inclined to help him. The images of touching her grew stronger.

When Lizzy didn't say anything more, he felt he should be the one to talk, to ease the uncomfortable silence that settled between them.

"Is anything wrong?" *Tell me,* he willed her silently. *Tell me that we didn't make love. Or that we did. Dear heaven, what happened? Where did the dreams end and reality begin?*

"What could possibly be wrong?"

"The boys, are they—"

"The boys are fine. Frankly, they've been a little upset to have you here."

"In the house?" he asked in confusion, not quite following her cryptic speech.

"In our parents' room. This used to be their bed."

He digested that statement before asking, "Where are your parents?"

"My mother is dead as well as the boys' mother—Sally, my stepmother."

"Oh." She made no mention of her father, but even as he waited, he knew she wouldn't be offering any more information. He'd only caused the quiet to grow even more unbearable.

Lizzy's manner became immediately businesslike. "There's an extra sheet draped over the bed. Wrap yourself in that. I'll send Crockett to take you to the privy, then come on in to the kitchen. By the time you get there, your bath will be ready. After that, you can eat." With that, she closed the door, offering him the same privacy she might offer a guest.

But he was not a guest, Micah reminded himself. He was her prisoner. And at that moment he knew beyond a shadow of doubt that he had also been her lover.

"What are you doing, Lizzy?"

Lizzy started when Johnny walked up behind her and

stood on tiptoe to stare out the window, searching the yard for the object of Lizzy's concern. Beyond the house, heading down the path toward the pump was Micah, followed immediately by Crockett and his rifle.

To be quite honest, the past three days had given her more than a scare. After her night of passion, she'd carefully schooled her emotions, repaired her defenses, and walked into the storeroom prepared to do battle. When she found Micah shivering, feverish, and delirious with fever, her heart had dropped to her toes. He'd been so weak, so ill. Even when she and her brothers had half carried him to the back bedroom, he hadn't regained his senses.

The next few hours had been torture for Lizzy, who had never really nursed anyone who was seriously ill. She'd been forced to try to remember each scrap of medical information that Sally had passed on to her. She'd bathed the man, kept him warm, and watched him for hours. Through it all, her primary fear had been that he would die.

She didn't examine why the life of a stranger, albeit an intimate one, should suddenly be so important to her. But she did have to admit that she had never been so afraid in her life as she was in the wee hours of the dark when his breath had rattled in his chest and his delirious mumblings had escalated to disjointed accounts of battle. Her relief had been overwhelming when the fever broke and he began to sleep. Really sleep.

But even then her worries had been far from over. They merely took a new shape as she wondered how long it would be before she would have to deal with what had happened between them. She'd schooled her emotions carefully. She had vowed to be stern and practical, a no-nonsense kind of woman, so that he would never know, never guess, how she'd melted in his arms.

"Lizzy?"

She jerked back to the present. To the hot kitchen and her worried younger brother.

"You keep staring out the window." Johnny pressed his lips together in disapproval. "At him."

"I've just . . . been thinking."

"About what?"

About the way he'd kissed her. The way he'd touched her. The way he'd loved her, all the while never knowing who he held in his arms.

"Nothing, really."

He stared at her in obvious disbelief. Within moments, seeing her and Johnny together at the window, Lewis sidled close, then Clark.

"That soldier's awfully big," Clark remarked, pressing his nose to the glass. "I bet he's like a bear in a fight."

But Micah could be gentle. Oh, so gentle, Lizzy thought unwillingly. He probably had the kind of shoulders that could hold up a world of problems and still be a comfortable place for a woman to lean her head. She only wished she had the right to investigate such a possibility.

"He's got funny hair," Clark said, standing on tiptoe to see over his twin's head. "It's white and grows all over his arms."

Soft, bleached by the sun.

"He's always growling and grumbling."

But he could moan too—low, guttural moans that turned a woman's knees to jelly.

"Lizzy?" Johnny tugged at the strap of Lizzy's apron, his eyes sparkling with concern. "Are you sure you aren't sick?"

"No! No, I'm fine," she said a little too vehemently. "It's just the heat."

Obviously no one believed her, so she turned away and began to busy herself near the stove. "I guess I'll do the baking this morning—the house is already hot enough to fry potatoes, what with all the kettles we've put on to boil. All of you run outside and play, now. Micah will be taking his bath as soon as he gets back, and I'm sure he doesn't need you gawking at him."

The twins did as they were told, but Johnny remained.

"Lizzy?"

"Mmm."

"Did that man hurt you?"

Lizzy whirled to face him. "What?" Her hands trembled, but she shoved them deep in her pockets. "No, dear. Why?"

"The last few days, while he's been sick . . . whenever you look at him, you get a funny expression on your face. As if . . . as if . . ."

"It because he's so . . ." She searched for some logical explanation and finally said, "He's so dirty. You know how I frown on that sort of thing. He's washed at the pump a time or two, but it's just not the same as an honest-to-goodness bath. I'll just have to see that he fixes himself up to my standards before the day is out."

With that, she busied herself at the pump, filling another pot to put on the stove to boil. But it was long moments later before Johnny headed outside and Lizzy could wilt in relief. She would have to be more careful. For pity's sake, she had to be more careful.

Micah paused halfway up the path from the privy to turn and survey the river below, the grassy banks, and the bridge.

It wasn't a complicated structure. He'd worked on dozens just like it during the war. The basic supports were there. All it needed was some fresh lumber to fill in the missing spaces. It would be an easy task if a person had a little time on his hands. In any other circumstances, Micah probably would have volunteered his help long before being put at the wrong end of a gun.

But he didn't really have the time. He couldn't afford to stay in this place. Not with Bean so close. Not with Union soldiers stationed somewhere in the area. Every minute he delayed was one more chance for the St. Charles treasure to be lost to them forever.

"Are you going to fix it?"

Micah didn't betray his thoughts by so much as a flinch when Crockett spoke.

"She's bound and determined it will be done, isn't she?" he asked the boy.

"Yep."

Micah looked at him then, met the dark concern in Crockett's eyes. "I take it she's always had a stubborn streak in her."

"A mile wide."

"I don't suppose you could talk some sense into her."

Crockett shook his head. "It wouldn't do any good. Besides, the bridge has got to be fixed, one way or another."

"What if I don't choose to be the man to do it?"

Crockett shrugged. "As long as you understand the consequences. Lizzy doesn't make idle threats. If she said she'd turn you over to the authorities, she will."

Micah pressed his lips together. "Even if I'm innocent of the crime she's accused me of committing?"

Crockett's lips twitched in the barest of grins. "She thinks you're guilty of something, that you're afraid of the authorities. Doesn't seem to me that it matters much whether she hauls you into town for raiding our farm or for something else. If I were you, I'd just take the easy route and fix the damn bridge."

"Crockett! Go on and do your chores." The shout came from the front porch. "You. Come here!"

When Micah didn't move, Lizzy held the screen door open a little wider. "There's no use pretending you don't hear me, Micah. I've lived through that response with the twins, and it doesn't work on me. I've set up a bath in the house just like I said, so if you want to clean up, you'd better come inside now while the water's hot."

She turned on her heel and stomped back into the house, leaving Micah to exchange wry glances with Crockett.

"Like I said," the boy warned, "it's a whole lot easier just to do what she says the first time.

Micah would have resisted, just on the grounds that he wasn't some dumb sheep to be led around by the nose. But after a second's hesitation, he had to admit that the thought of a bath, a real hot bath, was the bigger temptation.

He climbed the steps to the porch, taking a certain pleasure in the fact that he felt a little stronger than he had in some time. A little more able to cope. It was a confirmation of his own belief that the only thing to shake the recurring bouts of fever would be a few regular meals and several days of uninterrupted sleep.

"Stop there," Lizzy ordered when he'd climbed onto the porch. "You'll go no farther until you wipe your feet. I'll not have you traipsing mud inside."

"Yes, ma'am."

He dutifully made use of the rag rug by the door.

"That sheet will have to go too. You've managed to drag it through the mire." She held up a bath towel. "You can use this until you get inside."

When she didn't turn, didn't avert her head, Micah eyed her curiously, wondering if she wanted him to strip to nothing here in front of her. Judging by the earnest tilt of her chin so that she could see him eye to eye, she did.

The idea proved more interesting than he would have liked to admit. The mere thought of being completely naked in front of a woman—something he hadn't done since his wife died—caused a strange flash of excitement to race through his body.

"I beg your pardon?" he asked, sure that he couldn't have read her intent correctly.

"The sheet. Drop it."

She *was* serious. She meant for him to bare himself. The mere thought was enough to stimulate certain areas of his body that he had been trying to ignore of late, especially since he'd finally come to terms with the fact that he'd once caressed her, loved her. If only she would admit it or give him a chance to broach the subject.

"I don't think after what—"

"Do it!"

Sighing, he began to unfasten the knots he'd used to hold the sheet in place. She watched him dispassionately, her mouth pressed into a prim little line. He wondered how long that prudish expression would last. She might have had experience in taking care of her brothers when they were smaller, in caring for them, perhaps even in washing them. But somehow, deep down to his bones, he knew she hadn't had any such practice with a full-grown man. It was there in the ever so slight clenching of her fingers in the pocket of her apron, the faint flush that tainted her cheeks.

Once the sheet was completely unfastened, he shrugged free, clutching only a corner at his hips. The action only emphasized the fact that at least a part of him was fully invigorated by the process.

"Well?" he demanded, waiting for her to crack, to confess.

He was sure, quite sure, that her gaze flicked down. The fact caused the tingling that had gathered low in his belly to intensify even as he tried to will it away.

"Well what?" she snapped in return, but she gave nothing away.

"Can I have the towel first?"

Micah thought he could detect the slight blush deepening even more.

She handed him the worn bath towel, and he wound it around his waist, tucking the corner in next to his hipbone to secure it. Lizzy was openly staring at him now, and he feared the results of his own weak will if she didn't look away soon.

"You're going to have to get rid of this thing," he said, lifting his arm to reveal the manacle still fastened to his wrist. It was a token gesture at best, but he supposed it was meant to remind him that he could be locked up again at any moment.

"I can't bathe properly until I'm free," he said when she didn't respond.

"Free," she muttered more to herself than to him. Then, snapping to attention and yanking her gaze away from his chest she said, "Freedom is something you won't experience until you've repaired my bridge."

She turned to pick up a bucket from behind one of the porch chairs. A rather pungent aroma wafted his way. "I'll leave this here, but as soon as you've finished bathing, I want you to rinse with it."

"What is it?"

"Just never you mind what it's made of. I won't be having any lice in my house."

Lice? *Lice!* The woman was infuriating. Infuriating *and* insulting.

"I'll have you know I'm carrying no migrant wildlife on my person," he ground out between clenched teeth.

"Maybe, maybe not. I'll grant you the fact that you're cleaner than most of the fellows who've been wandering home, but you still need a good scrubbing. Now come with me or I'll dump it on you now."

Half believing that this willful young woman would do just that, Micah cursed the urge that had brought him to this place. Of all the locations where he could have taken shelter, heaven must have been frowning heavily on him to send him here.

"Lord, you're big."

He'd been trying to follow her as quietly as possible, but her sudden statement halted him midway through the door. He wasn't sure quite what Lizzy meant by her comment. He'd been careful to keep himself covered as much as possible. Although he might like to shock her if only to gauge the results, he was not about to humiliate himself in the process. But when he saw that she'd merely been commenting on the way he'd had to bend his head to get through the door unscathed, he realized she must be referring to his height.

"What did your mother feed you to make you grow into such an ox?"

"I am *not* an ox."

She paused to glance at him significantly, then began to stride down the hall. "Maybe not. But you're bigger than most men in these parts."

His lips twitched ever so slightly in amusement. If she only knew the ribald way her words could be taken, he was quite sure that Miss Lizzy Wilder would have shown some real signs of discomfiture. But before he could respond, she called, "Get a move on! There's a bath poured for you by the stove in the kitchen. I've set up the screen to hide you some, but don't be thinking you can do anything to get away. I've seen to it that all the pantry cupboards are locked and the tools tucked inside. Wash yourself with the dish of lye on the floor, then I'll bring you a bucket of clear water for rinsing. After that, you can head outside to smear that flea dip on you—and no lollygagging. We've got things to do besides coddle you."

"What about this?" he gestured to the iron band around his wrist.

She smiled sweetly at him—too sweetly—as if the size of his body didn't necessarily extend to his brain.

"Bathe with it on. It won't melt."

Chapter

9

The screen for Micah's bath had been set up in the kitchen area. He retraced the path he'd taken the first day, slipping through the sitting room and out the wobbly pocket doors positioned between a pair of horsehair chairs which—judging by the dust—hadn't been used in a very long time.

The kitchen, where he'd eaten breakfast before he got sick, was quite large with plank floors, a huge trestle table, a pine pie safe, an immense iron stove, and walls and walls of cupboards built from what looked like old barn siding. Unlike the rest of the house, this room was fairly tidy, scrubbed clean, and smelling of lye.

Clutching the towel at his hips, he rounded the warped pine and canvas privacy screen, then swore under his breath.

She expected him to bathe in that? *That?* The tub was no bigger than a large washbasin, to his eyes. He'd seen feeding troughs with more space.

"Great holy hell," he muttered, dropping the towel and gingerly testing the six inches of water that had been poured into the tub. He sucked in a breath at the scalding temperature.

"Hurry it up, Micah! I'd better hear water splashing and soap slathering in a matter of minutes."

As if to underscore Lizzy's orders, he heard the staccato rhythm of her boots stamping over the plank floor in his direction.

"This water is hotter than Hades, woman!"

"That's the way it gets when it boils."

His head shot up. "You put boiling water in my tub? *Straight* boiling water?"

"I told you I'd be killing any critters that might have walked in with you—it's bad enough that I've waited until now to do it. Now stop your bellyaching. That water's had plenty of time to cool. If you don't hurry it will be like ice."

He had his doubts about that. Seeing a bucket of water next to the stove, he dipped his finger in it, found it to be lukewarm, and presuming it was his rinse water, dumped a good measure in the tub. When the bathwater had reached a bearable temperature, he stepped into it and awkwardly sat down.

The cramped quarters forced him to nearly wrap his knees around his ears, but he supposed he should be glad that he didn't have an audience for this undignified experience. He could hear Lizzy working a few feet away.

Grasping the bowl of lye and a washing cloth, he hastily began to scrub, not trusting his hostess to remain on her own side of the screen. The lye concoction was slimy, not quite set up, and newly made, judging by the stench, but he couldn't complain. The stink managed to chase away the last of the wartime odors—moldering straw and human misery. He would rather smell like the strongest soap in the world than gunpowder and blood.

Washing his hair proved difficult, considering his wishbonelike position, but he managed to rub the soap into his scalp and lather his beard and face.

"Aren't you done yet?"

He barely had the time to cup the empty lye bowl over his privates before Lizzy pushed back the screen and glared at him. Wiping the stinging suds out of his eyes, he glared right back.

"Don't you have any sense of modesty at all?" he demanded.

"Living with little brothers kinda beats it right out of you," she retorted in that honey-sweet voice he was beginning to dislike. "Close your eyes."

"Wha—"

"Close them, or I'll be dumping the bucket over your head while they're open."

He did as he'd been told, and she flung the remaining rinse water over his head. "Now dry yourself off. I've got things to do."

At that, she tugged the screen back in place, leaving him alone.

Not trusting her to keep from storming in unannounced again, he scrambled to his feet in a rush of water. The sudden movement caused him to weave, the fringes of his sight bleeding to black, and he sucked in a quick breath to push the sensation away. He might be rested, but he wasn't completely well yet.

He dried his hair and most of his chest, then wrapped the sodden towel around his waist. None too soon, he realized, for Lizzy immediately stepped into view, her hands on her hips.

"You are a sorry sight, but I guess you'll have to do."

He had no real idea what she meant by that, but he thought it best not to ask.

"Come with me."

She led him over to the table where a man's threadbare robe had been folded neatly at the end. "You can put that on for now. It was my father's. It will be small, but it should cover anything that needs to be covered until we finish with you." She gestured to the table. "There's a pair of clippers there, and a comb." Her glance was stern. "If you'll use them for grooming purposes and nothing else, I'll let you borrow them long enough to trim your hair and that bush of a beard."

"I'd rather have a razor, if you don't mind."

"I'll just bet you would," was her only response.

When he realized he wasn't about to get a razor or anything approaching privacy, Micah waited until she'd turned away to tend to a lump of dough—only for appearance' sake. He would have liked nothing better than to drop his covering and shock the hell out of her. It would have served her right.

He was about to turn away himself when he noticed that Lizzy had grown quite still and was gazing out of the window. Could she see him reflected in the glass windowpane? Was that why she was staring, her breath coming more quickly?

He was suddenly struck by the inexplicable fact that he *wanted* to make her feel something for him. He *wanted* to make her notice him, to lose her concentration when she looked at him. He wanted some sort of reaction. Something besides irritation and anger. He didn't know why it was so important to him. But he needed for her to see him as something more than her captive, a laborer to rebuild her bridge. He wanted her to admit that he was a man.

The bath towel slid down the skin of his back, his hips, his legs. A tingling followed in its wake—because she was watching him in the windowpane. He *knew* she was looking at him. Unsure what he should do now that he had her attention, he paused, then held his arms over his head, stretching, feeling muscles he hadn't used for days growing taut, enjoying the sensation of his own cleanliness, the scent of soap-washed hair, the tiny dribbles of water slipping down his spine.

Sensing that to linger any longer would arouse her suspicion, he picked up the robe and shrugged it over his shoulders.

"Dressed?" she croaked when he loosely tied the sash.

Micah resisted the urge to grin. So she had been watching. "Yes, ma'am."

"Good." She slapped the dough into a bowl with unwarranted force and covered it with a cloth. "We haven't got much in the way of mirrors. Most of those we did have were broken long ago."

"By soldiers?"

"No. By boys." She wiped her hands on her apron, then faced him, but there was a flush to her cheeks, and she couldn't meet his gaze.

Outside, the twins began beating on a collection of pots they'd hung from the rafters and whooping. She paid them no notice.

"If you'd like," she began hesitantly, "I could help you trim your hair and shave off that beard, but I won't give you the razor to use yourself."

When she looked as if she would retract the offer, he quickly accepted. The hot water had caused a weakness to invade his bones. His hands were too shaky to control the scissors, and he didn't want her to know that he was still feeling the effects of his illness. Even more powerful than that, he wanted her to come closer, to drop her orneriness and touch him.

"Thanks."

She appeared startled by his acceptance, stammering,

"Well . . . well, I—" Then, taking a quick gulp of air, she motioned for him to sit in one of the kitchen chairs.

He was glad to take the weight from his feet, glad to feel the cool kiss of her fingers as they tucked a towel under the edge of his robe. There was something familiar about the routine. Normal. So what if he was dressed in nothing but a robe? So what if it gaped and shifted more than it should? He had this woman's attention. Her complete attention. A wary, sensual sort of attention.

"I'll trim your hair first."

"Fine." He didn't care. Now that he had washed himself with real soap and hot water and was cleaner than he had been in ages, he wanted to rid himself of the rest of the scruffiness. He wanted his life to become ordered again, sane.

She picked up the comb, a small silver affair with a worn filigree design on its spine. His hair was thick, matted, tangled, but she was patient, running the tines through the strands again and again, coaxing the snarls away until the waves hung past his shoulders. He was beginning to feel relaxed, peaceful, warm. The kitchen grew hot—too hot for the thoughts her touch inspired. The children's drumming from outside merely echoed the pagan, elemental urges he was experiencing.

"Don't your kind believe in haircuts?"

"My kind?"

"No-good thieves."

He sighed. "I'm *not* a thief."

"You look like one, and you refuse to tell me what side you fought with, so you must be a thief on the run. A criminal."

If she only knew how close she'd come to guessing, Micah thought, but he kept any sort of reaction from surfacing. "Anyone on his way home is going to look like a criminal. We've all been a long time away from the creature comforts."

Her hands grew still. "You've come from a far distance?"

He sensed a waiting in her tone, a barely submerged hope. "Yes."

"Where?"

"Mississippi." His voice grew hard before he added, "By way of Virginia."

She took the scissors and began to trim his hair with great care—more than was really necessary—the tugging and smoothing actions relaxing him to the point of near sleep. "My father was stationed in Mississippi. We haven't heard from him in ages. Not since he was listed as missing almost two years ago. Should he be home by now?"

In an instant he knew she was one of the most common casualties of war—a woman who had no idea whether a loved one had lived or died. If she hadn't heard any news to the contrary by now, her father was almost certainly dead. But he couldn't be the one to tell her that.

"Things are in a turmoil," he said. "Some men have horses, others have to walk. There are hospitals and churches and camps filled with soldiers just gathering their strength. It will take some time. Was he in the Union army?"

"Yes."

"Then it will take even longer. A lot of the soldiers are being kept on to help maintain order."

"I see."

Then she was quiet, and only the *snip, snip* of her scissors broke the silence. But his words must have comforted her somehow, because she took her time, performing the task with care so he wouldn't look as if he'd been sheared by a drunken sheepherder.

After she'd finished, she faced him, bending forward to work on his beard and mustache, her brow furrowed with concentration, the scissors soon replaced by an old razor.

Little did she know that her actions allowed him a glimpse of cleavage, a hint of lace.

"You never cease to amaze me with the extent of your skills," he said, tearing his gaze away.

She stiffened, obviously prepared to take his comment as an insult, but he touched her hand, pressing it against his shoulder. So soft and warm.

"You're far too prickly for your own good."

"What would you know about that?"

His thumb stroked her knuckles, and even in the heat of the kitchen, he saw the way her skin pebbled with gooseflesh. He knew there must be a streak of passion buried in her nature to cause such a reaction, and the very idea was more exciting that he had ever dreamed possible. What would it take to bring her emotions to the surface?

He strayed farther, touching her wrist, her forearm.

"Your skin's so soft," he whispered.

A slightly desperate light entered her eyes. When she would have backed away, he caught her hip with his other hand. "How do you keep it so silky?"

She shook her head slightly from side to side. When she refused to answer him, he took her palms, lifting them to his nose. "Such sweet smells. Fresh bread and . . . flowers." He couldn't help but smile. "You must have flowers on your back porch."

"I . . ."

"Sometimes I can smell them in your hair when you walk past me." He stood, crowding her, his bare shins brushing against her skirts. Still holding her hands, he bent, inhaling the natural perfume caught in her silky tresses.

"Do you know how enticing it is to catch a faint hint of roses?" He held her gaze captive, needing her to feel a portion of the emotions that burgeoned inside him. Why couldn't she admit what was happening? Why wouldn't she relax into his arms and ease his hunger to experience her body pressing into his again, consciously this time?

As soon as the thought formed, he drew her nearer, nearer. "Oh, Lizzy," he sighed, bending, touching his nose to the hollow of her ear, flicking the tip of his tongue against her neck.

She shivered in his arms, inflaming him even more. When he released her hands to wrap his arms around her waist, she pressed her hands against his chest, forcing him to look at her. There was an almost bruised quality to her expression.

He stroked her cheek. "You're so vibrant, so . . ."

"I suppose you're used to something different. Someone all perfumed and powdered and waited upon by a host of slaves."

His confused silence only angered her, and she wrenched free, dropping the razor onto the table. "Tell me? Is she really dead? This woman of yours?"

She stood, arms akimbo, glaring at him, but her manner wasn't entirely due to anger. There was something else in her expression, something undeniably hurt.

"What are you talking about? What does Lili have to do with all this?"

"You tell me, and don't think I'll accept some vague answer. I know she was your wife or your fiancée, or someone. Who is she? That woman in the picture?"

Micah's heart began to thud in his chest as a realization struck him. That night he and Lizzy had made love, he must have called out Lili's name.

"What was she like? Pale and squeamish? I bet she never had to surrender a life of privilege to slop the hogs or till a garden. I bet she never had to muck out the stalls, or harvest corn. She probably spent her days visiting, smiling vapidly, and sewing on table linens that would never be used. Is that what Lili did before the war? Is that—"

At the sound of his dead wife's name, Micah surged

toward her, grasping Lizzy's arms and shaking her. "Damn you, she's dead!"

"Is she? Is she really?" she shouted. "Three nights ago you called out to her. Don't you remember? You pleaded for her to come to you, but it wasn't your precious Lili who fell into your arms. It was me. Me!"

Chapter

10

The room shuddered in silence.

Lizzy's hands balled into fists as Micah stood still, staring at her, looking as if she'd slapped him.

"What's all the shouting about?"

They both started when Crockett ran inside, the rifle held firmly in his hands. "A body could hear you two clear to China and—" He stopped, seeing Micah's freshly trimmed hair and clean-shaven face.

Lizzy knew he must have sensed the ominous overtones in the room—how could he miss them? The air crackled with the energy of an impending thunderstorm. She was the first to react. Mustering her composure, she relaxed her stance, shoving her hands into her pockets, feeling the revolver she kept there. She wouldn't think about what had happened. She wouldn't think about the enticing glimpse she'd had of this man's shoulders, his broad chest, slender hips, and lower. She blinked. No, she wouldn't think about it. She wouldn't think about the silky cadence of his voice, his nose against her hair, his tongue touching her neck.

She wouldn't think about her blurted confession.

"Our soldier has had a bath and a shave, that's all," Lizzy said suddenly, jerking her thoughts into a proper line. "Take him to the bridge and see to it that he gets to work."

"No." The refusal came from Micah, and both Lizzy and Crockett stared at him.

"Crockett, go back outside," Micah commanded.

Crockett opened his mouth to retort, obviously not about to take orders from a man who was still their prisoner, but one steely look from the stranger caused him to reconsider.

"I'll just be gathering some of the planks from the barn." Crockett looked at Lizzy. "Call if you need me."

But she needed him now. She needed him to force Micah to avoid the line of questioning she had been stupid enough to open. She needed him to take Micah out to the bridge until she could gather her thoughts and think of something innocuous to say to divert this man's attention.

Crockett didn't wait for her answer. Turning, he walked away. The door slammed, leaving her alone with her captive.

The silence was overpowering, filling the room, invading the corners, making Lizzy tremble in an unaccountable fear. She should have kept her mouth closed—she'd meant to keep her mouth closed, but something had been pushing at her for days, something that wanted to be acknowledged.

She watched the way Micah stood before her—not quite the stranger he'd been, not quite familiar either. She saw the way his hands balled into fists, then released, balled, then released. A fierce frown creased his forehead, and those crystal blue eyes were intent on drilling right through her.

"Why didn't you tell me the moment I awakened?"

Lizzy had thought that Micah would hem and haw a bit, that he would dance around the issue at hand, that he would gently probe for information. Instead, he was almost brutal in his bluntness.

"I don't know what you mean."

"Dammit, Lizzy. Now isn't the time to be coy! I remember! I remember most of the nuances, the taste of your skin, the sound of your sighs. Don't you think you should tell me *exactly* what happened between us that night?"

She pressed her lips shut. Now that she'd forced the issue, she found the entire subject too embarrassing, too intimate to merely blurt out.

"Lizzy," he warned. "The truth. Dear sweet heaven above, you've got to tell me how it all happened. You must have known I wasn't entirely conscious of my actions. Why didn't you stop me? Why would you let such a thing occur?"

It was obvious that he'd wanted to ask those questions for so long, they nearly blurted free. But Lizzy merely shrugged, adopting a careless air.

"You talk as if something horrible happened between us," she said.

"That's what I'm trying to determine."

She folded her arms and marched to the window, staring sightlessly outside.

He sighed behind her. "Look, Lizzy, I don't mean to sound insulting or insensitive, but the memories I have of the last few days are a little disjointed. I think you owe me at least an explanation of what led to our lovemaking."

She turned, but didn't speak and the color drained from his face. He sank into a chair, resting his arms on his knees, not quite looking at her. "Did I hurt you?"

How could she answer that? "Only a little," she whispered. "At first."

The news did not appear to reassure him as she had intended. He rubbed at his brow. His chest expanded as he took a deep breath. "I'm sorry. There is no excuse for my behavior, none at all."

Lizzy didn't know what to say. She had expected him to blame her, at least in part, but he seemed prepared to take all of the responsibility himself.

For some reason she found that idea incredibly irksome. She wasn't a child or a simpleton. She didn't make a habit of melting at the first hint of emotional pressure. If she had truly wanted to stop him, she could simply have left the room.

"Lizzy, I—"

"How dare you?" she interrupted.

The color further drained from his skin when he misinterpreted her response.

"How dare you just assume that your charms were so intense, so magical, that I forgot all reason as soon as you kissed me!"

He stared at her in astonishment.

"What makes you think that I would be so weak, so gullible, as to let you force me to do something I didn't wish to do? For your information, I've lived for twenty-three years without making love with a man because that's the way *I* wanted things to be."

She took a breath to calm herself, but the anger burned even brighter. "Damn you! Did it ever occur to you to think of me? My thoughts? My motives? Of why I *allowed* you such intimacies?"

When he opened his mouth to respond, she continued on without urging. "Did it ever occur to you that I am a grown woman with desires and urges as strong as your own? I was to have been married, did you know that? But my fiancé, Bill, was killed mere days before our marriage. Did it ever occur to you that I might have been totally selfish in my actions? That I might have been seeking a little tenderness, a little comfort, from a man who was half out of his wits and hurting?"

"Hurting," he echoed, obviously peeved by her choice of words.

"You were moaning and groaning, thinking I was your dead wife."

"A fact of which you didn't bother to disabuse me," he retorted.

"As if I could have done such a thing. You *wanted* a woman in your arms, but somehow it sticks in your craw that *I* was the woman who fulfilled your wish."

He grabbed her arms, yanking her close. "Dammit, I thought no such thing!"

"How would you know? You didn't even remember a thing until now."

"I remembered," he growled through clenched teeth. "I just didn't think it would be gentlemanly to bring the subject up. I've been taught that a man and woman shouldn't talk about such things—even with a wedding band between them. How was I supposed to gently initiate this sort of conversation?"

"By being honest, with yourself and with me. By admitting that you didn't really want to acknowledge that you felt anything for me, even passion, because if you did, you would have to face the fact that Lili is dead. Dead and buried. And nothing on earth you can do will bring her back. Not even being a martyr."

The room echoed with her words.

Micah felt as if she'd struck him. A martyr? He hadn't ever felt that way. Had he? Sweet heaven, had he really lived the past few years thinking that if he suffered a little more, that if he bowed a bit lower to hardship, somehow Lili's death would make sense? That the pain he'd felt at her passing would go away?

Damn it all to hell, was this woman right? Had such emotions spread to every facet of his life?

The truth was nearly blinding. Yes. Yes, he had molded

himself into the perfect sacrificial lamb. It was the only explanation that he could give for allowing Bean to control him so completely. For the way he had dodged from battle line to battle line as if actually searching for death. It explained why he had purposely destroyed his own health, letting himself become a prisoner of another sort. He'd *wanted* to be punished. He'd tacitly *begged* to be punished.

Lizzy took another calming breath.

"I think it's time you went to work."

"No. We need to talk about this."

"As far as I'm concerned, there is nothing more to say. I will not allow you to touch me again. I have experienced all I want of the physical passions; of that you can be reassured. In the meantime you have your end of the bargain to fulfill. I want that bridge finished by the end of the month."

He studied her for long moments, testing her emotions, her mood, then he touched her cheek. "I *am sorry,*" he said again before abruptly changing the subject. "Where are your tools?"

"Crockett has them."

"Good." He didn't leave right away; his gaze filled with remorse and something more, a very tangible awareness. Then he went to the door.

"How long will it take to get the center planks filled in?" Lizzy asked, reasserting her role as captor.

"A few weeks, providing you have all the necessary supplies. The time will work to our advantage. That should be long enough to . . ."

"To what?"

He gathered his clothes. His eyes burned with an inexplicable heat. "Long enough to see if what happened results in a child." Then he went outside to change.

A child.

The thought was terrifying to Lizzy. Why hadn't she considered such a possibility? Why hadn't she looked beyond her actions to potential repercussions?

The idea haunted her for days. Lizzy tried to behave normally. She rose each morning at dawn, fixed her brothers their breakfast, sent one of them to fetch Micah and the rest outside to do their chores. But she could never really grow comfortable with the routine.

Micah continued to sleep in her parents' room. Crockett had insisted that the iron manacle be kept on his wrist for future use and since her brother couldn't be told the circumstances behind Micah's sudden change of heart, Lizzy had been forced to continue with the charade.

"Good morning."

Lizzy paused in the act of scooping eggs and pan gravy onto a plate. This morning she'd sent Boone to call Micah for breakfast. She'd been expecting him; her whole body had tensed for his arrival. Nevertheless, he had startled her. His low tone melted over her like sunshine.

She had to clear her throat to respond.

"Morning."

He took his place at the head of the table, alone. Vaguely, she heard Boone stomp out the front door.

Lizzy set the plate in front of him and returned to the stove. The distance she maintained between them whenever they were in the same room was part of an uneasy routine that they had developed over the past few days, one that was meant to ease the awkwardness of their relationship—that of intimate strangers. The effect was not as successful as Lizzy would have hoped. She still found herself tongue-tied and out of sorts, wondering what she could say that would ease the tension that thrummed between them.

"The bridge is coming along," she said when the scrape of his fork on the plate told her he had begun to eat. She busied herself with empty pans and soapy water in an attempt to look busy.

"The structure itself is sound."

"Good." After a minute she said again, "That's good. How have the boys behaved?" When Lizzy had caught them standing on the bank with Crockett, watching Micah develop a sweat, she'd ordered them all to help. Their work had been grudging at best.

"They seem to have the skill," Micah said after considering her question.

She pursed her lips in annoyance. "But they aren't applying themselves to the task at hand." The boys' attitude angered her. Didn't they realize how important the bridge was to the family's future?

"They resent me a little," Micah said as if he had read her thoughts. "They still think I was one of the raiders."

She gave up her busywork at the stove and turned to face him. "I suppose I could try to explain."

"Explain what? That I didn't rob your farm and take the pig? That I'm staying because I compromised their sister? I'm sure they'd take kindly to that."

Wiping her hands on a dish towel, she sat in the chair opposite Micah.

"I apologize for the way they've been acting," she whispered, but he didn't hear her.

Returning his attention to his food he said, "Give them time to work with me. A little hard labor tends to soften a person's attitude."

"You sound as if you know that from experience."

He poked at a crumb of egg with his fork. "I spent most of the war working on bridges just like that one."

"Blowing them up?" she asked tartly.

"No, putting them back together again. I was an engineer."

"For which side?"

His lips twitched at the familiar question. This time he deigned to answer. "The North."

Lizzy couldn't hide her surprise, and her reaction caused him to chuckle, a rich, almost rusty sound that made her wonder how long it had been since he'd really laughed.

"If you fought for the North, why didn't you just say so when I asked?"

"The war is over." The laughter dimmed. His expression became quite serious. "There are no more sides."

She let him eat for a few minutes, but now that she'd garnered this much information, she was not content to stop.

"Where are you from?"

He didn't answer right away, but finally said, "Virginia."

"Your people owned land?"

He nodded. "Before the war we grew crops on some of it, but most was used for grazing. My father bred horses." His fingers tightened, the knuckles gleamed white. "Now the animals are all gone. The whole lot."

"Stolen?"

"Stolen, requisitioned, destroyed. What does it matter how it happened? Solitude has been gutted and razed."

"Solitude?"

"That was its name. My grandfather came to this country from France. He said he wanted a home of his own, away from crowds and towns and noise."

"Such a place must have been heaven to him."

Micah nodded. "It was heaven, even two generations later. The house he built was imported brick by brick from Dijon. As a child, I was fascinated by this huge red building with its gleaming white shutters and open terraces. There were fireplaces in all of the rooms, imported carpets, secret passageways, and treasures from my ancestors' journeys to Africa and Arabia."

"It must have been fascinating." The words were spoken softly and with a tinge of wonder. Never would she have guessed that the scruffy, ill-kempt soldier she'd found in her barn could have come from such a privileged background.

Her own family, compared to those in most of the surrounding areas, had been considered quite well off, but in no way could their life have been compared to that of a horse breeder's son.

"My father was much like my forefathers, an adventurer of sorts, but his passion was horses. His only reason for traveling was to collect the finest specimens and bring them home. They were glorious animals, so full of pride and spirit."

The words trailed away, and unspoken between them was the fact that the horses were all gone.

Then she remembered that he'd used the word "razed" in describing Solitude.

"Was that how . . . Lili died? During the war?"

Lizzy knew she shouldn't have asked, but she had to discover the truth.

"No." He laid his fork down and pushed the plate out of the way. "My wife died before the war, of diphtheria."

"I'm so sorry."

"She was a beautiful woman. Sweet. Loving."

With each word, Lizzy felt a little more subdued.

"She would have liked you, Lizzy."

Micah's comment was unexpected.

"She always envied women like you—tall, spirited, able to speak their minds. Lili often scolded herself for her meekness, as she called it, her blind obedience to authority. Only once did she act defiantly."

"What did she do?" Lizzy asked, expecting some amusing anecdote.

"She married me."

Lizzy raised one brow questioningly.

"Her father was a very strict man. He wanted her to marry the son of a local banker. She defied him, left the school where she was teaching, and married me."

"Did you love her?"

"Yes. Lili was very easy to love. But in some ways, it

might be better that she's gone, that she can't see the man I've become."

"What man is that?"

He didn't speak for some time, but the way he held her gaze told her that he was mulling over how best to reply.

"I'm not the same as I was before the war."

"None of us are."

"I'm less patient, much more weary of life."

"She wouldn't have approved? I doubt that. I'm sure Lili would have been like thousands of other women who are just glad to have their loved ones home."

He didn't have an answer for that.

Lizzy glanced down at the dish towel she'd been twisting between her fingers. "I don't know you well, and I still have a few suspicions about your reasons for avoiding the authorities," she said pointedly. "But I haven't seen anything in your character that would cause a woman to fear you."

"I wouldn't think you, of all people, would say such a thing."

She shrugged. "Our lovemaking was not . . . unpleasant." He grew still, so still. "You allowed me to feel . . . pleasure."

Lizzy started when he laid his hand over hers.

"I wondered . . ."

"I should have told you earlier."

Which left him now with the inescapable conclusion that she had enjoyed their lovemaking.

"Why didn't you?" His question was punctuated with a slight squeeze of her hand.

"I . . ." But she couldn't tell him. She couldn't reveal, even to herself, any more of the secrets she harbored.

After several minutes he must have realized she wouldn't answer. After one more squeeze, he stood.

"I'd better get to work."

"Micah?"

He was halfway out the door.

"Your wife would have loved you still. No matter what

happened during the war." Her hand delved into her pocket, removing the key to the iron bands still fastened around his ankles. "Here. You'll be needing this," she said, tossing it his way.

It wasn't until he'd gone outside and she heard the *chink, chink* of his manacles being released that Lizzy realized she'd just argued the case of a dead woman. A woman he still loved body and soul.

For the rest of the morning, Micah thought about what Lizzy had told him, all of the information she'd unconsciously revealed.

He hadn't scared her away from passion.

That had been one of his greatest fears, one he hadn't dared ask her about. As a boy, he'd been taught to be a gentleman. At West Point, that code of behavior had been hammered into his character even more fully. He'd always thought that to lose control of one's baser instincts was one of the most serious crimes a man could commit. Little had he known that he would soon be guilty of abandoning his code and making love with a stranger.

It seemed incomprehensible to him that he could have done such a thing, even delirious and ill, but at the time, nothing had warned him to push back, to take a deep breath, to control his senses. Lizzy had felt so right in his arms. So damned right.

But how? He'd wooed Lili for years. On their wedding night, he'd spent an hour alone in the stable convincing himself that the time had come to consummate their marriage. How, in the space of two days, could he have taken such liberties with a stranger?

The screen door slammed, and he saw Lizzy come outside carrying a bucket of soapy water. She walked carefully away from the immediate area of the house and dumped it into a patch of grass. The entire action was quite simple, quite ordinary, but he couldn't help watching, noting the slim line of her arms, the slight sway of her breasts, that silly butter knife glinting in the sun.

She was an intriguing woman, to say the least. At a time when he should have been assuring Lizzy that he would never harm her again, *she* had been the one who comforted *him*.

Had she meant what she'd said? Did she truly think he was worthy of a woman's tender emotions? The thought caused him to stop short in swinging back the hammer. He'd spent so much time blaming himself, so much time acting like a hunted criminal, that he had begun to believe the charges himself.

Dear Lord in heaven, he thought, his throat growing unaccountably tight. Was there still something in him, some shred of decency, that this woman could find admirable?

"If you stare any harder, mister, your eyeballs are going to pop out and roll across the bridge."

The boyish comment caused Micah to jump, swinging the hammer down and mashing his thumb. Cursing, he stuck the offended digit in his mouth and stared at the boy who'd caught him unawares. Bridger. That was his name. The one who gallivanted around the yard and had a penchant for burning things.

"There's no use denying it," Bridger continued. "We've all seen it." He gestured to his brothers with a careless jut of his shoulder. Only Crockett remained removed from the group, standing a little way back, watching the confrontation with hooded eyes.

The twins crowded close, the chisels they'd been using to wedge the swollen boards into place held like daggers in their hands.

"We won't let you hurt her," Lewis said.

Clark nodded.

"So leave her be," Bridger warned. Then he threw down his hammer and stalked off, the twins following right away, then Boone, then Johnny, until only Crockett and a wide-eyed Oscar remained.

Oscar tugged at Crockett's pantleg. "He wants to hurt Lizzy?" he whispered, pointing at Micah.

"Run along, Oscar."

"But—"

"Run along! I need to have a talk with Micah. Go feed your chickens."

At the mention of the livestock, Oscar's eyes grew even rounder, for he apparently interpreted Crockett's remark to mean that the chickens were in danger as well.

Soon only Micah and Crockett remained on the battered bridge, the breeze soughing between them.

Crockett stared at him long and hard, measuring his character with such intense scrutiny that Micah found himself wanting to shift in discomfort. But he held himself still. Instinctively he knew it would be a mistake to show any kind of weakness.

"Leave her alone," was all Crockett said after some time. Then, with a gesture of the rifle he'd neglected to aim Micah's way all day he ordered, "Get back to work."

Micah didn't immediately comply. The boy was so naive, so infinitely trusting, thinking that a rifle pointed in Micah's direction would be enough to keep him in line. Didn't Crockett know that he'd been a soldier for years? That he couldn't remember the number of times someone had pointed a gun at him? It would be easy enough to lunge at the boy and slap the rifle away—or simply to drop into the river and swim to safety.

But he'd given his word to Lizzy that he would stay for a few more weeks. It was the least he could do.

Besides, Bean was out there—close, too close. Until he could figure out how to challenge the man, to prove his own innocence and avenge his family, he would be better off remaining where he was.

Turning back to his work, Micah ignored the boy behind him. The fire of retribution, which had nearly been extinguished by months of hiding and months of searching, began to glow in him again. He had to clear his name. He had to find the St. Charles treasure.

He needed it now more than ever before.

Chapter
11

Lizzy spent most of the day trying to avoid her own thoughts.

It wasn't an easy thing to do. Over and over again, her mind kept centering on one single issue: Micah. Her own behavior grew quite uncharacteristic. While sweeping, she made it a point to give the far corner of the porch special attention so that she could peek at him from under her eyelashes. While beating a rug, she placed it over the clothesline so that he could see her. And while she kneaded bread dough, she gravitated to the window again and again. When she caught herself staring at him quite openly, the dough forgotten on the sideboard, she could have kicked herself for such weakness.

She was becoming completely insane. That was the only explanation she could find for her actions. To stare at a man so blatantly, to visually caress the lines of his body, to imagine herself touching that skin, that hair . . . Yes, she had definitely lost her mind.

Never before had she acted this way—certainly not with Bill Hutchinson. He had followed all of the rules of a formal courtship. He'd begun by driving her home from church, then moved on to sitting on the porch while she served tea. There had been bunches of flowers, boxes of candy, an occasional brush of his hand. But none of it had affected her as much as a single glance from a soldier who'd strayed too far from home.

Was it only because she knew so much about Micah's body? Sensual details, like the way he closed his eyes when he kissed her, the way he made those soft little groans of pleasure.

She squeezed her eyes shut as a rush of sensation pooled deep in her loins. *Stop it!* she scolded herself. But try as she might, she could not push the feelings away. This man had done something to her; he'd done much more than introduce her to a few human pleasures. He had done something to her mind, to her heart. He'd made her remember what it was like to be young, to be a woman. To be alive.

But was there more to it than that?

She shied away from the very possibility. She mustn't even think of such things. In time, probably a very few weeks, he would be gone and she would be left alone again. Alone with her brothers and her farm and her sterile little life. It was the way her life had to be.

"Lizzy!"

She whirled, not realizing that Johnny had walked into the room. Her hand flew to her throat, her heart thumping.

"Don't scare me like that!"

Johnny scowled at her in displeasure, obviously guessing just who she'd been watching out the window.

"You don't like him, do you, Lizzie?" It was more of an accusation than a question. "That man killed our pig."

She opened her mouth to deny the charge, but Johnny continued heatedly, "Watch out for him, Lizzy. He's a bad man. Why, I bet he's the one who took Ruggles."

"Ruggles? What has that goat got to do with anything?" An immediate panic assailed her. Ruggles was their one source of milk and cheese, and when her kid was born, they would have something else to barter for food.

"She's gone. She's been gone all day." Johnny screwed his face up into a scowl. "Her rope was cut! Probably by that . . . that man!"

Johnny whirled and ran from the room, leaving her perplexed. Where in the world was that blasted goat?

Throwing a dishcloth onto the table, she stormed outside, marching purposefully to the barn. Sure enough, Ruggles's stall was empty, the rope dangling from one of the supports —not cut, as Johnny had claimed but clearly chewed apart.

Drat it all! The goat had escaped. Again. Unless she found out where Ruggles had wandered, the boys would blame Micah for the goat's disappearance.

She strode into the sunshine again. Standing with her hands on her hips, she surveyed the yard, wondering where the damned animal had gone now. They should have tied her up with a piece of wire or lightweight chain—anything she couldn't have chewed through so easily.

Desperately, she began looking for clues. Luckily, the ground had hardened up a bit since the recent rains, allowing her to see a trail of hoof prints that led into the woods.

The nanny goat was probably on her way to the garden right now.

Picking up her skirts, she ran to the plot they'd cultivated in a small clearing in the woods. Once there, she shuddered to a halt. The rows were undisturbed, the tops of the plants nodding listlessly in the breeze.

Where was that animal?

"Ruggles?" she called. "Ruggles, you'd better answer me,

or I'll be making a pair of shoes out of your hide." Nothing. "Ruggles!"

Naaa.

She whirled in the direction of the faint sound.

Naaaaa.

The pitiful bleat came again. Merciful heavens, was she having her kid? Here? Now?

"Ruggles!" Lizzy ran, leaping over rocks and dodging through overgrown trees. The goat's bleating grew stronger. "Ruggles, I'm coming."

After ducking beneath a particularly prickly bush, she caught a glimpse of the animal's pale hindquarters. Somehow, the goat had wedged herself into the small opening of a cave. Loose rocks had been piled from the ground up, but the goat had dislodged the makeshift covering and had tried to squeeze through the narrow opening she had created.

Lizzy paused to catch her breath. "Trust you to find the most impossible place to hide," she muttered as she grabbed the goat by the hips and tried to tug her out. The goat's pregnant belly prevented such an easy solution. She was going to have to lift Ruggles high enough so that the animal's body would clear the jagged rocks.

It took several minutes of squirming and grunting to move into a position where she could help the animal. Sweat beaded her upper lip as she wrapped her arms around the nanny goat and fought to lift her free.

Ruggles bleated in distress, her legs scrabbling for a foothold. Then her stomach moved free of the rocks, and she wriggled loose, running for home.

"Ungrateful animal," Lizzy said to herself. She was about to back away herself when a glint of light inside the cave caught her eye.

Silently chiding herself for being no better than the goat, Lizzy bit her lip in indecision, then slid through the narrow opening. The space inside widened to a large vaulted area and she blinked, waiting for her eyes to adjust. When they did, she could hardly believe what she'd found. Three huge wood-and-iron trunks had been jammed into the cave. They were obviously old, the hinges and hardware caked with rust and dried mud as if they'd been unearthed from somewhere else. The top of one had been dislodged, revealing a mound of leather pouches.

Her brow creased. Had someone hidden them here? She and Sally had buried the inn's silver by the riverbed a year into the war, but this cave was on Wilder land. Who would have brought the chests here?

She brushed at the dirt, revealing some painted words on the side of the trunk. Two names: Adam and Wilhemena. A date: 1843.

Gracious! How long had they been here? She'd never seen this cave before. For all she knew, the cases could have been stashed here years ago—decades! The cracked leather certainly attested to the age of the bags.

"Lizzy?" The call was faint, but the voice belonged unmistakably to Johnny. He must have taken it into his head to follow her.

"Coming!" she yelled, knowing she couldn't let the boy find her here. Unlike his other brothers, Johnny had a streak of the adventurer in his veins. She didn't need him to find another hiding place.

Sighing in annoyance at the fact that she couldn't have more than a minute alone each day, she snatched one of the pouches, intent on examining it later. But it was surprisingly heavy. Curious, she tugged it open, the old leather nearly coming to pieces in her hands.

Merciful heavens—*Gold.* Dozens of battered ancient gold coins!

"Lizzy?"

"Coming!"

Later, she told herself, shoving the pouch deep in her

pocket. It didn't belong to her, and she had no idea how long it had been there, but she was tempted beyond reason to use it and damn any future consequences.

But even as she ran to the house, she couldn't deny that the pouch in her pocket might prove to be the answer to her prayers.

This winter her brothers would not go hungry.

For several days Lizzy kept her distance from Micah, since she didn't want any more sparks to fly between them. That tactic calmed the boys a little, but it had the opposite effect on Lizzy. Saints above, she had never known that a woman could crave a man's company so completely. In avoiding the man, she became hungry for the sound of his voice, for the thrill of his gaze connecting with her own. At night she was haunted by dreams. Dreams of them touching, kissing, loving. Dreams she had never had before. Not with such clarity, such reality. They made her understand how Micah could have made love to her without really waking.

She still didn't know why she had abandoned her senses in such a fashion, but she no longer wanted to analyze her behavior. The man was here with her now. Before he left, she wanted a little more than dreams. Beyond that, she would not allow herself to dwell on anything else.

Finally, unable to stand her self-imposed distance any longer, she made her way outside. Midway across the yard, her determined stride faltered.

Rather than finding Micah working, as usual, she saw that he was stretched out on the grass, asleep.

Dear sweet heaven above, there ought to be some kind of rule against what he was doing. Not the slumbering, not the lollygagging from his chores, but the way he lay there, his hands flung over his head, his shirt left open, his chest laid bare, revealing the whirls of downy hair. Beneath the worn fabric of his underwear she could see each dip and hollow of his body, the formation of his stomach, the thrust of his pelvic bones, his . . .

She swallowed against the dryness that threatened to close her throat. My, oh, my, oh, my. Those first few hours when Micah had been her prisoner, she'd tried not to watch him moving around the yard wearing nothing but his underwear —mud-soaked, clinging, wet-at-the-hems underwear. Later, when he'd taken his bath, she'd tried not to look below his waist as she'd watched his contorted image in the depths of the windowpanes.

But today the temptation was undeniable. Somehow, when he was dirty and straggly and unkempt, she'd been able to keep a certain emotional distance. Now that he was clean, shaved, and almost . . . handsome, she couldn't stop her feet from slowing, her heart from lurching in her breast.

She approached Crockett first, trying to keep her eyes someplace, *any*place respectable.

"What's he doing?" she asked her brother.

"Sleeping."

She shot him a scornful look. "That's obvious. Why isn't he working on the bridge?"

Crockett shrugged. "He can't do much more until you get him some supplies. He told me he planned to rest for an hour or two until he could talk to you. He's still feeling a little tuckered by that fever he had."

"Rather bold of him, considering the fact that you're holding him at gunpoint."

"I didn't see any reason to keep him awake. As I said, he can't do much more until we get some lumber and hardware."

"I'll head into town tomorrow."

"We don't have any money."

Lizzy felt a niggling devil prodding her about the gold she'd found. No one could fault her for using it. Whoever had left it there was probably dead now. It had probably been there for ages. If its owners were still nearby, they would have retrieved it long ago.

"I'll think of something," she said.

"We don't have anything to barter either."

"Never you mind," she said firmly. "I'll find a way."

He shrugged at her optimism, but didn't press. "What do you want me to have him do while you're gone?"

"Surely there's something we need done that can keep him busy."

"I don't know . . ." Crockett hesitated. "Maybe you should let him go."

"What?" Panic welled up inside her like a black cloud.

"We can finish the repairs ourselves. He's done the hard part. We don't need him anymore."

No! No. He couldn't leave yet. Not yet.

"I don't think that would be wise," she said.

"Why not? What can he do that we can't?"

"Well . . . he's obviously more experienced than we are. We might run into some problems that only he could fix."

"There's nothing left to do but fasten some boards in place."

"No!" Her voice was a little sharper than she'd intended. "Not until I can ask a few questions around town. I won't be turning him loose if he's part of that band of thieves that stole from us before."

"Do you honestly think he was one of those men?"

No, she didn't. But she couldn't admit that to Crockett.

"Just wait until I get back from town. Wait until I can ask some questions." When Crockett opened his mouth to argue, she shot him a stern glance. Crockett might be close to adulthood, but she was still in charge. It was time he remembered that.

He wilted ever so slightly, a sign that he was willing to concede to her authority.

"Go on up to the house, Crockett."

This time he didn't protest. Wordlessly he handed her the

rifle, hiked up his pants around his skinny waist, and marched back to the house in barely concealed resentment at her tone.

Only after she'd heard the door slam did she allow herself to look at Micah. He'd shifted slightly, bending one knee, exposing a good length of leg. She was nearly overcome with the urge to touch him there, to explore the muscles, the bunching of his thighs.

She knew that she shouldn't allow herself to think such thoughts. They were far from appropriate.

But what did it matter?

The thought raced through her head with the strength of a bullet. The society and the rules that had governed her for so long were gone, blasted away by war. She was twenty-three years old, likely to remain alone, unmarried, the matriarch of her odd little family. Why couldn't she have this dalliance, this summer, to find out what her life *could* have been like? Why couldn't she forget that she'd vowed never to touch him again?

Without considering the consequences of her actions, she took a few steps closer, then sank onto the grass a mere inch or two away from Micah, laying the rifle aside. Then she drew her knees up under her chin and studied the man to her heart's content.

His features were so strong, so rough-hewn, that she couldn't resist. She had to touch him.

She laid a hand on his cheek. The skin was warm, sun-kissed. Her fingers slipped to his chin. There was the faintest cleft in the center. His neck was strong and surprisingly soft-skinned; the hollow between his collarbones enticed her.

Bill Hutchinson had never allowed her such freedom. He'd been a proper man, a strict man. Coming from a long line of religious people, he'd been kind enough to instruct Lizzy in how a woman should behave. He would've had a fit of apoplexy if he could have seen her now. But Lizzy realized she really didn't care. She'd never loved Bill Hutchinson. Not the way a woman was supposed to love a man. Theirs was to have been a marriage of convenience, a means of escape for her.

Escape. That was what she'd wanted. Even if it meant selling herself. Even if it meant giving up everything she'd had for something different. She'd been willing to do that simply because her life at the ferry landing had become intolerable. She hadn't known that she would also give up this chance to experience the unknown, to have an adventure, a few stolen moments.

She touched the crease in his breast, tracing it down, down, ever down, until she reached the dip of his navel. There she stopped, hovering in indecision, knowing that with the barest flick of her fingers, she could lift the edge of his drawers and trousers a bit and expose him completely.

A huge hand snapped over Lizzy's wrist, and she gasped, shrinking back.

Micah held her firm, his lashes flickering, his crystal blue eyes drilling straight through her.

Hastily she sought a way to explain her forwardness. "I thought you were feeling a little woozy again. I was merely . . . checking you for fever."

One of his brows rose. "Oh, really."

"You do seem hot."

"I do?"

"Mmm. But it could be the sun, so don't be thinking that I'm going to allow you to shirk your chores."

"I wouldn't dream of it."

She tried to yank away, but he held her fast.

"Suppose I told you I had other aches and pains. Would you investigate those too?"

The question was loaded with meanings that Lizzy chose not to explore.

"As far as I can see, you're as healthy as a—"

"Pig?"

"Perhaps even more so, considering the state of poor Rosie."

He chuckled softly at her tart retort, and she was glad. She loved to hear that sound bubbling from his throat.

She tried to pull away. "It's time you got back to your duties."

He shook his head slowly, deliberately. "I need supplies."

"I could give you a half-dozen other tasks to fill your time."

"Mmm," he said, but she knew he wasn't paying attention. He was watching the way the words formed on her lips. "Why have you been avoiding me, Lizzy?"

The question was direct and more disturbing than it should have been.

"I . . . The boys . . ."

"Have they been giving you problems?"

"No. But they regard you as a threat."

"Beyond that of a pig murderer?"

She nodded, then hurried to explain. "You have to understand. My brothers have been through a lot of hardship. First our father went off to war, then their mother died. I've had to see them through the nightmares, the clinging, the insecurity, the smothering protectiveness. I suppose they've sensed . . . something between us."

He cupped her cheek with his callused palm. "There is nothing between us."

"No. Of course not."

"Nothing at all."

Neither of them sounded very convincing. The truth was there in the way she couldn't look away, in the way his fingers spread wide to slip through her hair.

"We can't let anything more happen," Lizzy said breathlessly.

"I don't belong here."

"No, you don't," she agreed even as her heart skipped a beat.

"I came this far west for a reason."

"Yes."

"That reason has not gone away."

"I know."

"I've got to finish what I set out to do." He seemed to be trying to convince himself as much as her.

"Of course. You're an honorable man."

He became quite still at her remark, and she hastened to reassure him that she'd spoken honestly. "Everything I've ever been taught, every lesson I've learned about human nature in the past few years, tells me that I shouldn't trust you," she said. "But I cannot deny that you set out to prove to me with deeds rather than words that you were a man with a conscience. I can't ignore what I've discovered." She shifted slightly, forced to continue. "I still fear you a little. I would be lying if I said I didn't."

"Why are you afraid of me?"

"Because you still harbor so many secrets. Why did you come to my farm? Why are you so leery of the authorities? I'm not really sure I want to know the answers. But I do know that you are a man who would not hurt me or my family."

Her words touched him far more than she would have expected.

"Thank you, Lizzy," he said without warning. "You're been the first person to believe in me in years. You don't know what that means to me after all this time."

Then he pulled her down, his lips covering hers in a hungry kiss, one that held all of the pent-up frustration that Lizzy had thought she'd been alone in feeling the past few days.

She tried to remain a little aloof, to keep the embrace as innocent as possible, but within seconds it was she who melted against him, who encouraged his embrace.

Micah was astounded by her immediate reaction.

Never, even during his marriage to Lili, had he experienced the immediate, gut-wrenching reaction that he felt to that kiss. A flash of white-hot lightning raced through his body, igniting his blood and infusing his heart with a scintillating energy. All thought of caution fled from his brain as he reached out and drew her to him, closer and closer and closer, until her very body could have melded to his own.

Had he been alone too long? Had he completely forgotten what it was like to hold a woman in his arms? The dreams he'd had of making love to this woman were nothing compared to the reality.

He spread his hands wide, sweeping them over her body in hungry arcs, needing to absorb each bone, each muscle, each gentle curve. After all that had occurred between them, he was afraid of frightening her with the strength of his sudden desire, but he could no more control it than he could control the tide.

To his surprise she responded, hesitantly at first, her lips timid beneath his. It was obvious that she hadn't been tutored by any other man, for she didn't know where to put her hands, how to respond to the urging of his lips. But she was a swift learner, melting in his arms, slipping her fingers beneath his shirt, tentatively caressing him in a way that made him moan. Needing more, so much more, he opened his mouth and touched her with his tongue, bidding her to respond.

In an instant she grew still, stiff.

"It's all right, Lizzy," he whispered into her mouth. "You said you trusted me. Trust me now."

His head tipped and he began to teach her, showing her the pleasures that could be had between a man and a woman. His hands roamed her back, shifting her, bringing her over him, tightly pressing her against his hips.

"I need this so much," he whispered against her ear. "You don't know what it's like to feel alive again."

"But I do," she returned. "I do."

Her response was all he needed to drive him onward, clutching her to him as if she were a lifeline. He wanted to hold her, absorb her, love her.

It was Lizzy who broke away, inserting a measure of sanity. "We can't . . . the boys."

Immediately he knew her concern. Her brothers were already resentful of him and his interest in their sister. If they had proof of his intentions, they would be furious.

Lizzy scrambled to her feet, and he thought she meant to run into the house. Instead she reached out to pull him up.

"Come with me."

She led him to the springhouse, closing them both in the cool darkness. Her hands became urgent as they stripped his buttons free of their holes.

"I need to feel you," she whispered, and the words were like a match to kerosene.

His own fingers fumbled with the fasteners to her blouse, but after so long away from such feminine frippery, he couldn't manage the tiny things. Too aroused to deal with them, he settled for cupping her hips through the fullness of her skirts and pulling her tightly to him.

She became a wild thing, her mouth opening, her head tilting from side to side. He could barely keep up with her, with the passion that blazed between them.

When she pressed him down to the ground, he went willingly. When she began to unbutton his trousers, he could only gasp. Then she was straddling him, pushing her skirts out of the way.

"Come inside me," she whispered, her eyes glittering with such feminine desire that he could scarcely believe it was directed toward him. "I want to feel the pleasure again. I want to . . ."

He didn't allow her to say anything more. Not with the tenuous control he had at this point. Twisting them both, he rolled her onto her back.

It took all the strength he possessed to go slowly, to woo

her body into relaxing. She was strung so tightly with her emotions and the memory of their last occasion, that he feared he would hurt her.

He needn't have worried. As soon as he kissed her throat, the hollow behind her ears, she became languid and sensual in his arms, as if she had feared that he would not give her that which she desired.

Despite the barriers of their clothing, he did his best to woo her body into the realms of pleasure. He stroked her arms, her legs, that naked expanse of thigh above the tops of her stockings. Then, when she whimpered and shuddered against him, he reached up, up, parting the split covering of her pantalets and touching her intimately.

At the mere contact, she bucked against him, her mouth opening in pleasure, and Micah knew that he could not wait another minute. Positioning himself against her, he paused only a second.

"Are you sure?" he whispered, the words guttural and barely comprehensible.

"Yes." Her hands clutched his back. "Yes."

Then he was pushing inside her, feeling that warm, moist cavern that seemed to have been made especially for his own pleasure. He rocked against her, thrust, positioning his thumb between them in such a manner as to offer her the most sensation. When he felt her grip him and heard her gasp, her body beginning to shudder with her own release, he pressed into her one last time and took his own pleasure.

It was some time later before conscious thought returned, before he could roll to her side and draw her head into the pillow of his shoulder. She felt so right there, as if she had been fashioned to complement his own shape.

There were no words between them. There was no need for words. She lifted her head. "What is happening to us?"

It was a question he didn't know how to answer.

"I don't know."

"You're a stranger. A man who is wanted by the law."

He knew that was a guess on her part, but he couldn't deny the truth of her conclusion. "Yes. I am."

She closed her eyes. "What . . . sort of crime?"

He rubbed her arm, willing her to believe in him. The trust she'd so openly offered was still so fragile, so new.

"I have been accused of profiteering and treason."

"But the war is over," she said, echoing what he'd said to her more than once.

"Such charges don't go away when a war ends."

She took a deep breath, considering him for some time. "Did you do it?"

He shook his head. "No."

"Then this Bean person, the one you feared would find you . . ."

"He's the man responsible. He's the one who manufactured the evidence behind the charges."

"Why would he do such a thing?"

"His daughter, Lili, was my wife."

"He blames you for her death?"

"Yes."

She rubbed her brow. "What a mess. What an absolute mess."

"If Bean finds me, he will dispense with the formalities and have me hanged on the spot. He won't allow me to escape him again."

"How did you get away before?"

"One of my men created a diversion, and I was able to run." Micah's throat grew tight with sadness at the very thought. He had never learned what had happened to Wheeze, whether he'd died in the ensuing gunfight or had survived and been punished by Bean.

"So what do we do now?"

Micah could barely believe he'd heard the question correctly. When he realized that he had, and that Lizzy was serious in her intent to right the wrongs which had been done against him, he grasped her arm, pulling them both into a sitting position. "Nothing, do you hear? You will do nothing. This is my problem and I will solve it. You don't know Bean. You don't know the kind of hatred he feels for me. If he knew you were involved in my affairs, even remotely, your brothers would be the ones to pay."

She eyed him consideringly for some time, taking so long that Micah feared he hadn't been able to impress upon her the seriousness of the situation.

"Lizzy?" The call came from outside, from little Oscar. "Lizzy, where are you?"

"We'll see," she said again, rising to her feet. In quick, efficient movements, she tidied her blouse and brushed off her skirts. "We'll just see."

Then she stormed out of the springhouse, calling for Oscar's benefit, "Now you know where the springhouse is, Micah. Dip a pail of cool water for supper and then come into the house."

Chapter

12

The next morning Crockett escorted Micah into the kitchen for his breakfast, motioned him toward the table, and then went outside to do his chores.

"Here's your food," Lizzy stated, ladling the last of the pan gravy onto his plate. For a moment her gaze flickered, as if she wanted to say more. When he looked at her questioningly, she darted a nervous glance at her brothers.

Had they said something to her? Had the boys voiced their concern about the undercurrents that ran between her and Micah? Boone eyed him sulkily, Bridger stared. But that was nothing out of the ordinary.

The back door squeaked open, and the twins trooped in. "Sit down to breakfast, you two."

Collecting their plates from the sideboard, they complied,

taking chairs at the far end of the table and glaring at Micah suspiciously.

"What's your last name?" Lewis demanded suddenly. "Nobody's told me yet."

Sensing that perhaps, just perhaps, he might be able to pique the twins' curiosity and encourage their goodwill, Micah was swift to answer. "St. Charles. Micah St. Charles."

Clark shoved a mouthful of scrambled eggs between his lips and chewed thoughtfully. "Mica," he drawled between bites, his brow creasing. "They named you after a rock?"

"Oh, for pity's sake," Lizzy scolded. "Eat your breakfast and get out to the bridge. I'll be bringing some supplies home this afternoon, so you'd better get everything ready for them."

Clark's chin tipped at a stubborn angle. "We don't want to work on the bridge anymore. Not with him."

Lizzy dropped the frying pan onto the table. "Now, listen, you two. We need that bridge so that we can survive another year."

"Until Pa gets home?"

Micah felt an echo of the pain Lizzy must have experienced. Just by looking at her, Micah knew that she had given up all hope that their father would return. "Yes. We've got to get it built before Papa gets home."

Lewis scowled in Micah's direction. "But we don't want to work with him. He . . . he stares at you."

A faint hint of color touched her cheeks.

"He looks at you whenever you come outside. We've seen him ogling you like he didn't have anything better to do."

Lizzy opened her mouth, but she obviously couldn't think of anything to say to the twins.

Micah tried to focus his attention on his plate, but to no avail.

"We won't work with him. He stole our pig," Clark said.

"But—"

"Rosie was *our* pig. Pa gave her to Lewis and me for our birthday just before he left."

"I know that, but . . ." Lizzy's face was now completely infused with color.

"He stole her. Shot her and ate her, I bet," Lewis continued. "Didn't you?"

This time the accusation was directed at Micah.

"No." He could not hold back the truth. "No, I didn't."

"Why should we believe you? You're a . . . a pig assassin!"

"I'm telling you the truth."

The twins scowled at each other. "How do we know that?"

"You'd have to trust me, I suppose."

That answer didn't seem to sit well with either of them.

"Why would you stay here and work if you didn't kill Rosie?"

Micah set his fork down carefully. "Lots of men are accused of things they didn't do." He looked up at Lizzy, willing her to continue believing in his innocence. He was guilty of nothing more than loving a woman and helplessly watching her die. For so many years, he had longed to have just one person in whom he could confide that fact. One person who would proclaim him an honorable man. This woman had done so without any prompting on his part.

"Sometimes, after being accused, a man has to prove himself—even if some people think he's guilty for a time. But if he works hard, shows what he's really made of, then the truth will always come out."

The twins exchanged glances, clearly unconvinced. After a few minutes Lizzy bullied them into finishing their meal and rushing outside.

Through the window Micah could see Crockett, rifle in hand, on his way to the house. He was coming to fetch Micah for work. As the boy made his way into the kitchen nothing more could be said, even though he wanted to speak with Lizzy, kiss her.

"Tonight," he whispered as he rose from the table. "Tonight we'll talk some more." Then he disappeared into the hall.

Crockett didn't immediately follow his prisoner.

Seeing the accusation in his gaze, Lizzy hurriedly sought some way to elude the questions she feared he would ask.

"I'll be going into Catesby within the hour. Can you think of anything we need besides lumber and hardware?"

"We don't have any money."

Lizzy thought of the pouch of gold for the hundredth time that day. "I'm hoping the merchants will extend us some credit."

Crockett must have thought such a possibility was next to impossible. "I can't think of anything besides what I told you before, but I still think you should stay here. You shouldn't be traveling those roads alone."

"I'll take one of the rifles."

"Even so—"

"Who would you have me take for protection?" she interrupted. "You need to stay here. You're the only one who can shoot straight, and the other boys are too young to be left on their own. I'll be able to complete our errands much quicker without a chaperon."

Crockett agreed, reluctantly, and she hurried upstairs before he could change his mind.

Once there, she quickly began a ritual she'd abandoned so long ago, she was surprised she knew what she should do.

First, she powdered her body with perfumed cornstarch, taking special care with her face and arms, which the sun had darkened to an unfashionable brown. Then she delved deep in her armoire, taking out the few remaining garments from her trousseau.

She slipped into delicate batiste pantalets and a scoop-necked camisole. After tying the satin ribbons, she fitted a pink grosgrain corset around her waist, grunting and tugging until her torso had been tightened into a shapely hourglass, her breasts pushed brazenly against their restraints. Next, she donned pale pink cotton hose and leather boots, knowing she would never be able to reach her feet once she'd added all of the other paraphernalia needed by a woman of fashion.

After pausing to take several short, shallow breaths, she slipped into a lawn corset cover with a satin-stitched ivy design that she had embroidered the winter before her impending nuptials. This was followed by a knee-length petticoat with a similar scrolled handwork, a watch-spring crinoline, and two flounced petticoats. Last of all, she dressed in an ivory silk shirtwaist, a maroon-and-black plaid skirt, and a tight-waisted wool bolero.

As she paused in front of the mirror to sweep her hair into an elaborate coronet of braids held in place by her precious half-dozen remaining hairpins instead of the customary butter knife, she couldn't help but mourn how many things had changed in the past few years. Before the war, the bridge and the inn had provided enough money for this dress as well as the rest of her elaborate trousseau. A trousseau that had been worn beyond recognition or sold for food. Now the land could barely support a family of eight.

Pushing that thought away, she positioned a tiny bonnet over one brow and pinned it in place. She had a role to play today, one that these clothes would only serve to enhance. She would do well to remember there was no time for regrets.

It took her a moment to accustom herself to the full skirts and tight laces, but by the time she reached the kitchen, she felt she was in control of the masquerade—that of a woman without a care in the world.

Taking a key from the row of hooks on the wall, she paused. She'd spent most of the past morning debating her course of action. The time had come to commit herself, but the closer she got to the larder, the harder her heart began to thump in her chest.

Did she dare?

Why not? It was her only choice.

But it was wrong.

Pushing the voice of conscience aside, she unlocked the cupboard and removed the leather pouch from where she'd hidden it. No one would ever know if she used the contents. Even if the true owner came looking for them, she could plead innocence and eventually pay the amount back. She only needed a little money. Enough to make the shopkeepers think she was worthy of credit.

Before she could change her mind, Lizzy shoved the pouch into the pocket of her skirt, grabbed her reticule, and hurried outside.

"Crockett!"

Crockett and Micah turned at her call and, seeing her, grew still, quiet.

"Hitch Micah's horse to the buggy."

For a moment Crockett didn't move, then he hurried to do as she'd asked. Stationed by the pump, Micah continued to stare at her, heatedly, obviously.

For her brother's sake, she tried to make light of his response. "Is there something wrong, Mr. St. Charles?"

He shook his head. "Not at all. You're beautiful."

Her eyes darted to the younger boys, who were watching with rabid interest and varying degrees of horror. "Does that surprise you?"

"No. I knew you would look like this once you got rid of the butter knife."

She gasped, but he continued, "I've always thought you were pretty, even striking, but I never knew how completely beautiful you would be if you didn't have to work so hard to provide for your brothers."

Micah was studying her so intently that she felt as if he were actually touching her, caressing her. The boys looked as if they would like to bash him over the head with their shovels.

She tore her own gaze away and stared at the barn, the sky, the dirt, anything so that she wouldn't see him, so big, so beguiling.

Crockett approached with the horse and buggy, cutting off anything she might say. When she took the whip from her brother, Micah hurried toward her and offered his hand to help her into the seat.

"When you come back, Lizzy," he said in a voice so low only she could hear it, "I want to kiss you again. And I will. On that you can rely."

Then he walked away and returned to pumping water into a bucket, leaving her knees weak and her skin hot.

"When you come back, Lizzy, I want to kiss you again. And I will. On that you can rely."

The promise haunted Lizzy for most of the afternoon. The ride to town seemed much longer than usual, giving her far too much time to think, to wonder. To dream about a future.

A future? With Micah?

She squashed that thought as soon as it came into her head. It couldn't happen, she argued with herself. Ever. But she couldn't prevent the tingling sensation that began at her lower extremities and feathered up, up into her belly.

Sweet heaven above, what was wrong with her? Why couldn't she keep her heart and her mind where they belonged?

Her *heart?*

As soon as the word formed in her head, she drew back on the reins, stopping the buggy. But it wasn't the horse that was breathing hard, it was her.

Heart? Her heart wasn't involved in any of this. She was simply a woman doing what needed to be done. She'd captured this man, made him her prisoner, and forced him to do her bidding. How could that possibly be interpreted as anything other than . . . than . . .

Desperation?

For her family. She was desperate for her family.

But not entirely.

Drat and bother, why couldn't she silence that little voice inside her? The one that kept telling the truth.

Her fingers clenched around the reins, but she couldn't move, couldn't urge the horse to continue its journey. She was being pummeled by thoughts and sensations that, until a few days ago, she would never have allowed in her head. She was thinking of herself as a woman. Not as a sister, not as a surrogate mother, but as a woman with needs and dreams and wishes of her own.

Looking up at the brilliant sky, Lizzy damned the heat, not the heat of the day, but the overwhelming warmth that settled into her body when she thought of the stranger. No, not a stranger. Micah St. Charles. Her lover.

Whenever she was near him, she couldn't tear her gaze away. She wanted to study him, touch him, caress him. Even from a distance, he did things to her. When he wasn't around, she found herself thinking the oddest things—like how it felt to stroke his back, to run her fingers over the muscles of his arms.

These new urges were enough to make her crazy. She'd always been a level-headed woman. She'd entered her relationship with Bill Hutchinson calmly and methodically, knowing ahead of time its strengths and weaknesses. She'd been prepared to remain formal and cool, to call him Mr. Hutchinson for the rest of her life. In exchange, she'd known she would be given rewards of her own. A home. A new life.

A sterile existence.

Lizzy found herself panting as if she'd escaped a jail sentence. How close she'd come to imprisoning herself within the walls of respectability, just for a chance to escape. Yet here she was now, involved in one of the most complicated adventures of her life, and she had never felt so invigorated. So . . . aroused.

There was no way around it. This man had stripped away her defenses to expose the woman beneath. One who felt things too deeply, who responded to situations far too passionately.

So why couldn't she be a little selfish and fight for a future with this man?

Micah straightened from nailing a board in place on the chicken coop. Leaning against the wall for a moment, he struggled to catch his breath. He was gaining his strength back, but every now and again he felt a wave of exhaustion. Especially today.

"Maybe you need another drink."

He lifted his head then rued the abrupt motion as Lewis and Clark seemed to waver in front of his eyes. He was feeling so dizzy all of the sudden. Was the fever returning?

No, dammit! Now wasn't the time. He was hoping to use Lizzy's absence to his advantage. He wanted to speak privately with the boys and develop some sort of rapport. It was important to him that they didn't think he was a threat to their sister.

Lifting his head, he took short breaths to combat the wooziness that threatened to rob him of his equilibrium. He'd had the feeling for nearly a half hour. Ever since the boys had brought him some cider to drink. It had been a little on the hard side, true, but not strong enough to make him feel so unsettled.

"What's the matter?"

The question came from Crockett who still held him in the sights of Micah's own rifle. Beside him, Boone held the bucket of water they'd brought a few minutes before. Micah's vision seemed to jump and skip, but he was sure Johnny was there too.

Stumbling slightly, he leaned against the coop—not the strongest support, considering the state of the structure. Lifting his hand to his brow he said, "I don't know. I just feel suddenly . . . strange."

Crockett squinted at him, obviously suspicious. "You look kinda sick."

"I'll be fine in a minute."

"You don't look fine."

"We could give you some cod-liver oil," Bridger offered.

Micah shuddered. "No. Thanks. I don't suppose you know where Lizzy hid my saddlebags, do you?"

Again Crockett eyed him with distrust. "I might."

"I've got some medicine."

"Medicine?"

"Well, I've got some whiskey. It sometimes helps at times like this."

Crockett didn't move, and Micah allowed himself to wilt a little more against the coop. "Come on, boy, what would it hurt? The whiskey chases away the chills, that's all. There's not enough left in the bottle to make me drunk, or I would have asked for it long ago."

"Lizzy doesn't approve of spirits."

"Lizzy isn't here." He knew immediately that he'd said the wrong thing. "Besides," he quickly amended, "it's for medicinal use only."

Crockett's brow furrowed in indecision.

"I'm not going anywhere," Micah promised. "But if you don't help me, I might not be standing this well when she gets back." He wrapped his arms around himself as if warding off a tremendous bout of chills.

Crockett reluctantly nodded. "It will only take me a minute to get it. Don't you be trying anything."

"I won't." Micah held up his hand. "Honest."

The boy backed away, then turned and ran toward the barn.

Micah staggered forward, sinking onto the edge of a wooden trough. With each second that passed, he felt a little less sure of himself, a little more threatened.

He pushed himself to his feet.

"Crockett! He's trying to escape! Where's the gun?" The twins turned and thundered in the direction of the barn. Boone and Bridger quickly followed, shouting, "The house, get Lizzy's revolver."

Realizing they'd misunderstood, he stumbled to the gate. But he'd only taken two steps when a small figure rounded the corner of the chicken coop. Oscar.

Eyeing the little boy with his blond curly hair and piercing gaze, Micah froze.

Oscar frowned at him, lifting a tiny bow and a sticklike arrow. "Don't you move," he said, his voice high, childish. "And don't you hurt my chickens."

For the first time in hours, Micah became aware of the horde of feathered hens pecking the yard around him.

"Don't you kill 'em. If you do, I'll have t' shoot you."

Shoot him? With that toy bow and arrow? Micah knew he should be amused, at the least irritated. Instead, he found himself strangely touched. So small, so young, bearding the lion in his den to save a handful of ragtag chickens. His pets.

Micah knew he could outrun the boy; he knew the bow would prove to be no real deterrent. But he found that he couldn't move. If he made a defiant gesture of any sort, Oscar would blame himself for not being strong enough to stop him. He would never forgive himself for being less helpful than his brothers. Micah didn't have the will to put such a heavy burden on such tiny shoulders. This boy had been betrayed by politics and circumstance. He didn't have to be hurt further by a stranger who'd stumbled into the wrong place at the wrong time.

The weakness Micah had felt seeped into his limbs, and he sat heavily on the edge of the trough, praying that Crockett wouldn't take too long in retrieving his whiskey.

Then he had no more coherent thoughts at all as the world went black and he felt himself falling to the ground.

Chapter

13

Lizzy sashayed into Pickeney's General Store as if she owned the town that surrounded it. Mr. Pickeney was new to Catesby, having lived there for only eight months—ever since he'd lost an arm in the war. Lizzy intended to use his ignorance about her family to her advantage. She'd come to Catesby only twice since his arrival, so she felt sure the man wouldn't know she would never have this much money at her immediate disposal.

Plunking the bag of gold onto the counter, she sniffed in dismay and gazed carelessly around her. "I do hope you have what I need!" she exclaimed, exaggerating the feminine cadence of her voice until it was nearly a kittenish purr. "I've come all the way into town with a list, and I'm not sure where to find these things if you don't have them." With that, she dumped the contents of the pouch onto the counter and slapped her list beside it.

Mr. Pickeney's eyes grew wide and round. "Oh, my. Oh, my, oh, *my!*"

Just as Lizzy had suspected, he probably hadn't seen gold, real gold, since setting up his business. It didn't matter that the coins had strange antique markings or that some were bent or misshapen. With the war and all, most folks did their commerce in barter and trade.

"This is only a deposit, mind you," she said with a careless wave of her hand and a bat of her eyelashes. "I didn't dare bring it all on my person." She rested one hand against her breast, drawing Mr. Pickeney's gaze to the taut mounds of her breasts straining against her bodice. "I simply wouldn't dare."

"Of course," he breathed. "What will you be needing, miss?"

She pointed to the list. "Could you have these ready for delivery tomorrow?"

He lifted the paper and read the items in growing dismay. "I can get most of what you want, but I haven't a team to pull the wagon. If you could wait until the day after, I'll borrow one."

Lizzy pretended to ponder the problem. "I suppose that would do"—her eyes lighted on a basket in the corner—"if you throw in a pair of those boots." She thought of Micah's shoes, worn clear through the soles and stuffed with cloth.

Mr. Pickeney eyed her oddly at the unusual request, especially considering the size of the footwear she'd requested. But the sight of gold, real gold, persuaded him to overlook anything out of the ordinary she might ask.

"Yes, ma'am."

"Oh, and Mr. Pickeney," she murmured leaning close, "I'll be taking the boots with me."

Once Lizzy had left the general store and placed her

packages under the seat of her buggy, she paused, nibbling on her lip in indecision. She couldn't help thinking that there had to be something more she could do to help Micah. Mr. Ruthers had said that Ezra Bean was stationed here in Catesby, and even though Micah had ordered her not to delve into his affairs, she was sure he wouldn't mind if she asked a few discreet questions.

Her mind made up, she strolled down the block to the sheriff's office, which had been commandeered by a host of Union soldiers. She wasn't quite sure what she planned to say to them, but she wasn't about to back away from this challenge.

The effects of the war could be seen quite clearly here. Where once the office had been somewhat attractive, with pine paneling and high-gloss floors, now the place looked scuffed and worn and tired.

The front door opened as she approached, disgorging a pair of soldiers and then a stooped man cradling a sobbing woman—Mr. and Mrs. Ruthers? She paused, a tightness gripping her throat. They must have come here in search of information about Billy-Joe, their youngest son. He'd been missing since Vicksburg.

It wasn't until that moment that Lizzy realized there were worse things than not knowing for sure whether her father was dead or alive. She could have received a definite announcement of his demise.

She closed her eyes briefly in silent prayer. *Papa. Papa, come back to us.*

It took her a few minutes to gather her composure, to blink back the tears that stung her eyes. Even so, she couldn't tear her gaze away from that huddled couple heading down the street.

"Miss?"

She jumped, startled to find that she'd gained the scrutiny of an army officer, judging by the brass on his lapels. His uniform was bleached by the sun, too many washings, and dust, and his pants didn't match his jacket, having more of a grayish tone to them. His dark hair brushed his shoulders in an untidy windblown style. Much as Micah's had before she'd cleaned him up, she thought.

"Are you lost?"

She shook her head, jerking her attention back to the matter at hand. "No. No, I've come in search of some . . . information."

He must have seen where she'd been looking, at the sobbing shape of Mrs. Ruthers, and he nodded, assuming that she'd come for the same sort of news. Lizzy would have corrected him, but his assumption that she would soon be in similar somber circumstances caused him to shield her with his body a little as he ushered her inside. "Follow me."

"Do you work here?" she asked as he led her through a maze of halls.

"No, ma'am. But I've had a little business here myself, so I know where to go."

He led her to a desk heaped with papers. Behind it was a mousy-looking bald man who wore a pair of spectacles perched on his nose.

"Polnicek!"

The little man started, his hand brushing the desk and sending a sheaf of papers to the floor.

"Dammit, man," he snapped. Then he leaned forward to fiercely whisper, "I told you . . . I don't have anything else to say. If you want your brother, you're going to have to find him yourself."

The officer leaned over the desk, piercing the man with a powerful stare. "I'm not here on my own behalf. This little lady needs some help."

Polnicek primly pressed his lips together, but when he looked at her, his jaw became slack.

"Ma'am," he breathed, rising to his feet. "How can I be of service?"

Now that she had someone who could give her the

answers she sought, Lizzy didn't quite know what to say. "I-I need some information."

"About a loved one? Someone missing?"

Lizzy's heart thumped wildly in her breast as she envisioned Mr. and Mrs. Ruthers. She could ask about her father. She could finally find out for sure.

No. She didn't want to know if her father had been listed among the dead. Not yet. Not now. Let her live a few days more with hope, even if it was false hope.

"No. No, I had a visit from a neighbor the other day. He told me there was a man . . . a criminal . . . in the area."

Polnicek and her officer exchanged glances, and she realized she'd made a mistake. A horrible, horrible mistake. She'd thought to help matters, she'd hoped to gather a little information, but all she'd done was direct suspicion her way.

"Yes, ma'am. There is a man we've been looking for. Have you seen someone suspicious in the area?"

"No! That is . . . I'm not sure."

Polnicek blinked at her. She could feel the officer stare. Finally the clerk stooped and opened a file drawer. After rustling through the papers, he withdrew a wanted poster and handed it to her.

"Have you seen this man?"

On the poster was a picture of Micah—bearded, scruffy, not too skillfully drawn, but definitely Micah.

"I'm not sure."

"Think, ma'am. It could be very important."

Drat it all! How was she going to get herself out of this situation?

"I-I may have seen him. About a week ago. I saw someone . . . like him, sneaking through the woods about five miles from my home."

"Where is that?"

"At the ferry landing."

"You're a Wilder?"

She reluctantly nodded, although she'd hoped to keep her identity somewhat in question.

"What were you doing so far away from your own place?"

"My . . . my little brother and I were searching for berries in the woods."

There weren't many berries this time of year in this area of Ohio. She could only pray that Polnicek wouldn't know that.

"How far away was he when you saw him?" the clerk asked.

"A hundred yards. Maybe more."

"Why didn't you come here sooner?"

She shrugged. "I-I don't get into town often."

Polnicek sighed, looking at the officer who'd brought her inside. "One day. That's all I can give you."

Lizzy had no idea what he meant by such a cryptic statement, but the officer didn't wait. Donning his hat, he strode from the room, his spurs jingling against the floor.

"I'll have to take a statement."

She shook her head. "No, I can't stay. I'm expected back . . . and I have other stops to make." She was frantic now. She had to leave before she revealed too much. "I'm sorry I wasn't more helpful, but I saw him from such a long distance . . . it probably wasn't him at all."

With that she whirled, nearly running from the room, but she'd taken only a few steps when she slammed into a man coming the other direction.

Up, up, up, she looked, into cruel eyes and a cool expression.

"Colonel Bean!" Polnicek huffed behind her.

Bean. The name Micah feared. The same man that Lizzy recognized as being the leader of the men who'd taken Rosie.

Lizzy didn't wait to be introduced, didn't wait to be questioned. Lifting her skirts, she ran out into the sunshine.

* * *

As soon as she returned to the farm, Lizzy changed her clothes, not because she feared they might get dirty but because she'd been disturbed by the way Micah studied her in such feminine garb. She didn't want to feel that way again, all tingly and agitated, until she'd had time to think about her adventure in town.

"When you come back, Lizzy, I want to kiss you again. On that you can rely."

The mere thought of his promise caused her knees to nearly buckle. All day she'd done her best to push the memory away, but the words would not die.

Standing in the middle of her room, her empty, lonely room, she couldn't suppress the shiver that coursed through her body. She closed her eyes and tried to will away the thrumming of her pulse and the wanton heat that began to permeate her skin.

The first time she'd touched Micah's body, while searching for weapons, she'd felt this same bubbling expectancy. She'd vowed that he would not make her weak. To her surprise, the emotions he inspired had the opposite effect. She'd grown strong. Strong enough to know what she wanted. She wanted Micah. She wanted a future with him.

Her gaze strayed to the window, the yard beyond, looking for the man who dominated her thoughts. Yes, she wanted him, she admitted with a sigh. But not like this. Not bound to her out of guilt over a night of lovemaking that she had herself instigated. She'd already forced him to finish her bridge and stay on her farm, but she could never force him to care for her.

Removing the hairpins and replacing them with the usual butter knife, she adopted a stern expression, stormed out the back door, and marched to the chicken coop.

But the barnyard was deserted. Silent.

"Crockett?" she called, then added the other boys' names to her cries, but there was no answer.

An icy wave of panic rushed through her. Had the soldiers

followed her home? Had they come and taken them all? No. No!

She turned and ran toward the house. But at almost the same moment the sound of hooves thundering toward the house alerted her.

Stifling her concern, Lizzy ran to the front yard, intent on intercepting the rider before he could reach the house. As she darted around the house she saw the horseman and recognized him immediately. Although he'd abandoned his jacket and his brass markings, he was the same officer who had opened the door for her in town.

The man reined his mount to a halt, tipping his hat in Lizzy's direction. "Ma'am, I wondered if you could confirm where you saw that stranger."

"Stranger?"

"Micah St. Charles." He held out a copy of the same wanted poster she'd seen in town.

She pointed to a spot far away, near the tree line. "It was that way, five or more miles."

"Was he on foot?"

She was tempted to say no, but she thought that wouldn't sound very realistic. "Yes, on foot."

"Which way was he headed?"

"South."

The soldier frowned slightly. "Could you see what condition he was in? It would help me to judge how far he's traveled."

"I don't really know. He looked strong enough to me."

The officer didn't move, didn't speak. He stared at her intently, as if the word *liar* were printed across the bridge of her nose.

"Lizzy?" It was Crockett. She nearly wilted in relief, then stiffened again. If, by so much as a word, he revealed Micah's name or his whereabouts, Micah would be a dead man.

"I'm so pleased you're looking into this incident, Major."

"Captain," he corrected.

"I was so worried that no one would take me seriously. You will never know how you've eased my mind."

The captain merely nodded as if her compliment made him uncomfortable. "Is this the brother who was berry-picking with you?"

Crockett's brows rose.

"No! No, that's not him. I was with my little brother. My very little brother. Oscar. He's five."

"Then I don't suppose he would be much help."

"No. No, I don't suppose so."

"Well, thank you, ma'am." He touched his hat again, then rode off toward the tree line.

Crockett waited until the sound of hooves passed well out of earshot before demanding, "Berry-picking?"

"Just never you mind, Crockett. Where is everyone? You scared the life out of me when I came back to find you all gone."

Crockett didn't immediately answer.

"What's happened?" she asked, the fear returning.

"They drugged him."

"Who drugged whom?"

"Bridger, Lewis, Clark, and Johnny. They snuck up to the attic and got into Sally's medical bag."

Sally's medical bag. Drat it all! Why hadn't she thought of that when Micah was so sick?

"They put about a half-dozen medicines in some cider as well as a half a bottle of laudanum and drugged Micah out of his wits."

"What!" She was already heading toward the house. "Whatever for?"

"They were trying to protect you."

"Protect me? From what?"

"Him. *Him!* Dammit, Lizzy, can't you see what's happening here? He's got eyes for you, and I don't think it's proper. You were supposed to marry Bill."

She grew still. "Bill is dead."

"But you could find someone else to take care of you."

"For your information, I don't need anyone to take care of me. I can take care of myself." She stomped closer to her brother, pointing an accusing finger at his chest. "It may have escaped your notice, Crockett, but I am an adult. Perhaps I went into the war still a girl, but I'm a grown woman now. I don't need you telling me what to do."

Lizzy immediately regretted her outburst. Crockett had only been voicing his concern, but she'd nearly snapped his head off for it.

"He's in the barn," he said after several long, awkward moments. Then he stalked off, leaving her feeling very small and very mean.

Chapter

14

Lizzy wrapped her arms around her waist and stared down at the man in her parents' bed. Then she turned accusingly to her brothers who had spent the better part of a half hour loading Micah onto the twins' toy wagon and hauling him to this very spot.

"What did you do to him?"

They all looked guilty, but they would not admit they had done anything to the man who lay pale and sweating in the middle of the bed.

"I see. So he got this way all on his own?"

"Maybe he got that fever again," Lewis suggested, but she cut him off with a scathing glance.

"This is no fever and we all know it. Who is responsible? Tell me now, or I swear I'll be taking all of you to the woodshed no matter how big you've grown."

The threat had the right effect. They all began talking at once.

"Boone found the laudanum."

"Bridger put it in his water—"

"But Lewis gave it to him—"

"No, it was Clark—"

"Johnny gave him some too!"

When they'd finished spouting their information, she glared at them all in disapproval. It seemed that Crockett and Oscar were the only innocent ones.

"How could you?" she blurted.

"He wants to take you away!"

The cry came from Bridger, but at the immediate silence, she realized that he'd expressed a fear they all shared.

"Take me away?" she repeated in confusion.

They shifted uncomfortably, then looked at Boone, silently electing the shy, bespectacled boy as their spokesman.

"We know how much the two of you . . . like each other."

Lizzy could feel a blush rise into her cheeks, but she refused to think about it now.

"We knew it would only be a matter of time before he asked you to marry him."

"Why wouldn't he?" Bridger inserted. "*We* all know how wonderful you are."

She felt a lump form in her throat.

"We knew he wouldn't want to stay here after we made him work so hard. But we couldn't let him take you away. We didn't want to be alone."

The tightness in her throat made it impossible for her to speak for a minute. Then she sank onto the trunk at the foot of the bed and held out her arms.

"Don't you know I would never leave you?"

The younger boys rushed forward for her hug. Crockett and Boone held back, but she could see that they too were relieved by her statement. "This is my home, you're my family. I would never leave."

"Promise?" Johnny whispered, looking up at her with tear-filled eyes.

They could have squeezed her heart with their hands with equal results.

"I promise," she said, knowing as she wrapped her arms around their frail bodies that she could never go back on that vow.

Even if it meant losing the man who lay unconscious on the bed. The man to whom she'd willingly given her heart.

Micah didn't recover as quickly as she would have liked.

For several hours, he remained dead to the world. Then he began to shake, and the delirium he'd experienced during his fever returned.

It took less than twenty minutes of his mumblings for Lizzy to abandon her facade of casual concern, even around the boys.

"Why laudanum?" she demanded as she shooed them from the room. "Didn't you know that too much can be very destructive?"

The boys had no answer and she relented just a little. "Bring me a pail of cool water from the springhouse, then move some of your things into the barn for tonight. I won't have you disturbing him until he's well again."

"Yes, Lizzy . . . Yes, ma'am," they mumbled as they moved to do her bidding.

She took her place by Micah's side, alternating between heaping him with blankets when he shivered and picking them up off the floor when he became too hot.

When Lizzy found herself wringing her hands in distress, she huffed in irritation, scolding herself for acting like those weak-kneed, wild-eyed, fluff-headed women she'd seen in town who fainted at the first sign of a dogfight. No, she'd survived by being strong, and she would continue as she'd begun.

Feeling a little bolder, a little more confident, she closed her eyes, forcing herself to think. Think! Surely she could remember some of Sally's medicinal practices.

Sally.

Of course.

Of course!

She hurried up the attic where Sally Wilder's personal belongings had been carefully put away in trunks and stacked in the corner. She took two small metal containers off the pile, exposing a larger wooden trunk. Opening the lid, she retrieved her stepmother's medical books as well as the leather bag, which the boys had already raided in search of drugs. Then she ran downstairs again, pulled a chair close to the lamp, and started to examine the books.

Opening *Granger's Complete Guide to Medicine,* she found the language far too complicated for her, and since the binding looked new and the pages were crisp, she figured Sally hadn't used it much. Deciding that time was of the essence, she placed all the texts in a row, and chose the most dog-eared volume. It was a small book with a paper cover and smooth pages filled with tiny print. Not even bothering to read the title, she opened it and immediately began skimming the pages.

To her relief, she found that this was a layman's guide to medicine. In simple language it explained the most useful nursing techniques. The author listed the symptoms of the most common diseases, then suggested simple home remedies.

Breathing a little easier at having found some useful advice, she turned immediately to the section entitled "Laudanum" and read the instructions for treating an overdose.

The book was quite helpful. The author instructed her to place hot bricks in the bed to warm the patient and then to bathe him to lower his temperature again.

"Bathe him?" Lizzy didn't realize she'd said the word aloud until the sound of her own voice startled her.

Referring to the book again, she reread the first section softly to herself as if there had been some misunderstanding. " 'The patient should be bathed, dressed in flannels, and put to bed.' . . . Flannels?"

She glanced at the huge man on the bed. "You're just going to have to make do with what I can find. We haven't a thing made of flannel that will fit your frame. Wool's the next best thing, anyway. It's close to flannel."

Flipping through the pages, she found the instructions for "Invalid Bathing" and read:

> The person of ill health should be kept on the bed or pallet. Remove all clothing, using another sheet as a modesty screen, so that the nurse can wash beneath the shield. Spread another sheet over the right side of the mattress, ensuring that the sick one is kept to the left. Roll the patient to his stomach while centering him upon the taut sheet. Wash his body with a solution of one part soap, two parts vinegar, three parts weak chamomile tea, and ten parts hot water. Begin with the limbs and move inward toward the torso, paying careful attention to the shoulders and buttocks. Pulling on the sheet from the opposite side of the patient's body, roll the person again to his back. Wash the front portion of the body from the extremities to the torso, using small circular strokes and paying close attention to the genitalia where—

At the mere word, Lizzy's face flamed, and she slapped the book on the table. Her gaze bounced of its own accord to the bed, the man's thighs, and the sheet covering his . . . genitalia. A trembling settled into her knees, spreading outward through her body.

"Oh, my." She grew hot at the mere thought. She squeezed closed her eyes beneath the sensations storming her body. Sweet heaven! Was it possible that even now, after all they'd been through, she could feel a wave of embarrassment mixed with a healthy dose of anticipation?

Shaking herself loose from the tendrils of desire, she tried to focus on the matter at hand. She would follow the book's instructions to the letter and forget her own wayward tendencies.

Moving back into the kitchen, she checked the reservoir on the stove. To her infinite relief, it was nearly full and there were two clean buckets waiting nearby. Emptying the reservoir into a pail, she added some soap, dumped in a measure of vinegar and a bit of crushed chamomile, then carried the solution into the sickroom.

Her patient was still sprawled upon the bed, still mumbling incoherently under his breath. "If you'd just wake up," she said, "none of this would prove necessary."

He didn't answer. Not that she'd thought he would. But it helped to vent her worry and frustration a little. Unfortunately, as she pulled the sheet up to his waist, she knew the rein she held on her own control was tenuous at best. Blast it all! She had to get this man up out of bed and well enough to wash his own . . .

Nether regions.

An hour later Lizzy stepped into the sickroom again, rubbing at the aching hollow of her back. Never in her life had she thought that caring for one grown man could be so exhausting. Then again, it wasn't the bathing that had drained her energies. It was trying to remain detached, unaffected, while she soaped each muscle and counted the scars. Despite the hardships he'd suffered—or perhaps because of them—he was a beautiful man. More regular meals would make him even stronger until there would be no denying the symmetry and near-perfection of his form.

She stood in the doorway, looking at him, tracing the hills and valleys he'd made of the blankets, eyeing the way the wool clung to his feet, the shape of his calves and thighs, his hips, his waist. She wasn't sure, but she thought he appeared a little better.

A warmth stole into her veins, one that could no longer be pushed away. In the past few years she hadn't allowed herself to think of anything but the farm and her family, but lately she couldn't seem to bring them to mind at all. Micah filled her every waking moment. Secret, unbidden yearnings were tapping at the door to her mind, and she found it impossible to keep them at bay.

Did she love him?

The question whispered in her mind, then lodged there for good.

Yes. Yes, she supposed she did. How she had come to that point, considering the unorthodox course of their relationship to date, she didn't know. But she did love him. Utterly. Completely.

She crossed to tuck the sheets more securely around his neck, paused, then sank onto the edge of the bed.

"Why have you done this to me?" she whispered. "Why?"

Unable to stop herself, she reached out to touch his hair, soft, thick, fine-textured hair the color of ripening wheat. Then she slipped lower, exploring his forehead, his cheeks, his chin. His skin was different from her own, toughened by the elements and by experiences she would probably never understand. He had endured so many hardships.

"Micah?"

Her call was but a whisper of sound. She didn't know exactly what she meant to say, but she needn't have bothered. He didn't respond, and this caused the ever-present fear to return.

She'd done all she could for now, all she dared, but it worried her that he hadn't awakened. What if her simple home remedies weren't enough? What if she hadn't read far enough in the book? What if there was more she should have done? Lizzy had experienced enough death in her lifetime to know that she didn't like the natural phenomenon. Funerals gave her the shivers; sickness of any kind made her cringe. The blackness outside her window was so real, so thick, that she couldn't help thinking quite superstitiously that this would be an appropriate time for his spirit to take a walk.

Again she felt his forehead, his cheek. She tried to tell herself that he felt cooler, but she couldn't be sure.

"Micah?"

He didn't respond, didn't move, didn't wake.

"Micah? You can't die, do you hear me?" she whispered, bending lower so that the sound of her voice couldn't help but reach his ears. "The boys would never forgive themselves, and to be quite honest neither would I. Besides, I've got quite enough on my hands already—and there just isn't a good place to bury you. So you'll have to stay alive. Do you understand?"

She'd meant the words to emerge like an order, but they sounded more like a plea. Nevertheless, he gave no sign whatsoever that anything she'd said had sunk into his opium-dulled brain.

Standing, she pushed away her fears, her regrets, her sadness. Stiffening her spine, she said, "You will get better, Mr. Micah St. Charles. If I have to kill you to do it, you *will* get better."

Chapter

15

Mr. Pickeney delivered the supplies, grinning from ear to ear and telling her over and over again how he'd managed to find a horse a day earlier than expected.

Through it all, Crockett eyed Lizzy suspiciously, but she didn't bother to explain. Luckily, once the goods were unloaded and spread on the porch, the boys quickly lost interest in how she'd managed to pay for the items. They were much too excited about seeing honest-to-goodness supplies—lumber and nails and screws, potatoes and flour and cheese.

After they'd sampled some of the food, Lizzy put the boys to work on the bridge to divert their attention. Then she spent most of the afternoon making healthy broths for Micah. All for naught, it seemed.

It was late in the afternoon when Lizzy checked on him again. He'd been motionless all day. He didn't clutch the covers, but lay quietly. Soup. Maybe some soup would give him strength. Surely there was a way to drizzle it down his throat.

"Come along, Boone," she called to the boy reading in the chair. "Let's get him something to eat."

Filled with purpose, she hurried from the room.

He was alone.

Daring to open one eye just a slit, Micah searched the empty bedroom. A small smile curved his lips. That morning, after wakening with a skull-splitting headache and a few hazy memories of some acrid-tasting cider, he'd been able to piece together events enough to realize what had happened. They'd drugged him. Those little ruffians had drugged him.

Since then he'd been waiting for one minute when Lizzy was the only other person nearby, but invariably there was a boy in one of the chairs watching him sleep.

He wriggled a little deeper beneath the covers, enjoying the sensation of fresh linens against his skin, a soft feather mattress, plump, fresh-smelling pillows. Although he'd been sleeping in this same bed for some time, he didn't think he would ever grow used to such luxuries. As far as he was concerned, there were worse states for a man who was tired of riding, tired of sleeping on the ground, and tired of hating. If only he could resolve his business with Bean . . .

He heard the squeak of a floorboard outside his door and flung his arms above his head, closing his eyes, and moaning softly. First things first. He had to get Lizzy alone.

Once in the bedroom, she paused, gazing consideringly at her patient. He was sleeping, peacefully, mumbling a bit but not thrashing as he had before. Perhaps the measures she'd been using were beginning to work.

"Good," she said to herself, setting the tray with its bowl of soup on the bedside table. Boone marched in behind her, carrying a bucket.

"Put that on the floor, please."

He willingly complied.

"Where's Bridger with that mustard plaster?"

"He's coming."

Boone needn't have bothered with the confirmation. A pungent smell permeated the room long before Bridger arrived.

"Lizzy, this stuff smells horrible," Bridger complained, holding the bowl with the plaster at arm's length.

"Then be glad it isn't meant for you." She took the bowl from his hands. "Now get outside, you two."

They willingly complied, thundering from the room. Lizzy set the bowl on the table. Since the book's remedies hadn't worked as quickly as she would have liked, she had decided to use one of Sally's cure-alls. A full-strength mustard plaster.

Whipping aside his covers, she held the bowl over his chest. Evidently her patient got a good whiff of her concoction, because he coughed, his eyes opening, one broad hand snaring her wrist.

"Dammit all to hell, Lizzy!"

A rush of joy swept through her body. He was awake! He wasn't going to die!

She wanted to throw her arms around him and hug him close in delight, but not wishing to reveal the extent of her relief, she summoned her best school marm tone. "I am attempting to help you. Will you please hold still?"

When she tried to put the plaster on his chest, he turned his head away. "That smells awful."

"Yes, it does," she agreed tartly. "But it's supposed to help, and since it's brought you out of your stupor, I suppose it has."

He stared at her with narrowed eyes. "You didn't—"

"Kindly close your mouth and lie still," Lizzy commanded. If the past few days had taught her anything about herself, it was that she was not a patient nursemaid—especially now that the invalid was conscious of her ministrations, watching the way she washed him, feeling her touch him in places where she'd never explored a grown man overly much before.

Stop it!

The grip on her wrist tightened. "I'm awake. I've been awake for some time. There's no need to—"

"Shh! Great botheration! If you'd do as I say, you would be up and about tomorrow. I've been doing . . ."

Awake for some time.

Awake for some time?

"Awake for some time!" she finally said out loud, then clenched her jaw to keep from shouting again. The tension kept building in her, making her feel unaccountably weak. She was feeling quite inclined to sit down and cry—something Lizzy was never prone to do. So she did the next best thing. She smacked the mustard plaster onto his chest.

"Take it off, take it *off!*" He shot straight up in bed, grappling with the poultice. His feet churned, his body twisted, until he sprang from the bed, then stumbled and fell to the floor.

Lizzy smiled in satisfaction. There was no doubt. He was going to live.

"What in the hell are you doing to me, woman?"

"Quite obviously I'm making you well."

"*Well?* You've scalded me!"

"Such a fuss over a little medication."

"Medication my ass! You've flayed the skin from my body."

"It worked, didn't it?"

Her remark hung in the air, causing Micah to stiffen.

"Or did it?" Her eyes narrowed, her gaze becoming more intent, as if she had come to the conclusion that for a man who'd been at death's door, he was suddenly quite strong.

Finally she put her hands together and applauded. "Very convincing indeed. You should have made your career on the stage." The anger that had flared inside her grew brighter. "You might as well get up," she said, folding her arms. "The floor can be quite drafty," she added pithily, "and we wouldn't want you to catch a chill."

Her sarcasm was obvious. Micah must have noted it too, because he rose to his feet, bracing his back against the wall.

"How long," she ground out through clenched teeth, "have you been conscious?"

"Not long."

"How *long?*"

"Since this morning," he admitted.

"Was any of this"—she waved her hand at the bed, the medicines—"necessary? Were you ever really unconscious?"

"Your brothers were the ones who drugged me!"

"So at least *part* of your illness was genuine."

"I don't think I could have manufactured blacking out, do you?"

"I'm beginning to wonder." Her voice squeezed from her throat. "Damn you," she whispered, turning away.

Micah frowned, wondering why her shoulders were not quite ramrod straight. Why she seemed to . . . tremble.

"Lizzy?"

He was quite sure something was wrong when she didn't answer or try to goad him into admitting more about his charade.

Confused by her reaction, Micah approached her carefully. A sticky tension had flooded the room, making him instinctively wary. Something was seriously wrong. Lizzy wasn't baiting him, she wasn't arguing or prodding him—a definite sign of trouble.

"What's the matter?" He touched her shoulder. "Lizzy?"

She whirled to face him, wrenching away from his touch. Tears tracked down her face.

"You bastard," she whispered, but the word had no sting. "I thought you were . . . I thought you were going to . . . die."

She burst into sobs, and Micah stood rooted to the floor. This woman had been worried about him. She'd honestly cared. The fact shocked him to the core—although he supposed it shouldn't have. She was an amazing woman, capable of great tenderness, great empathy. Great love.

A tightness gripped his throat so that he could barely breathe. His lungs constricted; his heart grew heavy.

"Oh, Lizzy . . ." He reached out, pulling her close, wrapping his arms around her back. "I'm sorry. I didn't mean to frighten you."

His words were meant to comfort her, but they had the opposite effect. She gripped his back, sobbing even more forcefully.

Micah was at a loss as to how to soothe her. He tried to murmur tender little phrases in her ear, he stroked her back, kissed her hair. Holding her close, he rocked her in his arms, letting Lizzy purge herself of the fear he had unknowingly inspired. He let her weep until his chest was wet and his arms ached from supporting her weight. Then he lifted her, carrying her the short distance to the bed. He laid her on the tangled covers.

Climbing in beside her, he drew her close, absorbing the shuddering of her body, the lessening tide of her grief, the exhaustion of her spirit. As she fell asleep in his arms, he closed his eyes, but he didn't rest. He couldn't. The past few minutes had changed him, irretrievably. He could no longer shy away from the fact that this woman had done far more than chain him to a trunk and force him to rebuild her bridge. She'd also captured his heart.

Damn it all to hell. What was he going to do? He wasn't free to love anyone. Not until he'd found Bean. Not until he'd cleared his name so that he could offer it to another.

But even as he listed the obstacles in his head, he could not deny that he wanted to stay.

Chapter

16

From that day on, Micah was on his own a great deal so that he could rest. Lizzy saw to it that her brothers had a large hand in the recuperation process. Micah knew it was her own way of having them make amends as well as giving them the opportunity to get to know him a little better.

For the most part, the tactic succeeded. Boone, who loved to read, soon discovered that Micah was the only person in the house who could explain the meanings of some of the words he'd encountered in his reading. Bridger, on the other hand, after realizing that Micah had used explosives in the course of his engineering duties, began to pressure him for details. The twins continued to hang back, still suspicious. After seeing the way Lizzy had accepted him, Johnny didn't really seem to care about him one way or the other, but Oscar . . .

It was the highlight of his evening when Oscar came to see him. Evidently, when Micah had helped repair the chicken coop, he had somehow proved that he wouldn't hurt the boy's pets. So Oscar had begun to gravitate to Micah's room. Micah suspected it was as much through his need to be around a grown man as anything else. That was one thing which had been denied Oscar for most of his young life.

He started by helping Oscar fix a pull toy, then showed him how to tie his boots, then taught him how to shave with the spine of a comb. Then at night, when all was dark and the household was settling for the night, Micah would tell the boy a story. It didn't matter what the subject was as long as it somehow involved an adventure.

After running out of his meager supply of fairy tales and myths, Micah turned to his own family for inspiration, relating stories of pirates and explorers and a mysterious treasure buried deep in a well. His only regret was that Lizzy did not join them for the stories. In fact, since their last confrontation, he had not seen much of her at all.

That was why he eventually sent the boys on a pointless errand and went in search of her.

Micah paused at the doorway to the sitting room. Lizzy stood at the window, one hand on the curtain, the other resting lightly at her waist.

Did she know what a picture she presented? Did she know that the mere sight of her kicked his pulse into an erratic rhythm?

Micah knew he should have his head examined. This woman had stolen his freedom and his time. But he no longer resented his captivity. He was thankful. He no longer worried that Lizzy might carry his child—he would welcome such a fact should it occur. If she hadn't kept him here these past few weeks, hadn't made love with him, he would have ridden away, never knowing that his one hope of happiness lay here in this crazy household with this brave, audacious woman. He would have gone in search of Bean while he was still tired and weak, not strong as he was now.

Unable to help himself, Micah approached her. He knew that she was aware of his entrance; it was there in the slight stiffening of her body.

"You look pensive," he murmured when he was close. So close. He wanted to touch her. He wanted so much more.

"No, I was just thinking." When she realized what she'd said, she threw a rueful smile over her shoulder. It was at that moment, he knew he'd been forgiven.

Inching a little nearer, he saw what she'd been studying. During his illness, the boys had made quite a bit of progress on the bridge.

"They're doing well."

She nodded. "Thanks to the initial support work you did. I appreciate the way you've taught them how to handle Papa's tools." There was a beat of silence before she elaborated. "They've missed the influence of a man. Men look at things quite differently."

She was so earnest, so sweet, so unprepossessing.

So desirable.

"Yes. They do," he said, turning her to face him. "We men tend to see things quite, quite differently."

Drawing her to him, he dipped his head. She was so hesitant at first, so shy, but even now he could sense the way her body melted into his and how she clutched at his back.

"I want to kiss you, Lizzy. I've wanted to for a very long time. Since that afternoon in the springhouse. As I recall, I promised you a kiss on your return from town."

"Yes." It was a bare whisper of sound.

"Do you want it now?"

She was trembling, her fingers digging into him. "Yes, oh, yes."

Unable to resist a second longer, he touched her lips with his own.

In an instant, passion flared, an aching, burning need. But as he pulled Lizzy close and wrapped his arms around her back, plundered her mouth with his tongue, and absorbed the mewling sounds of delight that seeped from her throat, he realized that this was no pretty vase, no fragile figurine, as he'd been taught females were. She was a woman. A strong, passionate woman with needs and desires as blazing as his own.

He shifted to bring her tighter against his hips, rubbing against her, feeling the bunch of her skirts against his groin. A moan escaped from his throat. So long. It had been so long since a woman had felt this way in his arms. It had been . . . forever. No female had ever felt this good. This right.

His hand slid between them to cup her breast. She gasped against him—soft, kittenish sounds that inflamed him even more. He pressed his thumb against the taut nipple. Even through the layers of clothing she wore, he could feel the tender button responding, growing tighter, harder. Not wanting to frighten her, he moved down to her rib cage, her hips, her waist.

Their mouths parted, and both of them panted for breath. Lizzy's eyes grew wide, shining with flecks of molten gold. She took his wrist, and he thought she meant to push him away, but instead she brought his hand back up to her breast.

"Touch me there again. Please."

Moaning, he took her lips once more, needing her. Dear heaven how he needed her—the taste, the smell, the feel. His free hand slid down to cup her buttocks through her skirts, tipping her hips up to his own, bringing her flush against that part of him that ached for possession. He'd grown greedy for her. He never wanted to let her go.

"Lizzy!" A door slammed and a pair of childish feet pounded down the hall.

The two of them sprang apart. But even as Lizzy hurried

to intercept Bridger at the door, Micah knew, just by looking into the fire of her eyes, that there would be no turning away from what had occurred between them. Neither of them had the strength or the will to do so.

The next morning it was Micah who arose at dawn, pulled on his shirt, and made his way out to the bridge. By the time the others began looking for him, he'd already finished a good portion of the center section.

Lizzy was the first to come running from the house. He saw her panic, sensed her desperation, and knew that it was because he might have taken it into his head to go after Bean without telling her good-bye.

He paused in his work to study her. She must have come straight from bed, because her hair streamed down her back. She'd thrown on a wrapper, but hadn't fastened it, and her feet were quite bare.

Seeing him on the bridge, working quite diligently on his own, took her a little off guard. She lifted a hand to her hair, smoothed some of the strands into place, then backed into the house again as if embarrassed that she'd been caught with the tresses streaming around her shoulders instead of caught with the usual butter knife.

A few minutes later she emerged, completely dressed, her hair plaited and tamed and wound in a coronet around her head. He liked it that way. It gave her an almost regal appearance. But after the glimpse he'd had of her disheveled and sleepy, he wanted to see her that way too. After another night of lovemaking. He could only pray that it would happen again. Soon.

Sweet heaven, he was a cad to think so. He should content himself with a simple courtship, holding hands, bringing flowers. But the world had grown far more complicated in the last few years, and the old rules didn't apply.

The hammer in his hand hung motionless, forgotten, as he watched her step from the porch and make her way down the path. Her skirts swayed, the breeze toyed with her collar, allowing tempting glimpses of her throat. He wanted to kiss her there. He wanted to touch that skin with his tongue.

"You didn't go." She stated, referring to the way she'd come looking for him earlier. "No."

Her steps slowed as she neared the bridge. "I . . . brought you something to eat."

It took a few seconds for his brain to push aside the sensual images that had formed.

"Not eggs, I hope." His voice was husky, telling.

Her smile was timid. Since his illness and her own trip into town, none of them had seen much in the way of eggs. She must have stocked the larder after her visit to Catesby, because they'd had a variety of foods lately, canned beans, salted meats, and preserves.

"No. No eggs."

Micah grinned, setting his hammer down and meeting her halfway across the bridge. She gave him the basket, then stood self-consciously, clasping her hands behind her back.

"You came out to work all by yourself."

"I thought it was time I finished the job."

She nodded, obviously not knowing what to say.

"It should be finished in a day or two. Of course, you will need to make other repairs even after the bridge is passable."

"I see."

But when she looked at him, he knew her mind wasn't on the bridge or the resulting tolls. It was on him.

Him.

The blatant desire in her eyes was disconcerting. She obviously wasn't accustomed to hiding such feelings. Micah was glad of that. He didn't think he could have borne it this morning if she'd played the coy maid. He wanted her too badly. There was no room in the emotions they shared for each other to play games.

"I've . . . got to return to the boys."

She didn't move.

"I suppose you should."

She remained.

Looking at him.

Wanting him.

Inflaming him with a glance.

"I wish you would kiss me," she finally whispered. Her words were like a punch to his gut.

When he would have taken a step closer, she stopped him with a shake of her head. In the distance he could hear the twins warming up their war whoops. They would be coming outside soon.

"Have I ever told you how you make me feel when you kiss me?" she continued.

To Micah's surprise, the words had as much power to excite him as an actual caress.

"A burning starts deep in my body," she went on. "It swirls into my chest, my stomach, and lower, pooling there and gathering into this charged ball of need. Sometimes I wonder if that's what lightning feels like just before it streaks through the sky. Does it experience that same tension? Does it feel a building, a gathering, an aching want until it can't bear the suspense any longer and explodes in a silent shriek of passion?"

Dear heaven, what was she saying? How could any woman put such things into words with such vivid imagery?

"I feel a storm building between us, Micah."

"Yes." The word was gruff, barely recognizable.

"Like any force of nature, it will have to be dealt with eventually," she said. "I see no other way."

Then, without allowing him the chance to respond, she turned and walked back to the house.

Chapter

17

At noon, Micah ate lunch on the back porch with the boys. She could hear them chattering and laughing, and with each minute that passed, a greater shame built in her heart.

She had done this man a disservice. She had accused him of crimes he had never committed, she had bent him to her will, and even now, after all that had occurred, she still hadn't freed him completely.

It shamed her to the core when she realized that through it all, the lovemaking, the bantering, the arguments, she'd kept his picture of Lili, knowing instinctively that it was a symbol to her. He had promised he would not leave without it; by keeping it, she was keeping her own emotional hostage. But the time had come to rectify her actions.

When she heard the boys leave the porch and make their way to the bridge, Lizzy knew she couldn't avoid the issue a minute longer. Micah had to know that he had her complete and utter trust.

She paused, pushing aside the curtain to study the man who sat on the top step, his plate balanced on his knees. Oscar approached him, holding out one of his toy arrows, and Micah put his meal aside to help him. It was a touching picture that would be engraved on her heart no matter what the future brought.

The future.

Could she and Micah have a future together?

She prayed so with all her being.

The breeze that came through the open window was cool and fragrant, redolent of the roses and honeysuckle that grew over the trellis spanning the back of the house. From now until the end of time, those smells would remind her of this man, this summer.

Sighing, she dropped the curtain, and opened a small drawer in the plant stand to clutch the cool leather portfolio she'd hidden there. *Go on,* a little voice urged. *It's time.*

She dropped the photograph into her pocket and reluctantly made her way to the back porch. Oscar was still there, sitting on the middle step. Micah was showing him how to repair the fletching on his arrow with a piece of thread. A tenuous bond had been forged between the two. Lizzy feared the results of a parting.

"Oscar?"

He gazed up at her with wide blue eyes.

"You haven't gathered the eggs yet today. I need them for later. Scoot."

He nodded, waiting for Micah to finish the repairs, then grinned, suddenly throwing his arms around Micah's neck.

Micah blinked, his own hands settling on the boy's back so slowly, so carefully, that it was painful to watch. Then Oscar wriggled free and bounded down the path and into the chicken coop.

Lizzy waited until the door slammed shut in his wake.

"You have a natural way with my little brother. He's warmed up to you quite a bit lately. He usually won't talk to anyone but family."

Micah didn't immediately answer—a curious reaction, she thought as she settled on the porch beside him. He merely sat with his elbows on his knees, staring out toward the river. At first she thought he was looking at the chains, which the twins had retrieved from his room and draped over the railing to contain Ruggles earlier that day. But she soon realized he was looking inward, not outward.

"I always wanted a son like him."

When he spoke, the words were so low, so quiet, that she almost believed she'd imagined them.

"Did you and Lili have any children?" she asked weakly, feeling even more remorse and guilt. Why hadn't she ever bothered to ask? She hadn't dreamed that by holding him here she'd separated a child from his father.

The silence grew heavy, prolonged. Then Micah said, "No." The confession was obviously painful. "But Lili was in the family way when she died."

Lizzy didn't know how to respond. She'd never known what to say to a person in mourning. She invariably remained quiet, feeling incredibly awkward. Just like now.

"I went back, you know. I'm sure I told you that I did."

"To Solitude?" she asked softly when he didn't elaborate. She felt slightly breathless. As if she were about to discover an important piece of the puzzle to this man's identity.

"Yes. Home. I went home." He sighed, leaning back on his hands and staring up at the wisps of clouds in the sky. "The whole time I was running from Bean, I thought about that place. I even dreamed about it at night. It was my one link to sanity. I used to plan the crops in my head and inventory imaginary stock."

He stopped again, and she waited several minutes before he continued.

"But, as I told you once before, Solitude was gone." The

words were said matter-of-factly, but she saw the way his knuckles gleamed near-white. "All gone. Bean destroyed it completely."

Lizzy's heart lurched at the stark pain she sensed, even though Micah had told her of Bean's perfidy once before. "The war was very . . . unkind." They were hollow words.

"But it wasn't the war that was responsible. It was one man's hate. Ezra Bean burned the house, stole the livestock, terrorized the caretakers, salted the fields. Then, to make matters worse, he stole an inheritance meant to be divided between me and my two brothers."

"Do you mean the land?"

"That and so much more. Before the war my family buried several trunks of valuables. Jewels, silver, gold."

Lizzy felt a tiny twinge of unease at that piece of information, but pushed it away without analyzing it. "The stories," she whispered as recognition dawned. "The stories you told Oscar."

"All true," he confirmed. "The chests of gold, silver, and jewels exist. You know," he continued. "I had plans for my share of the treasure. I was going to build more paddocks, an addition to the house. It's ironic that I didn't know until all our funds were gone that my heart was never really involved in developing the family estates. I was always expected to do it because I was the eldest son." He clasped his hands together. "Such things don't matter anymore. If there were anything left, I think I'd turn Solitude over to Bram's care. He always loved the place. Then I'd make a new start somewhere else. Maybe out west."

Lizzy pleated her apron with her fingers, growing more and more agitated. He had made no mention of staying in Ohio, of spending time with a crazy woman who'd chained him to a trunk, or of a little boy named Oscar who had begun to adore him.

She sat quietly for several more minutes, trying to convince herself that the night had not become that much blacker. After some time, she sighed, removing the photograph from her pocket. "Here," she uttered in a choked voice, pressing the picture into his hand. Then she turned and ran inside.

She wouldn't watch him go.

She wouldn't be able to bear it.

Micah stared down at the leather case in his hand as if it were some sort of foreign object he'd never seen before. To be quite honest, he'd forgotten that he'd given the portrait to Lizzy. He'd forgotten how much it had meant to him, how the thought of losing that last link to his home would have been a mortal blow. But after so long in this place, he'd learned to put the past where it belonged—in the past. Why hadn't he ever bothered to examine his own feelings? He would always love Lili. He would carry the happy memories of her in his heart for an eternity. Lili had loved him, but she was dead now. And Micah still had a lifetime of his own to finish.

He glanced up at the chains wrapped around the railing. The links in those chains were all but rusted through, squeaky, brittle. A good blow with the hammer and they would have fallen free. But he'd kept them on, kept the manacles on, until Lizzy gave him the key. Now she had offered him the last symbol of her control.

He could have laughed, but it would have hurt too much to do so. Didn't she know that she had a far more subtle hold over him? One that could not be eradicated? Or did Lizzy *want* him to leave? Was this her way of saying that things between them had gone too far too fast?

He stood, walking forward, touching the cold, rusting chains. Until coming here, he hadn't realized that his own heart had grown rusty and incapable of anything but anger. Now the very sight of them made him feel somehow weightless. Free.

For long moments he held the links. Then, still wondering

about Lizzy's motives, he dragged the chain free, weighing it in his hands. Lizzy had released him, body and soul. He could go in search of Bean without recrimination.

Curiously, he felt no sense of relief, no wild jubilation. He knew he should be jumping to his feet and running to saddle his horse. He should ride all day and into the night and resume his search of his nemesis as if nothing had happened to delay him. He was so close to his goal. Why couldn't he move?

Staring into the shadows, he watched Oscar and the twins skirt the back of the house and tramp out to the privy. They took turns inside, not bothering to latch the door, jabbering to one another about something that sounded vaguely like flying frogs. Then Lewis helped Oscar with the buttons of his trousers, and the three marched back to the chicken coop, Oscar pausing before disappearing from sight to wiggle his fingers in Micah's direction.

He might as well have wrapped those fingers around Micah's heart.

Exactly when had it happened? When had he succumbed to this odd family's charm and become a prisoner of another sort? What had caused him to cease being angry, irritated, and ready to throttle them all, to become a man who . . .

Loved?

Damn.

Why hadn't he been more careful? Why hadn't he remembered he had other responsibilities?

He had a home.

It was gone.

He had his brothers.

Grown men now.

The gold . . .

Stolen.

Lili.

He couldn't live for the dead.

Freedom.

The freedom to stay if he wished.

He clenched his hands, and the iron bit into his skin. Did he want to remain here after all that had occurred? True, he had developed a yearning, a fondness, a . . . desire for Lizzy. But maybe that would prove to be temporary, the result of too many years away from the creature comforts of civilization.

But even as he thought such a thing, he felt an echoing hollowness in his soul. A sadness. And he realized that for the first time in years he felt alive—really alive! It wasn't just because the war had ended. That had honed his wants and needs, true, but he'd been looking for something long before the fighting ended. A purpose, a grand reason for living. He'd found that here, of all places. There were people who needed him, worthy tasks, and with a little luck maybe Oscar wouldn't be the only Wilder male to look favorably on him.

He shook his head at the vagaries of fate that had brought him here. Then, roaring, he threw the chains into the bushes. Turning his back on the iron links and all they represented, he shoved the photo into his pocket and strode into the house, pushing the door open with such force that it bounced against the wall.

Lizzy, who'd been on her way to the back of the house with an armload of dish towels, whirled to face him, dropping the towels, and pressing a hand to her breast. Standing that way, poised in front of that huge stuffed bear, bathed in the afternoon light, she looked as if she was about to be eaten alive.

Micah held out his hand.

"Come here," he ordered.

She shook her head.

"Now."

She approached with obvious reluctance. As soon as she was within arm's reach, he hauled her close, kissing her with all of the pent-up frustration he'd felt for hours, days. His hands greedily roamed her shoulders, her hips. His tongue traced hers, tangled erotically. Then he withdrew it so that he could run his lips down her throat, taste the hollow at the base of her neck. He drew back once, saying fervently, "I won't be leaving. Not until *I* decide it's time to go." Then he kissed her again, fiercely, passionately, knowing that if he held her many more times like this, he would never be able to leave.

The horsemen appeared on the road about five.

Lizzy didn't know what made her look up from her washing pot which had been set outside near the barn. She simply recognized, in an instant, that something was wrong.

As soon as she saw the Union uniforms, she knew who had come her way. Bean. The officer he'd sent must not have found any sign of the deserter she'd supposedly seen, and now these men were about to retrace his steps.

"Johnny!"

Her little brother stood next to her wringing out clothes, and she poked him in the ribs.

"Johnny, run to the bridge and tell Micah to hide."

"What?"

"Just do as I say. Then tell your brothers to stay away from the soldiers. If they ride toward you and start asking questions, you haven't seen anything or anyone, understand?"

It was clear that Johnny didn't, but she pushed him toward the bridge. "Go!"

As her little brother ran toward the structure, she could only pray that his movements wouldn't draw attention. Taking a basket, she began moving toward the laundry-laden line strung in front of the house, an action that would allow the men to see her first and hopefully ride to intercept her.

Her breath was coming fast and shallow. She didn't dare turn to see if Micah had been able to find cover. She could only grip the wicker handles of the laundry basket and pray that she wouldn't bring more suspicion to him than she already had.

The group of about ten men drew to a stop a few yards from where she'd come to a halt, and she put the basket down, raising a hand to shield her eyes from the glare of the dipping sun. She studied Bean, in the center, then, one by one, she recognized the others who had come to steal from her family. Micah had never been responsible for the robbery. It had been committed by *these* so-called officers and soldiers.

"Good day, Miss . . . Wilder, isn't it?"

Bean was the one to speak. The man who'd led the raid on her home Lizzy was flooded with the same impressions she'd had when she encountered him a second time at the office. Here was a person who was cold and withered with his own bitterness. So this was Lili's father! She could only pity the young woman. For the first time, Lizzy could understand how hard Lily's decision to marry Micah must have been. She must have known that her father would react quite vehemently to having his will thwarted.

When the man continued to wait, Lizzy knew she should speak, but her throat had become so dry that she feared any sound would emerge as a croak.

"I'm Colonel Ezra Bean. I believe you spoke to one of my men in town. A clerk by the name of Polnicek."

Again she nodded.

"He said that you had seen someone in the area who might have fit the description of a known traitor."

"Yes," the word was barely audible. "As I told one of your officers later that day.—"

"My officers?"

"Yes, he was intent on following the man's trail."

Bean's eyes narrowed. "I'm afraid that you have been misled, Miss Wilder. None of my officers have been here."

Lizzy's stomach flip-flopped with nerves. *None* of his officers? Then who was the man who had come to look for Micah St. Charles?

"I would like you to confirm where you last saw the traitor."

She pointed to the same spot that she had shown the captain days before. "Over there."

"Was he on foot?"

"Yes."

"And how quickly was he moving?"

"I-I couldn't say. A brisk pace, I suppose."

Bean turned to mumble an instruction to his men. In an instant, all of the soldiers but Bean were reining their horses toward the tree line and urging them to a trot.

As the sound of hooves thundered away, Lizzy stood trembling. Why had Bean sent them away? Did he suspect her of lying? Did he intend to punish her?

"Miss Wilder, I hope we haven't inconvenienced you."

She shook her head.

"If you should happen to see the man again, you must notify my office immediately. It is of the utmost importance. The man we seek is a known traitor, a profiteer, and a dangerous criminal. Do not try to apprehend him yourself."

"No, sir."

His eyes flicked to the bridge, and she froze. Had Micah found a place to hide? What were her brothers doing? She prayed that this man would not go near her brothers.

"You've made progress on the bridge since I was here last."

"Yes. My brothers have been working night and day."

"Hmmm." It was clear that Bean didn't think that such young boys could have that much of an effect on a dilapidated bridge. She tucked her hands into the pockets of her apron as they began to shake. Did he suspect that they'd had help? That they'd had the expertise of an engineer to aid them?

"I don't suppose your brothers could add any more information?"

She shook her head, being careful to keep the motion from becoming too emphatic. "Only Oscar was with me at the time—my smallest brother. He's much too young to be of any help."

"I see."

Again she had the eerie sensation that Bean didn't believe her, that if her story didn't hold true, he would be back.

But if that was the case, he didn't say so immediately. He merely touched a finger to his hat and said, "We'll be in touch, Miss Wilder. Good-bye."

He turned his mount and galloped away, but even after he'd disappeared into the trees, she didn't dare move for fear he was watching her from somewhere.

"Lizzy?"

She nearly jumped a foot when Johnny tugged on her skirt.

"Where's Micah?" she asked immediately.

"In the water under the bridge. He lashed himself to one of the supports."

"Go tell him to stay there. I don't trust those men. They might still be watching."

"How long will he have to keep hidden?"

Her mind whirled madly, but she knew there was only one choice. "Until dark. Tell him he'll have to stay until dark. In the meantime I want all of you to work like the devil on that bridge. If anyone is keeping tabs on us, it's got to look like we were able to finish all the repairs ourselves."

Chapter

18

The night was dark with only a glimmer of moonlight when Lizzy dared make her way to the bridge. She had to pick her way over the uneven ground and down the bank, afraid to light even so much as a match to reveal her movements.

"Micah?"

He didn't immediately answer.

"Micah!"

"Over here."

To her relief, the sound did not come from the water.

"Where are you?"

"Down the bank."

She followed his voice, nearly stumbling over his supine form. Dropping to her knees, she felt his arms, his shoulders, assuring herself that he was unharmed.

"What happened?" she said.

"As soon as it got dark, I tried to swim to shore. The current carried me a good half mile downstream."

"You're cold as ice!" she said touching his cheek. "Why didn't you just come to the house?"

"I didn't know if it was safe."

"Come on. We need to get you inside."

Since he was wet and a little shaky from fighting the current, she slipped her arm around his waist. But they both knew it was only an excuse. An excuse to touch, to reassure.

Once in the house, she carefully drew all the blinds, then lit a single lamp.

"You've got to be starving. Sit down at the table. I've got soup and bread and cold meat. Use one of those bath towels on the counter to dry yourself off, and I'll heat some water for washing."

"Thanks."

He grabbed one of the towels, drying his face and hair and hands. By the time he'd finished, she had his meal on the table. He sank into a chair, hungrily reaching for the food.

"What happened?" he asked between bites.

She sank into the chair next to him. "Bean came."

"I gathered as much. What did you say to him to make him go away?"

She looked down at her hands, knowing that she would have to tell him the whole truth.

"He came looking for me, actually."

Micah stopped chewing and shot a piercing gaze her way. "Why?"

"Well . . . when I went into town, I thought I might try to help you."

"Help me?"

"So I went to the army office to ask about the man Mr. Ruthers had warned me about. When the soldiers got a little too nosy about my motives for asking such questions, I lied and told them that I'd seen a man who fit their description. I explained that I'd spotted him about five miles away from here and that he was heading south."

"They didn't believe you."

"I guess not. This is the second time someone has come to confirm my story."

"The *second* time?"

"Yes. Another officer came first. A captain. He rode to the farm right after I returned from town, but Bean denies that the captain was one of his men. Who could he have been?"

"A bounty hunter, probably."

"A bounty hunter?" she gasped.

"There's a price on my head."

"How much?"

"Five hundred dollars."

She stared at him in astonishment. "It's a good thing I didn't know that the day I found you in my barn."

"You would have turned me in?"

"For five hundred dollars? In a heartbeat."

"What about now?"

"Never," she whispered fervently.

Micah stared blankly at his food. "Damn. Bean's men will be coming back. As soon as they realize they've been sent on a wild-goose chase."

"What are we going to do?"

"*We? We* aren't doing anything. I've got to get out of here. I can't endanger you and your family."

"But you can't go tonight! You'll need supplies first, clothes, water."

"All of which can be gathered in a matter of hours."

She grasped his hand, not afraid to let him see that she was desperate.

"Not tonight. Please. It's the only thing I'll ever ask of you. Not tonight."

His body remained tense, rigid, but then he relented. "I'll leave tomorrow at sundown."

Her eyes filled with unexpected tears at the reprieve. "Thank you."

He finished his meal in silence, but Lizzy didn't move. She sat with him, touching his thigh, watching him, absorbing the little nuances of this man whom she had come to love.

"What will you do?" she asked when he rose to put his plate on the counter. "What will you do after you leave?"

He was still, quiet, his back to her for long, agonizing minutes. Then he said simply, "I'm going to stop Ezra Bean."

"How?"

He looked at her then. "I've thought about this for a long time. I've cursed myself for not going after him earlier; I've damned myself for allowing him to go this far. But it wasn't until I began tracking him this last time—following an obvious trail that he'd left me so that I would come—that I realized one thing."

His chest swelled with a deep breath. "There is no way for me to clear my name unless Bean himself confesses to his crimes."

While Micah went to his own room to wash, Lizzy dug into the bottom of her bureau drawer for the one remaining garment from her trousseau. It was fitting that she wear it tonight. For Micah. In minutes she was dressed in nothing but a delicate batiste wrapper interspersed with insertion and ivory satin. Tying a matching ribbon around her hair, she blew out the lamp and made her way into the hall.

Moonlight pooled on the bare plank floors, dancing there as the breeze toyed with the ivy that had grown over the outside of the windows. As she walked down the hall, she ran her hand along the chair rail. The wood felt cool against her heated flesh.

The door to the back bedroom moved easily against her

touch, and she pushed it open, smiling when the hinges remained silent, allowing her to surprise him.

Micah lay on the bed, the covers draped low over his hips, his arms flung overhead. The regular rise and fall of his chest was even, comforting, enticing. But he was not asleep. She knew that instinctively.

Something must have warned him of her presence, because he shifted, his eyes flickering open.

"I don't want to sleep alone tonight," was all she said, her tone soft, yet filled with an inestimable yearning. Then she fingered the sash to her wrapper, sliding it loose, slowly, carefully, temptingly. Once the bow had dissolved, the edges of her robe parted. She could sense his heated regard, feel the passion radiating between them as he realized she wore nothing beneath.

Smiling, she slid her fingers under the soft material and shrugged out of the garment, allowing it to pool on the floor at her feet.

For long moments Lizzy stood there, proud, motionless. She kept thinking that she should feel shame. No man had seen her behave so brazenly. Yet here she was, baring herself, offering herself.

He didn't speak. He didn't need to. He merely held out a hand, inviting her closer. Inviting her into his bed.

It began slowly, the brush of his hands against her cheeks, light hummingbird kisses that skimmed her jaw, her ears, her neck. She lay at his side, ensconced in the softness of his bed while he leaned over her, his chest rubbing against her arm, his hands strumming across her ribs.

She closed her eyes, arching in delight, absorbing the sensations—the incredible mind-drugging sensations. Her whole intent had been to make this a night that he would remember, but she found she couldn't concentrate. She could only close her eyes and *feel*. He touched her shoulders, her waist, before one finger slid up, circling her nipple, causing it to pebble and harden.

Lizzy became aware of the thudding of her heart, the warmth pooling into her veins. There were sounds, the soughing of his breath in her ear, the rustle of cloth, her own kittenish moans. He leaned closer, the hair on his chest abrading her skin, setting it on fire, encouraging Lizzy to begin her own exploration. There was so much to learn. So much to know. So much to remember. There were tastes— his lips, his skin, his hair. The feel of him, the texture of him, the weight of him. All of it inundated her mind, rendering her incapable of coherent thought. Yet when he began to stroke her, exploring more deliberately each hollow of her body, her back, her hips, the areas behind her knees, there was no longer a need for thought. She became a creature of instinct. A woman of desire.

Pushing him onto the mattress, she bent over him. She needed to satisfy her yearnings for all those little touches, little gestures, that she had denied herself up to now. She wanted to drown herself in excess.

She began by plunging her fingers through his hair, that soft, thick hair, feeling its weight, its warmth. Then she kissed his brow, his cheek, his jaw, reveling in the differing textures of his skin.

"I've wanted to do this for ever so long," she whispered, trailing her mouth down his throat. She paused to suck on his collarbone, then to lick and make amends. "I've watched you in secret, denying even to myself the need to do so." She peeked up at him, offering him a shy smile. "Now I discover that you will not refuse me."

His eyes glowed. "Never."

"Good."

She rubbed at his chest, his stomach, dipping to lick his nipples, to rub her cheek against the dusting of hair on his breastbone. Her thumb flirted with his navel, and then she delved lower, lower, until she encountered that most amazing part of him, which she had never dreamed she would hold so freely. She caressed, explored, delighted, then placed a brief kiss on its tip.

He shuddered, taking a deep breath and closing his eyes. Lizzy marveled at the power she felt from so elemental a response.

"Perhaps I should chain you up again," she murmured, crawling up so that she lay full length on his body. "I could make you my own personal slave."

He opened his eyes, and even in the semidarkness, she could see the way they glowed. "I don't think the chains will prove necessary." He covered her hand, drawing it low. "All you have to do is look at me the way you are now."

Then, without giving her a chance to protest, he rolled over, pressing her into the mattress. His lips covered hers, becoming hungry, demanding.

She moaned, wrapping her arms around his neck, parting her legs, parting them until she could feel the heat of him, the strength of him against her moist womanly core. She found herself straining against him, needing more.

"Please," she whispered next to his ear. "Love me."

The plea meant so much more than the merely physical act of lovemaking. She wanted his heart. She wanted his soul. But when he propped himself up on one hand and reached down to ready her, all coherent thought vanished. She could feel the tip of him pushing against her, pressing. Then all at once he slid deep inside her, filling her, warming her from within.

Automatically she lifted her hips toward him, wound her legs around his thighs, and she whispered, "Give me my pleasure, Mr. Micah St. Charles."

As if her words had unlocked the invisible chains that bound him, he began to move, slowly at first, then quicker and quicker, inspiring a frenzy of need. The world whirled away as she focused on her body, on his, on the miracle of their joining. Then all thought dissolved completely, and she became a hungry creature, bucking against him, kissing, scratching. A familiar tautness was building low in her belly, an indescribable pleasure. She urged him on with her legs, her arms, soft guttural sounds. Then she was tensing, tensing, tensing, her muscles straining before her loins began to shatter in a flurry of passionate vibrations.

Above her, Micah stiffened, thrusting into her one last time. A moan was wrenched from his throat, and he squeezed his eyes shut, spilling his seed into her womb.

It took a long time for reality to return. When it did, Lizzy became aware of the heat of his skin, the weight of his body, and she smiled.

How she loved this man.

She wrapped her arms around his waist, hugging him tighter and tighter, praying that this would be enough to satisfy a prisoner of fate and convince him that his future lay here.

With her.

She woke much later to find him standing by the window, staring out at the night.

"Micah?" It was a whisper of sound.

"It's so peaceful here."

She didn't know what to say, so she remained silent, allowing the evening's stillness to flow around them. A warm sort of quiet had settled over their shoulders. One that didn't need words.

"You'll go after Bean tomorrow night?"

"Yes."

"How long will you be gone?" Lizzy asked some time later.

"I don't know." The admission was hesitant.

"Will you come back?"

He sighed, saying again, "I don't know. I wish I could offer you more reassurance, but my brothers will be waiting for me at Solitude."

"I prefer your honesty."

"I want to stay here, but . . ."

"You've been kept from your own pursuits for too long."

"Bean has gone too far. I can't let him hurt anyone else." He looked at her then. "Especially not you."

"I see."

"Will you notify me immediately if you discover you're with child."

She seemed to flinch, but nodded, not bothering to hide.

"You're being very understanding."

She gazed down at the sheet she was twisting between her fingers. "No. I'm not. I want to beg you to stay, but I can't. I'm selfish enough to admit that if you come to me, if you decide you want a future with me, it must be a decision you've made of your own free will. In the meantime, at least you've given me a little hope. For now it's enough."

He sat on the bed, pulling her close, but even through five years of war she had never felt this uncertain, this afraid. It was a sure sign of how much she'd grown to care for him.

Micah shook his head. "Nothing turned out the way I thought it would," he said, moving to frame her head in his hands. "What about you, Lizzy?" He bent closer, his lips hovering above her own. "What kind of a future did you dream about?"

"I had no dreams. Until I met you."

His eyes squeezed shut as if her words had gone straight to his heart.

"Surely there was something," he prodded, his voice rough. "I want to give you something, grant some sort of wish to repay you for making me *feel* again. Love again."

His admission was all that she needed. Love. He *did* love her. But looking at him now, she knew that he had his doubts as to whether or not that love would last.

"If you could have had anything you wanted these past five years, what would you have asked for?"

She thought carefully before saying, "I always wanted to dance."

"Dance?"

"I was only eighteen when the war broke out. My fiancé didn't believe in such frivolous activities, and before I met Bill, my father wouldn't allow me to spend time with the boys in town. He didn't want me marrying as early as he and my mother had, so he was very strict about letting me attend socials of any kind."

"You were very young when your fiancé died. Surely no one would have blamed you for going to the parties then."

She shrugged. "I suppose . . ."

When she grew silent again, he urged her on with his eyes.

"But by that time, there were no dances, no boys."

He rose to his feet, reaching for her. "Then dance with me now."

She stepped willingly into his arms, into his embrace. He had obviously been trained in ballroom techniques, because he knew how to lead an unskilled pupil such as she, humming a waltz in her ear the whole time. But soon there was no need for fancy footwork, no need for music. Phantom tendrils of passion whirled about them, binding them together, pulling them close, until they barely swayed, holding tightly to one another.

At least she had this, Lizzy thought. Pulling his head down for a kiss, she closed her eyes and prayed. Prayed that this man would be happy. Prayed that he would find a purpose in life.

And prayed that the destiny he sought lay with her.

Chapter

19

Micah waited until just before sunrise, not wanting to leave any sooner than necessary. But the minutes had rushed out of his grasp, leaving him with nothing but one last kiss, one last caress.

He stepped into the bedroom and in the moonlight saw the woman cuddling the pillow he'd substituted for his own body. She would be angry when she awakened. He'd promised to stay for another day, but he knew that to do so would put her family in more danger than she could imagine. He had to leave now, while there was time. He wouldn't be able to live with himself if anything happened to her or the boys.

Leaning close, he placed a kiss on her cheek. She smiled slightly in her sleep, but didn't wake, a fact for which he would be eternally grateful.

She was so young, so lovely. She'd given him life, infused him with a feeling of well-being. So much so that he had hesitated in the pursuit of his original goals and had thought for a time that there could be a normalcy to his existence. He could only pray that somehow, some way, he could claim her love again. Genuinely. With honor. In the wee hours of the night, he had come to that inescapable conclusion. He didn't want to be this woman's lover; he wanted to be her husband. Her soulmate. The father of her children.

Bending low again, he kissed her ear and whispered, "I love you, Lizzy. More than life itself." Then, placing a red rose on the pillow beside her, he stood and turned, forcing himself to leave the room while he still could.

Once in the kitchen, he gathered the supplies he'd taken from the cupboards earlier that hour after washing at the pump and cutting a rose from the arbor by the back door. He had food and water, as well as a blanket, his revolver, and a new pair of shoes. It would be enough to get by.

The kitchen door squeaked slightly as he opened it.

"Micah?"

He froze, the boyish voice drilling straight into his heart. Oscar. Little Oscar.

Turning, he saw the boy's confused expression.

"Where are you going?"

He didn't know what to say. He didn't want to lie to the boy, but he didn't want him to wake Lizzy either.

Kneeling, he gestured for Oscar to come close. As soon as he was in arm's reach, he ruffled his hair. "Tell me," he said, hoping to divert the boy's attention. "How did you get the name Oscar? All your brothers are named after explorers, aren't they?"

Oscar grinned. "Yes, sir. But I'm named after Pa. His name was Oscar too, and Ma figured he was the greatest explorer of them all. She said"—his brow furrowed as he fought to find his mother's exact words—"'it took a man of vision to find me in a sea of women, and for that he deserves a namesake.'"

Micah chuckled. "Your mother was a wise woman." Unable to stop himself, Micah held the boy close in a snug embrace, needing to imprint this moment on his memory. Then he drew back, turning Oscar and swatting him on the behind. "Now get on back to bed."

"We're still sleeping in the barn."

"Then get back to the barn. You've got hours yet before Lizzy puts you to work."

Oscar held up a tin cup. "Will you get me a drink of water first?"

So that was what had brought him to the house. Leaving his bundle in the shadows, Micah took Oscar's hand and led him to the pump. He filled the cup and waited patiently while the boy drank, then escorted him back to the barn.

"'Night, Micah," Oscar whispered as he stepped inside.

"Good night, son." The word slipped free, the endearment, but Micah would not have retrieved it for the world.

Then, ruing the fact that the sun had already begun to rise, he gathered his bundle from the house and hurried across the bridge.

As he crossed the planks, he felt a niggling unease. He stopped. Turned. But the yard was quiet, serene.

They would be fine now that he was gone, he told himself. As long as he got out of sight as soon as he could.

A booming noise split the early dawn. Lizzy jerked awake, automatically reaching for Micah, but he was gone. The linens were cool. All she encountered was a single red rose.

She smiled. Micah had left it. Did he know that red roses symbolized love? Yes. She was sure he knew.

Sweeping the covers back, she jumped from the bed, tying the wrapper firmly around her waist, meeting her brothers in the hall as they ran in from the kitchen.

"Lizzy, did you hear it?"

At that moment she remembered the distant noise that had awakened her. Immediately she grew panicky.

"Where's Micah?" she demanded.

The boys shrugged, gazing at each other.

Another explosion rocked the house, causing the windows to rattle. Holding her ears, Lizzy could scarcely believe that the noise was real, that it wasn't some sort of dream.

"What a blast!" Bridger shouted above the din. "It sounded like cannon fire."

Fear swept through her body. "Stay here."

"But—"

"Stay here!"

Hurrying to the door, she wrenched it open, stepping onto the porch. She watched in horror as timbers from what remained of the bridge were still settling in the water and on the banks. Black smoke and dust rolled into the breeze.

"Merciful heavens, wh—"

A hand whipped around her body; the muzzle of a revolver pressed into her temple. "I've got her, Colonel!"

Men on horseback appeared, circling the house, weapons raised. She recognized Bean's group immediately, but their appearance was even more menacing in the dim light of dawn.

"Well, well, Miss Wilder," Bean proclaimed from where he remained mounted on his horse mere yards away. "We meet again."

Lizzy's eyes closed briefly in horror. Her thoughts became jumbled, disjointed, whipping from her brothers' safety to Micah's whereabouts.

Bean folded his arms over the pommel of his saddle and bent close, spearing her with that icy gaze she was beginning to loathe.

"I believe you have some information we require."

Even though she had never felt fear so intense, so all-consuming, she forced herself to talk. "I told you everything I know."

His lips pursed. "I don't think so. In fact, I think you made quite sure that you *didn't* tell me anything but lies."

He straightened, gazing around the yard with mock idleness.

"You see, I have proof the man is here. Somewhere. I've had a pair of men watching you for hours."

"No."

He continued as if he hadn't heard her. "They saw Micah go into your house late last night. You really should take care not to stand in front of the blinds in your bedroom when the lamp is lit."

Lizzy couldn't control a betraying flinch.

Bean smiled. "I knew the minute I heard your story that you were lying. Micah St. Charles would never head south. Not when *I* am so close." His voice grew harsh. "He's searched too long for me to give up now. I'm the man who destroyed him, who brought his life down to this." He made a disparaging gesture to the farm. "Besides, I had only to look at that bridge to know he'd been here. The man's craftsmanship is like a signature, you know."

"He isn't here," she repeated more forcefully.

It was obvious Bean didn't believe her.

"Search the house!"

His men dismounted and stormed up the front steps. Lizzy tried to free herself, but the arms that restrained her were too tight. Soon, as the sound of crashing glass and splintering wood filled her ears, she ceased struggling. It was all too horrible to believe. She expected her brothers to be dragged out by their hair at any minute.

"He isn't inside, Colonel," one soldier shouted from an upper window.

"Look again!" Bean ordered.

The soldiers must have been tearing the house apart

board by board, but after another quarter hour, they emerged. Lizzy could only thank heaven that the boys had been wise enough to run out the back door and hide.

"He isn't here, Colonel," the same soldier said as they emerged.

"Search the premises. He's got to be here somewhere."

The men scattered in all directions.

"Wouldn't you like to save yourself and your home? Just tell me where he is," Bean said.

Lizzy took a deep breath then stated, "I would rather burn in hell forever."

Micah was little more than a hundred yards upstream on the other side of the river, on his way to Catesby, when he heard the explosion. As he was thrown to the ground, he squeezed his eyes closed and was inundated with images of another bridge, another detonation.

"Run, Captain, run!"

Wheeze's call echoed in his mind, infusing him with energy. By hell, he'd had enough of this. Bean had gone too far.

Dropping the bundle he carried, he took off his shoes and waded into the river, knowing that his only chance of helping Lizzy and confronting Bean lay in his ability to swim. But after his experience the night before, he already knew the currents were swift and dangerous.

He had no other choice.

Taking a deep breath, he plunged into the water. Almost immediately he felt the rush of the undertow beginning to tug at his body. He allowed himself to flow with it for a time until it took him to center stream, where he began swimming with all his might. Within seconds he had been drawn past the bridge supports. Grasping a floating board, he kicked toward shore.

The water was cool, muddy. His head kept bobbing below the surface so that he wasn't sure when it was safe to breathe. He was whirled around and around, but time and again he reassured himself that he could make it to the other side. Lizzy waited for him there.

Lizzy. The very name infused him with strength. Their relationship would not end with his drowning. She had faced too much pain, too much hardship. He would not allow Bean to destroy her peace of mind as well. The man demanded too much for the death of his daughter. Too much!

He kicked harder, harder. Something caught at his pants, and he grasped the root of a tree that had grown down into the river.

Immediately, his headlong journey downstream halted and he gasped for air, realizing that he'd made it to the other side. He'd made it!

But there was no time for self-congratulations. Dragging himself onto the bank, he forced his rubbery limbs to obey his command. He dodged into a screen of bushes at the top of the rise and crouched there, assessing the situation.

Bean had come to the Wilder farm with eight men. Two had been stationed on the hill with a cannon and were probably responsible for the destruction of the bridge. Another soldier held Lizzy at gunpoint while five more dismounted and hurried inside to search the house. Even from his vantage point, Micah could hear the sounds of destruction that came in their wake.

Dammit, what was he going to do?

And then he saw them. Seven boys clasping rifles, revolvers, and a host of makeshift weapons, hurrying toward the barn.

Micah ran to intercept them, keeping low and to the shadows. Johnny, the last in line, was the only one who had not entered the barn by the time Micah caught up with them. Before the boy could get inside, Micah caught him fast around the waist, covered his mouth, and swept him around the corner.

When Johnny saw Micah, the fear in his eyes disappeared beneath a glimmer of hope.

"Go get your brothers. Tell them to bring their weapons and meet me in the bushes behind the springhouse."

Johnny didn't need a second push. He was already running toward the barn door.

Soon the Wilder boys were crowding close, dropping their weapons on the ground behind the springhouse so that Micah could take inventory.

It was a sorry arsenal indeed. A rifle, two revolvers, a cast-iron frying pan, three pots, two carving knives, a slingshot, a peashooter, a rope, a dozen bottles, and a can of kerosene. But with a little luck, it would be enough.

"All right, men," he said as if the boys were a squad under his command. Their shoulders straightened a bit in pride at the distinction. "Listen to me. I only have time to outline our plan once. Then we'll have to put it in action."

As soon as the boys were in position, Micah loaded the revolvers, stuffing one into the back of his trousers and handing the other to Crockett. The rifle lay on the ground at his feet.

"Can you shoot straight?"

"Yes, sir."

"Good. Your sister's life may depend on it. Just remember, don't hit Bean—the tall man in charge. I need him alive."

"Yes, Micah."

"Have you hitched up my horse?"

"She's hooked up to the buggy and waiting."

Micah slapped him on the back in a companionable male gesture, knowing that Crockett was too old for a hug but that he needed a gesture of approval and trust.

"Very well, then. As soon as Lizzy is safe, I want you to take her and all of your brothers out of here. Drive as fast as you can into town. Go immediately to the church and demand sanctuary. Even Bean won't come after you there. As soon as you can, tell the minister you want to talk to an army officer from another state. Don't settle for anyone less than a general. Explain what happened. Make the general believe that your family was forced to take me in, forced to defend me. It's the only way you'll be left alone."

Crockett nodded to show he understood, but a blatant fear shone in his eyes. Micah checked the rifle one last time and held up his hand in a signal for the boys to begin.

"Do you think this will work?" Crockett whispered.

"It has to work."

Bean's men were spilling from the house, heading into the barnyard, just as Micah had supposed they would.

"Here they come."

The first wave of defense depended entirely on the younger boys. Micah had known that the only chance they had for success was in a stealthy attack until the numbers could be brought down.

One of the first soldiers headed for the chicken coop, Boone's territory. Micah's heart pounded heavily in his chest as he saw the boy waiting on the far side of the building, saw the soldier walk closer and closer to the corner. As soon as he rounded the edge . . .

Clang!

Boone whacked him over the head with the skillet, and the soldier slumped to the ground. In seconds Boone had commandeered the man's weapons and pulled him out of sight.

"One down."

A second soldier made the mistake of moving toward the springhouse, Bridger and Johnny's location. After his signal, the two boys had hidden inside and crouched on either side of the entrance. The soldier undid the latch, swinging the rough plank door outward toward him. Without warning, it was propelled toward him with such force that it struck him in the nose and sent his revolver flying into the retaining pond.

Johnny, who'd been responsible for hurling himself full tilt into the door, picked himself up and whipped a rope around the man's hands, hog-tying him. Meanwhile Bridger incapacitated the man for good by kicking him in the groin. Then, straddling the man's chest and holding a butcher knife to his throat, he allowed Oscar to stuff the soldier's open mouth with the same rag that had once served as Micah's gag. Then the three boys dragged him into the springhouse.

"Two down," Crockett counted.

Lewis and Clark were next to begin fighting. Seeing three more men heading across the compound in the direction of the barn, they pushed open the hayloft door. Lewis began hurling rocks with his slingshot, while the other boy lit the fabric wicks they'd shoved into bottles of kerosene and threw them into the yard. Micah had to give them credit. They were excellent shots. One squat, bowlegged soldier was hit in the center of his forehead with a stone and went down first thing. The next soldier dodged one flaming volley, but the next hit him in the arm, setting his sleeve on fire; the other hit his leg. As he was showered with rocks, he began screaming, running toward the river in an effort to douse the blaze. The third man, seeing the state of his companions tried to run, but a chunk of brick hit him in the temple and he stumbled and lay still.

"Now!" Micah yelled to Crockett.

They both jumped from cover at the same time, Crockett running toward the rear entrance of the house while Micah streaked around the front.

At the first sign of chaos, most of the army horses had bolted, leaving only Bean and the man who held Lizzy, plus the two men by the cannon who had mounted their horses and were riding toward them.

Micah paused in mid-flight, held his rifle straight out from his body, and fired. One of the men on horseback flew backwards, a red stain flowering from his chest.

A bullet smacked into the dust next to Micah's foot, and he ran again, zigzagging, ducking behind the porch for cover.

Almost immediately the shooting stopped and an eerie silence settled over the yard.

"Micah St. Charles!" Bean called.

Micah remained silent.

"I know you're here. Come out. Come out now and surrender yourself and no one will be hurt."

That was a lie. Micah knew that Bean couldn't afford to leave anyone on the Wilder farm alive.

He forced himself to remain calm, to think only of the adversaries who remained. Bean. The man who held Lizzy. One horseman.

A shot rang out and he squinted. It hadn't come from the house or from Bean. Damn it all! Was the last soldier shooting at the boys?

Filled with anger at men who had become beasts and would prey on small children, Micah lunged from his hiding place, his revolver primed.

But the barnyard was empty. The other soldier who had abandoned the cannon and begun riding toward them was sprawled in the grass, his horse running away.

Micah didn't have time to question how the man had been shot. He turned his attention immediately to Bean.

"Tell your man to let her go."

Bean reined his horse to face him, a slow smile creasing his lips. "So . . . the traitor is captured at last."

"Not quite, Bean. Let her go."

"Why should I?"

"Because if you don't do as I say, just as I tell you to, I'll shoot you."

"What? And ruin your chance for some sort of miracle?

After all, I'm the only man who can prove or disprove your innocence. If I die, you remain a traitor."

"I'm willing to take my chances."

Bean cocked his head. "Indeed." Immediately he focused on Lizzy. "You would do that? Bargain away your own life to save her?" A patently cruel light entered his eyes. "Does she know that you killed your first wife? Does she know that to love you endangers her very existence?"

"Lili died of diphtheria! How many times do I have to tell you that?"

"Never, never will I believe a man like you! A murderer! Drop your weapon."

"No, Micah!" Lizzy shouted.

"If you want the woman to be released, drop it now."

Micah sighed and dropped the revolver, holding up his hands in surrender.

"No!" Lizzy cried again, but no one paid her any mind.

"Release the girl, Sergeant, and apprehend our prisoner."

As soon as the sergeant stepped away from her, the front door opened and Crockett snagged Lizzy's wrist, dragged her inside, and slammed the door shut. Neither Bean nor his man had an opportunity to react.

Bean turned his horse toward Micah. "Very clever. Very clever indeed."

"Did you actually think I would believe your lies about leaving them alone?"

Bean shrugged. "It was a thought."

"They'll be gone before you can hang me."

That idea seemed to upset Bean a little.

"Perhaps."

Even as he uttered the word, the barn doors were rolled open, and Bridger and Boone led out the horse and buggy. As instructed, the rest of the boys had gathered at the buggy. They had only to collect Crockett and Lizzy before escaping into town.

"You thought of everything, didn't you, St. Charles?"

"You gave me no choice."

The sergeant was striding more quickly toward Micah now and Bean threw him a rope. "String him up from that tree by the river."

"No!" The cry came from Oscar. "No, you can't kill him. You can't!"

Lizzy was hurrying to the buggy from the rear of the house, but even she wasn't quick enough to grab the little boy as he jumped from the seat and ran toward Micah.

"Let him go! You're mean men, both of you. Let him go!"

Micah tried to dodge forward. A shot rang out from somewhere on the hillside, and the sergeant fell to the ground, a gaping wound in his chest.

Someone else was shooting at them! Dear heaven above, would the killing never end?

Bean must have realized that someone other than the Wilder family had opened fire. Whirling his mount toward Oscar, he galloped forward, scooping the little boy up, and tossing him over the saddle.

"Micah!" Lizzy ran forward, clutching Bean's pant leg, but he whipped her with his quirt, then rode back in Micah's direction, bending low over his horse and leaning sideways to slash him.

"Micah!" Lizzy called again.

In the scuffle, Micah's revolver had been kicked under the porch, and he looked around him in panic, searching for something, anything, to use as a weapon. Seeing a glimmer of metal in the grass he rushed forward, retrieving the iron chains he'd thrown there not so long ago.

Seeing that Micah was running away from him, Bean raised his free hand and slashed down with his quirt.

Micah dodged the blow, then whirled to wrap the chain around Bean's throat. The horse reared, and Bean fell to the ground. Oscar stayed on the animal by clutching the saddle horn, but the horse soon burst into a gallop and bolted toward the trees.

Micah barely noted the fact as he began to grapple with Bean, pummeling him with blows. It was Lizzy who ran to calm him.

"Stop it!"

She grasped his wrist. There was no way she could have prevented the blow, but she distracted Micah enough to make him look up.

"Stop. There's been enough violence, enough killing. We'll deal with him our way."

The anger in Micah's gaze slowly faded, as did the savagery. Although he trembled with the need to exact his own measure of punishment, he reluctantly agreed. He had to go in search of Oscar.

"Crockett, unhitch that horse. The rest of you boys tie this man up so he can't get loose."

"How?"

"As I recall, there's a very heavy trunk nearby. Chain him to it."

Crockett was leading the horse toward him when the sound of hooves alerted them all.

They whirled, expecting another of Bean's men to appear, but it was a lone horseman. Another tattered soldier with scruffy hair and a sun-weathered uniform. In front of him, straddling the saddle, was a familiar curly-headed lad.

"Is anyone here missing a boy by the name of Oscar?"

Micah saw the way Lizzy froze at his side, and in an instant of hearing that voice, that low, musical voice, he knew immediately what she feared. That this was another of Bean's men. The one who had intercepted her in town.

Slowly he walked forward, squinting at the rider. His breath locked in his throat as a familiar set of dark eyes waited for him to respond. The moment recognition dawned, Micah moved quicker, then ran. The soldier lowered Oscar to the ground. Vaguely, Micah patted the boy on the shoulder, then brushed past him, grabbing the soldier by the shoulders and hauling him from the saddle to the ground, wrapping his arms around him.

"Bram! What are you doing here? Is Jackson with you?"

Then he was wrestling his brother to the ground and they were rolling playfully like the two boys they'd once been.

"Do you suppose they know each other?" he dimly heard Oscar ask.

"So it would seem," Lizzy answered. "So it would seem."

Chapter

20

It was much later, when Lizzy went outside with a basin of warm water and a cloth to bathe a gash over Micah's eye, that introductions were made.

Bean was still chained to the trunk, and Boone was forcing him at gunpoint to haul the toy wagon with its burden of Sally Wilder's rocks all over the yard, picking up broken planks from the bridge. Crockett had herded the wounded soldiers into the root cellar and he and the other boys were checking their bindings and doctoring their wounds.

"Lizzy, this is my brother. Abraham."

The tall, rangy soldier rose to his feet, taking the basin from her hands. "Call me Bram," he said smiling. It was a warm smile, a natural smile, the smile of a born seducer, but somehow it seemed at odds with the creases of worry and hardship that lined his face.

"Dammit, Bram, how did you get here?" Micah asked as the basin was passed to him. "Where's Jackson?"

"I haven't seen him or heard from him. I arrived at Solitude not a week after you did. The caretaker told me where you'd gone and why. Hell, after all the trouble I've gone through, I couldn't let you get shot up, now, could I?"

Micah frowned. "Trouble. What trouble?"

Bram grinned and walked to his horse. He withdrew a folded sheaf of papers from his saddlebags and handed them to his older brother. "This is an official nullification of your supposed crimes as well as a copy of the documentation that proves all of the charges against you were manufactured."

Micah stared at him in disbelief. Then he opened the documents and scanned the contents. "But how in the world—"

"Did I get those? I couldn't let my brother hang, could I? When word of the charges reached me, I knew someone was trying to frame you. The very thought of my older brother turning traitor was preposterous. I apprehended one of Bean's men nearly a year ago and elicited from him a confession of sorts. There has been a Pinkerton on your case for a good six months piecing together the lies Bean told. The detective has enough evidence to prove that—unless you were in two states at the same time—you couldn't possibly have made half the expeditions into Confederate territory that Bean claimed you did. Once I had the documentation I needed, I called in a few favors from my superiors."

"Favors? I was told you had fought for the Confederacy."

"Appearances can be deceiving," was all Bram said, a glitter embedded deep in his eye. "I worked for a much higher authority."

Micah stared at the signature on the last page. "Lincoln?"

"He signed this document last December, months before he was assassinated. I was part of the new secret service corps."

"Good hell! You? In the secret service? A spy?"

Bram became grave. "The war was especially fierce when seen from the Confederate side."

Micah nodded, evidently at a loss for words.

"But now, like most people, I'm officially unemployed. Once I've taken Bean back to Washington to be court-martialed and most likely hanged for the profiteering crimes he blamed on you, I'll be heading home to Solitude again . . . after I take care of some business in Baltimore."

"Marguerite?"

"Yes." Bram's expression became hard. "My beloved wife is about to discover that her husband has risen from the grave. Unfortunately, that means my time here with you will be limited." He turned to Lizzy. "If I could beg a little food and some fresh water, I'll be on my way by morning."

"Of course," Lizzy jumped to her feet. "I'll start heating some water for a bath as well."

"A bath," Bram sighed. "You are a dear, dear woman. I'll just take my horse to the barn and curry him, then I'll accept your kind offer."

He was about to walk away when Micah stopped him with a hand on his arm.

"Just a minute. We have one last item of business that needs attention."

Lizzy saw the way Micah was staring hard at his former father-in-law. Dropping the cloth he'd been using to wipe away the blood caked on his cheek, he approached the man, his carriage proud, his expression ominous.

Sensing an impending conflict, the boys began gathering from their various positions in the yard.

"Where is it, Bean?" Micah's words were filled with unspoken rage.

Bean tried to ignore him, continuing to pick up charred

pieces of wood, but Micah's hand shot out, grasping a fistful of Bean's uniform and forcing him to look up.

"Where is the St. Charles treasure?"

Bean became defiant. "Ask all you want, but I'll never tell you—you or your brother," he spat.

Micah's grip tightened. "Damn you . . ."

"You're the one who's damned. Damned in hell for what you did to my daughter. As for your stupid treasure, all you need to know is that I hid it—three huge trunks of it—in a cave somewhere in the state of Ohio. You'll never find it. Never."

With that he wrenched free, and Micah let him go without a fuss, his shoulders dipping ever so slightly in defeat. Even Lizzy knew there was no arguing with the man. His attitude proclaimed quite clearly that nothing could persuade him to reveal the location of the cave. This was his final revenge.

Bram approached his brother, clasping his shoulder and saying, "It doesn't matter."

But it did matter, Lizzy realized. The treasure was their legacy. Their hope for a future. It had to be somewhere . . . in a cave . . .

A *cave*.

The realization of what she knew, what she'd done, washed over her.

"Micah?"

Micah turned.

"Do you know anyone by the name of Adam? Or Wilhemena?"

"My parents."

"I see." The sinking sensation intensified. "This treasure. Were there any bags of coins?"

He nodded and she shifted uncomfortably, then shrugged saying, "I don't suppose you would be in any sort of a mood to discuss the *temporary* loan of one single bag. Would you?"

* * *

It took far too long to get the boys settled and in bed. They wanted to tell Lizzy all they'd seen, all they'd done in minute detail. She would just get one child settled in, with the covers tucked around his shoulders, when another one would pop up, kneel on the blankets and mattresses, and launch into a noisy, detailed description of his day. All the while, Crockett kept pacing the length of the room saying, "We routed them. We *routed* them!"

After nearly an hour of this, Lizzy stamped her foot, extinguished the lamp, and muttered, "Good night! All of you!" closing the door behind her.

The ploy worked. Silence reigned—for about a minute. Then they began whispering and giggling, but by that time she was too tired to care. They would exhaust themselves soon enough. In the meantime the noise would obscure any conversations she and Micah might share.

Micah.

She leaned her shoulders against the wall and squeezed her eyes shut. It had been a long time since she'd prayed—not that she'd ever actually abandoned God. She just thought that he'd probably had greater worries than hers for an awfully long while. But tonight she couldn't prevent a whispered, "Please, please let him stay."

There was no reason for Micah to remain here any longer. He'd found everything he'd sought for so long—his brother, the St. Charles treasure, the man responsible for the destruction of his home, even his health. At the very least, he would want to take the gold back to Solitude. Perhaps if things were different, he might have asked her to accompany him. But she wasn't free. Her brothers depended on her, and they would for a very long time. She couldn't leave them. But as much as she might want to chain Micah up again, she couldn't force him to stay. He had a life of his own to lead. One that had been denied him for so long.

Opening her eyes, she fought a foolish urge to burst into tears. Not here. Not now. She would cry later.

Holding her breath for several seconds, she straightened her spine, smoothed her apron, and adjusted the butter knife that held her hair in place. Marching determinedly to the rear bedroom, she pushed open the door.

"I hope you're hungry, I . . ." The words died on her lips. He was packing. Micah St. Charles meant to leave tonight.

Her knees began to tremble. Even her hands and her chin were quaking. Clenching her jaw, she suppressed the reaction.

He finished stuffing his clothes inside his saddlebags. "I'll be needing some new shirts and such. I hope Bram won't mind too much if I take my share of the gold right away."

He was leaving.

The stark finality of the fact hit her like a thunderbolt, making her weak and hollow.

"Then there's another horse and such, but I suppose that can wait. Can you think of anything else I'll need to get?"

Me. Take me! But she couldn't say the words aloud.

"You'll be wanting some bread and cheese."

"In a minute."

"I'll wrap some in a dish towel. You'll want to take some with you."

He looked up then. "You think so?"

"Mmm."

He shrugged with an apparent lack of concern over taking needed supplies. A sign that he was truly anxious to go.

"What about water? Do you have a canteen to carry it in?"

"I'm sure I can find something to drink when the need arises, Lizzy."

"If you think so."

His brow creased, and he straightened, planting his hands on his hips. "What's wrong?"

"Wrong?" she echoed vaguely. She wouldn't beg, she wouldn't plead. Even though her heart cried out: *Don't leave me. Please.*

"You look rather glum, considering the circumstances."

Glum? She was breaking in pieces.

"I suppose you're tired," he said, his eyes resting on her in a way that was warm and familiar. "That's too bad."

"Too bad?" she couldn't seem to do much more than repeat everything he said.

He walked toward her, slowly, deliberately, those crystal-blue eyes becoming hot, burning a path from the tips of her toes, up, up, inevitably up, caressing her each inch of the way.

"I'd hoped that we could . . . spend a little time together this evening."

Before he left.

It occurred to Lizzy that she should be insulted. He didn't care enough to live with her, but he wanted one last bit of kiss and cuddle. But she was so distraught at his departure, so needy, she didn't care.

Melting into his embrace, she wrapped her arms around his neck. She wanted to whisper, "Love me, love me," but she could only hold him tight, breathing in his scent, absorbing his warmth, cataloging each feature to remember in the lonely days ahead.

"Hey," he whispered next to her ear. "What's this?"

She shook her head, unable to speak past the knot in her throat and the stinging moisture flooding her eyes. Shaking her head, she hoped he would be satisfied with the nonverbal reply, but he drew her back, tipping her chin up.

"It's over. There's no need to cry."

No need to cry? When he stated quite baldly that their relationship had passed its term of usefulness?

"Things will be brighter from now on, you'll see. Bean blew a hole in the bridge, but it shouldn't take too long to fix. Soon the tolls will be piling up. You can get Boone some new spectacles and buy him the books he needs, and Crockett can go back east to school if he wants to. Bridger can go to West Point and learn how to blow things up properly, and the twins can join the cavalry and see some real Indians. Of course, they'll all be around for a while, but—"

She burst into tears. She couldn't help it. The boys had a future—a wonderful shining star of a future—but she was going to be . . . she was going to be . . .

An old maid.

The sobs came even harder; she was completely inconsolable. Micah obviously didn't know what to do. His arms hung awkwardly at his sides, and then he patted her back saying, "Shh, shh. There's no need to cry."

She sobbed again, louder, gripping fistfuls of his shirt.

"Shhh, Lizzy. We can make this work. You'll see. Shh."

We?

She grew suddenly quiet. "We?" she said, as she lifted her tear-streaked face.

"I assumed," he said, "I mean, I . . . hope I didn't just take for granted that we . . . that we would . . . marry."

"Marry?"

He frowned. "Damn. I shouldn't have said that. I don't mean to push you into anything. I just thought that you and I should make things all nice and legal and permanent."

"Permanent?"

"Of course, you might want a church wedding." He scowled. "Hell, I should have considered that. I was just thinking that a judge would be a little quicker. That way Bram could stay for the ceremony, and I wouldn't have to spend so much time in the barn."

"Barn?"

He held her cheeks between his palms. "Lizzy, you've done nothing but repeat everything I've said. Haven't you been listening?"

"Lis . . ." she nodded, swiping the tears from her cheeks. "You're going to stay?"

"Well, of course I'm going to stay. After today, where else would I go?"

Where else? West, east, north, south, anywhere but here.

"But you're packing."

"So I can move into the barn for the next few days. I don't want Bram to know that we've celebrated the wedding night before the nuptial ceremony. Besides, I don't want to do anything to hurt your standing in the community. It wouldn't look right for me to stay here in the . . ." His words trailed away. "You thought I was leaving? For good?"

She could only nod.

"Oh, Lizzy. My poor little Lizzy, trying to be so brave." He drew her into his embrace, rocking her, soothing her. "I thought today had made things clear for me and for you. Don't you know? Haven't you guessed? I love you, body and soul. When I confronted Bean, I realized the past wasn't important and my only future is here. I could never leave you. Not willingly. Not unless you force me to go."

"Never," she whispered against his chest. "Never in a thousand years."

"Then we seem to have made a decision."

"Mm-hmm."

"You'll marry me? Be my bride?"

"For all time."

When he would have said more, she drew him down for a hungry kiss, knowing that all further discussion could wait until later. Much later. Right now she needed to feel this man next to her, pressed as close as two bodies could be.

"Love me," she whispered in his ear.

"But—"

"My reputation be damned," she murmured against his lips.

"The boys—"

"Won't notice. After the day they've had, they'll fall asleep in a minute or two and won't wake until noon."

"But—"

"No buts, Micah." She watched his eyes begin to smolder. "I want you here, in my arms. I want you to love me and make love with me until the wee hours. I want to feel the

236

lightning, the white-hot lightning, deep in my body. And I want you to feel it too."

Micah needed no further encouragement. Sweeping her into his arms, he carried her to the bed, then laid her on the quilts as if *she* were a precious treasure. Standing back, he stared at her, making her feel so beautiful, so beloved.

He undressed her, starting at her feet and working his way up, touching her, kissing her, setting her skin on fire. By the time he reached the butter knife, pulling it free and spreading her hair over the pillow, she had no more control, no more patience.

She tore the shirt from his back, heedless of the buttons that scattered across the floor. Fumbling with the fasteners of his pants, she pushed the trousers down his legs to the floor, freeing him, exciting him. Then she was pulling him down to the bed, tugging his body over her own. Their passion held a new dimension, a tenderness, a reverence, each caress that much more meaningful because it was to be a foundation for a future together. Lizzy held on to each moment as if it were a precious gift. And when he filled her, loved her, possessed her, she closed her eyes, hearing the words she'd thought he would never say.

"I'm home, Lizzy. I'm home."

Epilogue

March 1866

The moon was beginning to rise over the eastern hills when Lizzy stepped outside to wave good-bye to the townswomen who were starting their journey home.

"Tomorrow," she called. "Tomorrow will be our big day! Thank you for staying so late!"

The women laughed and waved as they clambered into wagons and buggies and headed toward Catesby. They would be back again at dawn to work, glad of the jobs the Wilders were providing, just as Lizzy was more than happy to pay for their help.

She jumped down from the porch, ran a few feet down the path, then turned to study the repairs that had been made on the house over the last few months.

In the glow of the gas lamps that hung in each window, the

inn looked like a fairy palace. Thanks to Micah's share of the St. Charles treasure, the exterior had been scraped and painted a cool blue-gray, the shutters had been stained a rich dark brown before being rehung, and the porch railing and supports had been repaired and whitewashed. Inside, a bevy of townswomen had worked most of the winter to polish woodwork, paper the walls, and clean the rugs. Furniture had been reupholstered, new plants were thriving in front of freshly curtained windows, and every surface gleamed with a good scrubbing.

All their hard work would soon be put to the test. At ten o'clock sharp, the bridge would be christened and then the inn would be officially open for business. The women had been baking and ironing for days in preparation for the event. The entire area was permeated with the smell of fresh breads, cookies, pies, and cakes.

Lizzy nodded her head in satisfaction. Who would have known that she would find her niche in life purely by an accident of fate? As a youngster she'd thought only of escaping this place, but she had since learned that she loved organizing the inn, planning the meals, arranging deliveries, and keeping the accounts. Never had she felt so useful, so filled with purpose. All because Micah had convinced her that if she wished to stay at the Wilder farm, she should do things right and return it to its original purpose.

Abandoning her study of the house, she looked across the river. For the past hour or so, wagons had begun to camp on the opposite bank. Travelers who were planning a trek west had been more than content to wait a day to use the nearly finished bridge rather than opting for the more hazardous ferry crossing. Micah had reserved one of the fields for their use as a campground, and now the grassy knoll glittered with a half-dozen fires. It wouldn't be long before stages would be stopping on a regular basis, and if Micah was able to complete his negotiations successfully, there were even plans for a railroad spur midway between here and Catesby.

She sighed. Life had never seemed so right to her before, so happy. She and her family still struggled, there were days when they missed their father beyond reason, and Micah sometimes longed to see his brothers, but on the whole, they were all mending from their wartime scars.

Wrapping her arms around her waist to ward off the cool breeze, Lizzy gazed at the bridge, unable to dampen her pleasure, at seeing the men in her life hard at work. Together Micah and the boys had worked side by side since the snows had melted enough to safely navigate the bridge and brave the swirling waters that sometimes dashed over the planks. She could not claim that heaven had descended on the household. There were still spats and squabbles. But with the presence of a grown man, her brothers had begun to relax. They'd begun to be boys again. Even now, with the wind ruffling their hair, they looked so carefree.

Micah must have felt her regard because he looked up and waved, his hair gleaming in the light of the lamps they'd strung overhead. "Is it quitting time already?" he shouted.

"Past time. Come in and eat," she replied. "What you haven't finished can wait until morning."

For some time, she'd been taking all their meals to them outside, but tonight she and the other women had fixed a special dinner, put flowers on the table, and even taken a jug of apple cider from the springhouse. They would eat like a real family for once.

Her brothers didn't need a second prompting. Whooping and hollering, they took a pair of lanterns and headed to the back of the house, where they would wash at the pump before going inside.

Micah, taking the last lamp, made a detour in Lizzy's direction.

"How's my baby?" he whispered, lightly touching her stomach. There was no apparent swell there yet, but soon . . .

"Fine."

"And how's my wife?" he asked, tipping her chin up for his kiss.

"Happier than ever before."

"You still love me?"

"More and more."

He hugged her close, kissing her until she swatted him away. "You're going to have to do some washing at the pump yourself before you get another sample of that," she teased. "You're covered with paint and sawdust."

"How do you like the railing? I tried to copy your father's original pattern as best I could."

"It looks wonderful. Papa would have been so pleased with what you've done." It was still difficult to talk about her father, but time was beginning to ease the hollow ache in her heart.

"I didn't do it alone. The boys helped."

She rubbed his waist. "But you were their mentor. Before you came, they couldn't hammer a nail."

"Practice," he said. "All it takes is a little practice."

She thought his view on the subject was a little too modest, but she didn't press.

"If I wash up, will you kiss me?"

"After supper."

"As long as I can have all I want tonight," he leaned close to whisper next to her ear. "After all, there's still a little interest owing from your loan," he said before brushing past her on the way to the house. It was a long-standing joke between them that she would be forever in debt for stealing that first bag of gold coins from the St. Charles trunks.

"You told me I'd fulfilled my obligations," she said, trailing him.

"Not yet. Maybe in ten years. Twenty. When we're old and gray and rocking on the porch, then perhaps I'll consider the issue. Until then . . . I think you'd better keep me satisfied with your dedication to my every whim."

"Every whim, indeed," she mumbled, then they both grinned.

Naaa!

Lizzy paused, seeing that Ruggles was gazing soulfully into the underbrush on the other side of the barn.

"Snuggles must be loose again," Micah said, referring to the nanny goat's kid. Although the baby had long since been weaned away from its mother, Ruggles seemed to miss her offspring's company whenever he strayed too far.

"I'll get him. You go wash up."

Taking the lantern from Micah, Lizzy walked toward the trees, knowing that she would probably find Snuggles in the little meadow over the ridge. The kid had taken to escaping there since he had discovered the first shoots of ripening grass on the creek banks.

Naaa.

"I'm hurrying, Ruggles, I'm hurrying," she chided the mother goat. But as she grew closer, her brow knit in confusion. Snuggles was there, curled in a bed of straw sleeping.

Naaaa! The nanny goat became more insistent, straining at her tether. *Naa-aaa-aaa!*

Lizzy felt a hint of unease, and the hairs prickled at the back of her neck. Granted, things had changed since she'd married Micah. She slept a little easier now, felt a little safer, but that did not mean that she'd completely forgotten the lessons she'd learned during the war. Even though Bean had been tried and hanged for war crimes, she had her moments of fear. Especially when things seemed a little too perfect.

There was a rustling in the trees.

"Who's there?" she called suspiciously, holding the lamp high, her eyes narrowing as she tried to pierce the shadows. Drat it all, she should have asked Micah to come with her.

The snap of a twig caused her to jump.

"I know you're out there! Show yourself."

For a moment there was no noise. Then she heard a scuffling, and the leaves trembled. A dark shape moved out of the foliage, then stood hesitantly, stooped.

Lizzy took a cautious step forward, allowing the light from her lantern to slip down the man's length. Like that of most wanderers, his clothing was old and threadbare, barely recognizable as the remnants of some kind of uniform. He wore a floppy hat that kept most of his face hidden. What she did see was covered with grizzled whiskers.

"Who are you?" she demanded again, wishing that she still carried a revolver in her apron, but there'd been no need for such measures in months.

"I wondered . . . if you could spare some water."

His voice was a mere croak, barely recognizable. Catching a glance at the red welts of new scars that crisscrossed his throat, Lizzy knew he must have been wounded during the war.

She didn't speak right away. Most of the soldiers had found their way home by now. Very few still wandered the area. But now and again a stranger would pass down the lane on his way somewhere, anywhere, after discovering that his family was missing or his farm was in ruins.

"Follow me," she said quietly, turning and making her way back to the house. She felt a slight twinge of irritation. This was to have been a special night with her family. They were probably waiting for her—or, more likely, they had begun eating without her. She would simply have to get this man his water and hurry him on his way.

Pausing by the pump, she filled the ladle kept hooked on the handle. She turned to face the stranger, only to discover that he had paused a few feet away, just out of the puddle of light. Judging by his stance, he was looking at the house. Following his line of sight, she saw that he must be reading the sign, which had been rehung from the porch eaves. She handed him the ladle, but he seemed distracted as he drank.

"A ferry crossing . . ." he said, after he'd wiped his mouth of a few stray drops. "How wonderful."

"Yes, we open tomorrow."

"The bridge was damaged?"

"By war, by misuse, by hate."

"Bean . . ."

Lizzy frowned at the whisper of sound. Surely she hadn't heard this man say "Bean."

"What?" she asked.

"Bean came here?"

Lizzy felt a cold finger trace down her spine.

"What did he do to you? Dear heaven, I didn't tell him who I was, but he must have known. He must have guessed."

A hand seemed to close around her throat so that she could barely breathe. She took a stumbling step.

"How do you know about Bean?" The words tore from her chest.

The stranger lifted his head. He reached up to pull off his hat.

Lizzy stood speechless, staring at the face of her father. She blinked, sure she was suffering from some delusion.

"Papa?" she whispered. No, it couldn't be. This man was old. His hair was long and matted. His face was scarred, the left side pulled drastically down and nearly lifeless.

But the eyes. She would know those eyes anywhere. They were the same golden brown that stared back at her each morning from the mirror. They were Crockett's eyes, and Boone's.

"Papa!" She hastily set the lamp on the trough, then ran to him, feeling his frail arms wrap around her shoulders in a death grip.

"I never thought I'd see the place again, Lizzy girl," he sobbed next to her ear.

She had never heard him cry before, had never felt him tremble as he held her. He was so weak, so frail, so aged, but she didn't care. This was her father. Her *father!* Alive and back home again.

"How . . ."

He shook his head, unable to speak for some time. When he did, his gruff voice was barely intelligible. "I spent two years in prison, Lizzy. It should have killed me, would have killed me, but I wanted to see you all just one more time. The conditions, the worry, the strain. It was all a little much, I suppose, because I had a stroke. The doctor didn't think I'd pull through. But I showed them that a Wilder is made of sterner stuff. It took me some time to learn to talk again and to get around. But I'm here now."

"Oh, Papa." She clutched at him, understanding now why it had taken him so long to return, why there had been no news. "We had all but given up hope." Her fingers curled into his coat, and she pulled him after her. "Come inside. The boys will want to see you."

He didn't move. It was as if, seeing the house so close in front of him, he didn't dare believe it was real. "How . . . is everyone?"

She knew immediately that he wondered how much of a family he had returned to.

"You heard about Sally?" she asked gently.

He nodded, blinking his eyes against the tears, which he obviously despised but could not control.

"We buried her on the hill overlooking the river," Lizzy offered, wanting to give him some comfort. "Do you remember how she used to go there each morning to count the geese?"

"Yes. Yes, I remember. And . . . the boys?"

"All of them are fine, Papa."

"*All* of them?"

"Yes. I nearly had to tie Crockett and Boone to a post to keep them from running away and joining the army, but they stayed here to help."

"Thank God." It was a sigh of thanksgiving.

He was a little shaky, and she drew him to the watering trough, helping him to sit down.

"I prayed you would all be here, but I never thought . . . I never . . ."

She knelt in front of him, taking his hand. "I know, Papa. So much has happened since you've been gone, so much will seem strange to you. You've got years of catching up to do, but don't you see? It doesn't matter. You're home. That's all you need to think about."

"The house . . ." He gazed up at it, and she saw the way the gaslit windows illuminated his face. "How did you manage . . ." His hand made a weak gesture to the repairs.

"We've had some help, Papa. A very special man came into our lives." She squeezed his hand. "I'm married now."

"Married?"

"Mm-hmm. For months now."

"My!"

"Yes, and come fall, you'll have a grandbaby to spoil."

He stared at her in astonishment, and she realized she was overloading him with too many details. There would be time for all this later. Much later. When he was stronger.

"Come inside," she urged. "We're about to have dinner. You'll join us, talk to the boys. Then we'll put you in one of the beds in the back where it's quiet. You look worn out."

He took a deep breath. "I am, Lizzy girl. But not for long, now that I'm home."

She wrapped her arm around his waist and helped him stand.

"Papa," she said after a few steps. "How did you know about Bean?"

"He was the one responsible for these," he said, gesturing to the scars at his throat. "When I refused to die from my wounds, he put me in prison."

"But why?"

"Because I dared to save the life of a man who had once saved mine."

"I don't understand."

He patted the hand she'd wrapped around his waist. "One of these days I'll have to tell you how I plunged headfirst into this sorry mess. But first"—he sniffed—"is that pie I smell?"

"Yes, it is. Mrs. Ruthers has been making her famous dried apple pie."

He smacked his lips. "Now, there's a memory that doesn't leave a man right away, don't you think? Why, I remember when—"

"Lizzy?"

The back screen door squeaked open, and Micah poked his head out. "What's taking so long? Did the blasted goat . . ."

He stopped, the words trailing into silence as he squinted into the darkness.

Lizzy's father stumbled and grew still.

"Micah, you'll never guess who this is!" Lizzy cried.

"Wheeze?" he whispered, then called out joyously, "Wheeze, is that you?"

Her father began to laugh, huge chest-resounding chuckles that filled the air with his mirth. "Well, I'll be double damned! Captain St. Charles, what in the name of heaven above are you doing in *my* home, with *my* daughter?"

"Captain?" Lizzy eyed them both in confusion. "This is Micah. My husband."

"Your husband!" He climbed the steps and held out his hand. "By thunder, it's good to see you alive!"

Micah ignored the hand and hauled him close for a bone-crushing embrace. "All thanks to you, old friend. If you hadn't created that diversion at the bridge, I would have been a dead man."

Suddenly it all became clear to Lizzy. Micah had told her how he'd managed to escape arrest, how one of his men had led a suicide charge to create enough of a diversion for him to run away. That man had been her father!

Rushing into the house she called, "Boys! Come quickly! Papa is here! He's here!"

They stared at her as if she'd lost her mind, forks and spoons and pieces of bread suspended midway to their mouths. But when Micah and her father entered the room, they forgot their meal and jumped to their feet, scrambling toward them.

Only little Oscar held back, sidling close to Lizzy's skirts. "That's my Pa?" he whispered. "The one I'm named after?"

She ruffled his hair. "Yes, Oscar. That's our father. You haven't seen him since you were a baby."

He shifted, but did not budge.

"Will he love me as much as Micah does?"

Lizzy felt a lump lodge in her throat. "Oh, yes, Oscar. He'll love you just as much as Micah does."

"Will Micah have to go away now that he's back?"

She understood his fears. He'd known only one man in his life who had treated him like a son. Micah. Now he feared that another person would take his hero's place.

"No, Oscar," she said, kneeling beside him and hugging him close. "Don't you see? We're a family. A great big, rousing, bursting-at-the-seams family. No matter how many people join our circle, there will always be room for one more. And no matter what happens from this day forward, good or bad, our love for one another will never die. It will just grow and grow and grow."

Standing, she gave him a little nudge, pushing him toward the other boys, who were jostling for their father's attention. When he reached the fringes of the group, a slight hush occurred. Then the old man, weary from battle, from imprisonment, and from deprivation swept Oscar into his arms, holding him close, tears trickling down his face.

Lizzy put a hand to her mouth, choking back a sob of gratitude at a picture she had thought she would never see. She and her loved ones had survived the war and its aftermath. But even more, they had grown strong, indomitable.

Micah's arms slipped around her waist from behind, pulling her close when she began to tremble. He didn't speak. He didn't need to. He knew instinctively that her only desire was to stand close to him and revel in all that had happened. And at that moment Lizzy knew her world was complete. She had her home, her brothers, and her father together in one place.

But most of all, she had Micah. A man who had joined her in a sweet dalliance, then had been willing to trust her enough to give her his heart, his soul, and a lifetime by her side.